KRISTINE KATHRYN RUSCH

an imprint of **Prometheus Books**
Amherst, NY

Published 2012 by Pyr®, an imprint of Prometheus Books

Cover illustration © Dave Seeley
Cover design by Nicole Sommer-Lecht

Inquiries should be addressed to
Pyr
59 John Glenn Drive
Amherst, New York 14228–2119
VOICE: 716–691–0133
FAX: 716–691–0137
WWW.PYRSF.COM

16 15 14 13 12   5 4 3 2 1

Library of Congress Cataloging-in-Publication Data

Rusch, Kristine Kathryn.
    Boneyards / by Kristine Kathryn Rusch.
        p. cm.
    ISBN 978–1–61614–543–9 (pbk.)
    ISBN 978–1–61614–544–6 (e-book)
    1. Life on other planets—Fiction. 2. Space ships—Fiction. 3. Interplanetary voyages—Fiction. I. Title.

PS3568.U7B66 2012
813'.54—dc22

                                                                                2011037543

Printed in the United States of America

For Sheila Williams again
This series wouldn't exist without you.

acknowledgments

*T*hanks on this one go to Lou Anders for understanding my method, Dean Wesley Smith for reading more versions than he probably wanted to, and all the readers who have let me know how much they like the stories in the Diving universe.

SECTOR BASE W

ONE

*R*ubble everywhere. Dust. Debris. I feel filthy and we've only been inside this room for fifteen minutes.

If you can call where we are "inside." Most of the rubble around us comes from caved-in rock destroyed not by time, but by some kind of blast.

We're here because Coop has finally tracked the location of Sector Base W, the base that was under construction when he and his Dignity Vessel, the *Ivoire*, left their timeline and got caught in foldspace. Five thousand years have passed for him, which is hard enough for me to grasp, but must seem impossible to the crew of the *Ivoire*.

Not all of them have dealt with it well. Maybe none of them have dealt with it well.

But some are dealing better than others.

I like to think Coop is one of those who is dealing with the loss of his friends, family, and universe quite well.

It's cold here, the kind of cold that I associate with failing environmental systems on spacecraft instead of with planets. Some of us are wearing our environmental suits (without the helmets) so that we can stay warm. Others—the planet-raised for the most part—are wearing layers of clothing.

That doesn't matter to me at the moment. At the moment, we're not going to do heavy work. But when we decide what heavy work to do, I'm going to make the ground team wear environmental suits, just for ease of movement.

Technically, I am running this mission. Coop has hired me not as the CEO of a now-huge corporation called the Lost Souls, but in my former capacity as a wreck diver. He has decided that he needs my expertise, and I have decided that I need to return to basics.

We have brought quite a crew with us. My three main divers—Mikk, Roderick, and Tamaz—are on the team, along with the Six. The Six are civilians who have a genetic marker that allows them to work in stealth tech. Or, at least, they were civilians. They've now worked in and around stealth tech for five years.

Archeologist Lucretia Stone, historian César Voris, and scientist McAllister Bridge finish off my team. Coop's team includes military officers from the *Ivoire*, a cadre of linguists, and a large group of scientists who specialize in what we have come to call Lost Technology, even though we should probably call it Found Technology, given the circumstances.

We have one large ship in orbit, *Nobody's Business Two*, although it's not large by Dignity Vessel standards. (A Dignity Vessel can house a thousand people somewhat comfortably, although it's designed for five hundred.) The *Two* is large by *my* standards. Even though I have run a huge corporation for almost a decade now, I still think of myself as the woman who ran a small diving operation out of a ship barely big enough to hold the team on this ground mission.

Most of our crew is not on this ground mission. Most are still on the *Two*. We wanted a small team down here—well, *I* wanted a small team down here—to assess what we need to launch some kind of study of this place.

The ground mission isn't risky the way that some of my wreck dives have been risky. We're not operating in the vacuum of space, and we don't have any inexperienced tourists with us. We're operating in the remains of a mountain on a planet with normal gravity.

But the ground mission is still difficult, and not just because we're working in the unstable remains of a mountainside. We have strange levels of command here, and even stranger levels of emotion.

For Coop, this place must seem surreal. He had looked at the schematics of the sector base before it was built, approving the design in a large meeting with the other captains of the Fleet. In his mind, Sector Base W is both a place that's still under construction and a place that was ruined centuries ago.

It represents a hope, now gone, that he will find his people again—or what remains of his people, five thousand years in the future.

For me, Sector Base W is a curiosity, albeit one that has a firm grip on my imagination. I want to know what happened here. History always captures me, and now that I'm working beside living history, I'm even more captivated.

But I'm worried as well. No matter how often I do planetside missions, I hate them. I prefer to explore in zero gravity, so that I can float around the problems, propel myself forward with my arms alone, look at everything from top to bottom without climbing anything.

I have learned that ground-based missions are not my strong suit, which is why Lucretia Stone is actually in charge of the physical part of this trip.

Stone, one of the most highly regarded archeologists in both the Empire and, now, in the Nine Planets, has perfected the art of ground-based exploration, and I was foolish on our very first mission not to trust her experience.

In the five years since, I have rectified that. Stone has proven herself time and time again to be an able group leader. I'm just not a very good follower, and neither is Coop.

He's beside me now, standing on the wreckage of a platform with the word "Danger" written on it in Old Earth Standard. He is tall and broad shouldered, with dark hair and intense blue eyes. If I had to tell someone years ago what a captain of a Dignity Vessel looked like, I would have described a man like Coop. The square-jawed hero of legend.

Only Coop's not a legend, and at the moment, he looks heartbroken.

I want to slip my arm around him, but I don't dare.

Right now, he has assumed his professional persona, that of Jonathon "Coop" Cooper, captain of the *Ivoire*. Captain Cooper remains strong for his troops, even when there aren't many of them around him. Only two of his people have joined us on the ground. Joanna Rossetti, small and tough, has moved closer to Stone, trying to see deep within the rubble. The *Ivoire*'s chief engineer, Yash Zarlengo, stands beside Coop, hands clasped behind her back.

Yash's face is always hard to read. She was raised planetside by an engineering family at one of the sector bases and has the thick muscles and firm bones of anyone raised in real gravity. Coop has them too, although not everyone on his staff does.

Yash should be back at Lost Souls, working with one of my teams on the various *anacapa* projects. The *anacapa* is a specialized drive developed by the Fleet, something no culture has replicated in five thousand years. Initially, my people thought the *anacapa* was stealth technology. It functions that way sort of, but really, it's much much more. Yash heads *anacapa* research in Lost Souls, but she, like Coop, wants to solve the mystery of the Fleet. She wants to know where her people are, even if they are her people no longer.

The condition of Sector Base W, however, has all three of them upset.

"A lot of this damage could just be caused by time," says Stone.

She's in the very middle of the debris field, trying to look through the boulders and the broken rock at the remains of the room beyond.

I have been inside a sector base before, albeit one long shut down. The main room of a sector base is huge, big enough to hold several Dignity Vessels. The floor is smooth, and there is lighting everywhere. In the very back, there should be apartments for visiting workers and storage rooms. The ceiling is high, and in some sector bases, should open to the planet above.

If you didn't see the Old Earth Standard word "Danger" on the platform

Coop is standing on, you might not realize that this is a man-made cavern. The door is long gone, the corridors leading to the room have collapsed, and there is no equipment that I can see.

Of course, I've learned from Stone that time adds to our problems in understanding what happened. Over time, dirt and debris and basic garbage cover the ground layer, burying the path that people walked on five thousand years ago in centimeters, sometimes meters, of material.

Plus, planets change. They're living things, just like we are, and they expand, contract, and alter as their atmospheres and environments wear on them each and every day. That doesn't count what humans do to planets, carving them up for bases or building roads. Nor does it count things that impact planets from the outside, like large asteroids that don't entirely burn up as they hit the atmosphere.

Stone assured me before we came into this part of the mountain that mountains age like everything else. Old mountains—like old humans—grow shorter with time. Sometimes mountains implode from within. Sometimes rain and other forces wear at mountainsides, and those tumble away. If the mountain is filled with caves or is, like this one, mostly hollow thanks to the work Coop's people did on it five thousand years ago, then that rock slide, that tumble, might lead to a cave-in, which could lead to something like this.

It looked, as we landed, like someone had taken a scoop and carved an opening in this mountain, then left all the debris to gather at the base. Some on my team—away from Coop's people, whom we're treating very delicately— made a variety of comparisons: a half-eaten grapefruit, a shattered ball, a wall display punched by a gigantic fist.

Despite our work with archeologists and geologists and land-science people, most of my team isn't used to working planetside. We live in space, we function in artificial environments, and we know that if anything happens to our tiny worlds, that anything is usually caused by malfunctioning systems, mismanagement, acts of war, or something else that can be blamed on human beings.

Arguing whether part of a mountain came down over five thousand years because of natural causes just seems strange to me, and I wonder if it seems strange to Coop.

After all, he was born in space, to a culture constantly on the move. The Fleet never went backward. It only moved to the next system, the next sector, solving problems and meting out its own version of justice.

It did stay in an area for a designated period of time, building bases along the way for ground repairs and other such things. The Fleet cycled back and forth in that designated area until it was time to move forward again, and then it did, sending teams to build bases ahead of the core of the Fleet, and letting older teams close the bases too far back for the Fleet to ever easily return to.

Sector Base V, the base where I first encountered Coop, where the *Ivoire* appeared one magical day when our blundering saved his people from their trap in foldspace, was one of the bases that had been properly shut down. The last of the equipment, five thousand years old, still thrummed with a bit of life, but most of the tools, all of the furniture, records, and important items, were long gone. Sector Base V had not only been abandoned, it had been forgotten by the people who lived on the surface. No record of the base existed in any of the histories—our histories, anyway—and nothing, not even legends about it, remained on the surface.

When we discovered that base, it was as if we had found an entire world that no one, not even the people planetside, had known existed.

There is no one planetside in this part of Ylierr, and according to the planet's various official histories from all of its cultures, there has never been a community on this location. Ylierr was settled one thousand years after Coop's people touched the place.

No settlement—that we've found anyway, and granted, we've only just started to search the various databases—was ever established on this site. We don't know why yet, whether the destruction we see before us was already here, or if the mountains—which are formidable—scared the other settlers away.

Stone believes the other colonists looked at various places on Ylierr's eight continents and found those places more amenable to settlement: closer to water, arable land, an abundance of plant life.

Coop believes the other colonists looked at this location, saw ruin, and decided to go elsewhere.

Both of them could be right, but I haven't said that. Even though I lead this overall mission, I don't see it as my responsibility to settle an early argument with two invested adults. The histories will eventually give us the information we need. Histories, and the stories the land itself tells.

But right now, we're just guessing.

There appears to be a makeshift path through the rubble leading to the still-intact back wall. We seem to be standing on the platform closest to that wall, but I am not certain.

Yash has a touchpad with the schematics that the Fleet approved for this base before a battle trapped the *Ivoire* in foldspace. She holds the pad up now, trying to find something that corresponds.

Stone has devices that overlay holographic images on top of such sites, but she didn't bring it at the moment. She doesn't want us to go into the area yet, but Coop does.

"I can answer this debate with one simple check," he says to Stone. "Let me go back there."

"You don't know how to move in an unstable environment," she says. "You could send the entire rock pile down on yourself."

He gives her a withering look, so intense that it makes my breath catch. There's a reason he was chosen to command five hundred people at such a young age. He has a power, an *authority*, I have never ever encountered before.

"I'll be fine," he says flatly.

Stone is oblivious to his power. Stone is oblivious to a lot of human interaction. It is both her weakness and her strength.

"You don't decide what rocks do," she says. "They decide. No matter what happens, Captain, the natural environment will triumph over the human spirit every single time."

He does not argue with her the way a lesser person would. He was raised in space; he knows that human will cannot conquer everything.

But in this instance, it does not matter to him. I can see it in the set of his jaw, the look in his eye.

Mikk, one of my divers, who has come down here not to dive or explore (since this trip is truly informational), but for muscle in case something horrible does happen, gives me a sideways look. I can read Mikk's expressions after decades of working with him.

He wants me to step in and settle the conflict between Coop and Stone.

Technically, I should step in. But I suspect there will be a lot of interpersonal battles on this trip, and I am not going to risk my authority arbitrating a fight I will lose.

Stone is right, of course: Coop should not go in there. But Coop has spent the last five years coping with loss and change that would devastate most people. I am not sure he cares if the rocks slip and he gets crushed.

"You do realize," I say softly to him, "that if you're back there and injured we might not be able to help you."

He gives me the same withering look he gave Stone. He realizes it, and as I suspected, he doesn't care.

"You have my permission to abandon me for the sake of the mission," he says.

The words have just enough sarcasm to anger me. But I don't let that out. He's baiting me when he's really angry at Stone for treating him like an idiot.

"What are you trying to find back there?" I ask, pretending like his previous words don't matter to me at all.

"Evidence," he says.

"That's what the prolonged investigation is for," Stone says.

"I don't want to have a prolonged investigation if we can settle this in a few minutes," he says in a tone that vibrates with frustration.

They have had this argument before, clearly not in my presence, and they still haven't settled it.

Now Yash is the one to give me the sideways look, but not before Stone starts down the argument's familiar road.

"You can't determine what happened from guesswork," she says, not trying to hide her frustration either. "Sometimes I think you don't understand what five thousand years really means in terms of the toll it takes on everything from buildings to mountains."

Her words echo in the rock-strewn space, and then she blanches. She has just realized what she has said.

"Captain, I'm sorry—"

"No, you're not," he says. "I'm going in there."

And then, he stomps into the small corridor made by those rocks.

I curse silently. I had asked what he was looking for so that I would have an idea of how long he would be back there. I want to know if we're going to need to worry. It's a simple precaution we use on space dives—timing everything, giving limits because they ensure that the diver remains focused on the task at hand.

I take a deep breath to calm myself. Of course, Coop will stay focused on the task at hand. He's the one who has been focused on this mission from the very beginning.

Still, reflexively, I glance at my watch, then move to the mouth of that corridor. Stone grabs my arm and moves me back a dozen centimeters.

"I don't want you to get hurt if those rocks fall," she says quietly.

She seems resigned. Maybe, like me, she has always known he would go in there and that there would be little we could do to stop him.

I want her to reassure me that he will be all right. I want her to tell me that ground accidents are rare. I want her to say that we're not silly for letting him go alone.

But I know she will say none of those things. I wouldn't say them if we were on a real dive.

Instead, I beckon Yash to my side. "Let me see those schematics," I say.

She taps the pad, zooming in on the part of the room that she believes we're standing in.

Just like I thought, we're near the back of the gigantic room, not too far from the doors that open onto the apartments and the storage areas.

If, of course, the Fleet built Sector Base W according to these schematics and didn't change the design as they worked on the site. Yash, who was raised on a sector base to a family of technology specialists, says that often the design will change as the engineers discover problems inside the base's location.

She often discusses a base she apprenticed on, a base that had to make all kinds of alterations because the presence of methane threatened the entire build.

"What's he looking for?" I ask her.

She shrugs, but I recognize her expression. She knows. And she's not willing to tell me.

She assumes everything is confidential. Coop is still her commander, and she operates as if everything he tells her is under the seal of that command.

I don't have that attitude. Coop and I have had a lot of go-rounds since we met, many of them over who is in charge. It took me months to get him to call me Boss, which is what everyone calls me. I don't acknowledge my so-called "real" name, not because I dislike it or even because my father was the one to christen me with it, but because that name no longer applies to me.

It hasn't applied to me for decades.

Coop finally gave in one afternoon over coffee. He shook his head, and said to me, *I can't avoid your name forever. I have to call you something. I'll just pretend "Boss" is your given name. After all, it's not like I'm using that word in my native language.*

His native language, our joint linguists have figured out, is one of the parents of my language. Even the language has twisted and altered over five thousand years, so much so that when we first met, we couldn't speak to each other.

I know Stone's accusation is a false one: perhaps more than the rest of us, Coop knows how long five thousand years is. He deals with it every single day.

And just when I think he has the knowledge—and the feelings it engenders—under control, he does something like this.

TWO

We crowd around the opening in the rock pile, which is probably not the smartest thing we can do. But Stone and I are standing only about a meter away, and when Yash joined us, it became an unspoken invitation for everyone else to join us.

Mikk turns on the wrist lights on his environmental suit, lights that can imitate bright flares, and he aims them at the opening. He looks, to the casual observer, like an insecure man flexing his muscles. Mikk already has more obvious muscles than most people I know—something that has come in handy in more than one crisis situation.

"I don't need any damn light," Coop says from not too far away, but he doesn't ask Mikk to turn them off. Coop is still surly from the power struggle with Stone, and is probably regretting his impulsive decision to go in there without inspecting the area first.

He's usually a lot more cautious than this. His uncharacteristic impatience is a testament to how long he's waited to come here, how much he has given up these last few years.

"Do you need a damn tiny person?" Rossetti asks in a tone that would have bordered on insubordination if she had been on the *Ivoire*.

To my relief, a chuckle floats out of that opening.

"Probably," he says, sounding a lot more like himself. "But there's no sense in risking you. I'm almost there."

I move a little closer and look inside that pile of rock. I can see Coop, outlined in the light from Mikk's suit. Coop is crouching as he makes his way through, turning from side to side to avoid outcroppings of rock.

He really is too big to be inside that opening, but he's going to go through with this now—not out of stubbornness, but because there's something he needs to know for himself, and it's not enough to have someone else tell him. He needs to see it in person.

I've only seen Coop act this way one other time before, and that was the day we joined forces. The *Ivoire* had been trapped for weeks, first in foldspace and then in Sector Base V, and Coop couldn't quite believe what all the evidence was telling him. I think he hoped, deep down, that I was lying to him, that the evidence was lying to him, that he had ended up at the wrong base in the right time period rather than the right base in the wrong time period.

Whatever his motivation, he nearly got everyone on my team arrested for treason by the Enterran Empire. Only some quick thinking and even quicker action on his part and mine saved all of our hides.

I hope his impulsiveness now doesn't cause another emergency. I've been inside rock fall only once before, and I hated it. I'd rather die in the vacuum of space than be crushed underground by a pile of rock.

He slips around a corner, and I can no longer see his entire frame. Now I only catch glimpses of him as he moves along.

At least he's moving carefully, and so far we haven't heard much from within, not even the tinkle of a falling pebble.

Yash holds the pad out as if staring at the schematics will help. Rossetti has moved even closer. Mikk still stands with his arms raised. Stone has her arms crossed, and she glares at the interior of that opening.

She doesn't understand why I let Coop go, why I didn't rebuke him. We all know he would have listened to me, however reluctantly.

But I understand, maybe better than anyone else on my team, what he's going through. He's been remarkably patient so far.

He has waited years for this moment.

I don't know if I could have waited that long.

Coop spent his first year upon arrival at Lost Souls learning. He learned our language; he learned a broad general history of the sector; he learned our customs. He also spent the rest of his time dealing with his own crew.

The shock of moving so far forward in time devastated everyone. Some coped by resigning their commissions and leaving the Fleet altogether, claiming they never wanted to experience travel under an *anacapa* drive again. Others worked even harder on maintaining the *Ivoire*, shoring up discipline and acting like the ship would rejoin the Fleet. Still others offered to work for the Lost Souls Corporation, helping us with scientific research.

And a few, a hopeless despondent few, found ways to take their own lives.

Those people, including Coop's first officer, Dix Pompiono, challenged everything the crew of the *Ivoire* knew and believed about themselves. The members of the Fleet don't give up, Coop kept saying to me, even though their own history, by his own account, belied that.

The Fleet simply had methods of dealing with those who could no longer travel, and were no longer up to the rigors of military life aboard such a ship. The team always had the option of remaining planetside at any planet they visited, or they could leave their ship and volunteer for duty in a different ship. They could join other cultures, or become ground crew at sector bases or leave the Fleet altogether, at any point.

But the handful who died believed themselves trapped here, in a way that Coop didn't entirely understand. For Coop, rejoining whatever remains of the Fleet five thousand years out is like rejoining family. Many of the others believe the same thing.

Those who died, however, knew they would never see family and friends again, and couldn't cope with that loss. So they imposed yet another loss on the survivors of the time shift, a loss that made Coop angrier than anything else.

"He's been out of visual range for a long time," Mikk says softly to me.

I glance at my watch. At least fifteen minutes have passed since I last saw him through the gaps in the rocks.

"You want to send someone in?" Mikk asks, which means he's saying, in Mikk-speak, that he's volunteering to go inside because he believes it crucial.

"Not yet," I say.

The rocks haven't fallen. We would have heard it. But I've talked to Stone enough about the risks to know that Coop could be in danger even if the rocks haven't fallen. He could be stuck in a tight area, one he wedged himself into and now can't get himself out of.

"The amount of time that has passed is relatively insignificant, given what he's trying to do," Stone says, letting us know that she overheard us and that she should be the one making the decisions on what happens next.

"We're not sure exactly what it is he's trying to do," Mikk says.

"He wants to see if shutdown procedures were followed," Yash says.

I look at her in surprise. She hasn't been willing to answer that question until now. I can't tell if she's speaking up at the moment because she's worried about Coop or because she's tired of our arguments.

"Even if he finds your equipment, which I don't think he will," Stone says in her snottiest tone, "he won't be able to tell how it was shut down."

"You don't know our equipment," Yash says in an equally snotty tone.

"I do know that in an undisturbed environment it can survive," Stone says. She was with us at Sector Base V, even though she was never allowed inside. "But this environment has been open to the elements for a very long time."

"Yeah, I know," Yash says dismissively. "He does too."

I look at her. She knows even more than she's saying. But I don't ask. I figure it'll all play out shortly.

I move closer to the opening. I don't see him any longer. This time, Stone doesn't try to stop me.

Mikk glances at me, still worried. I shrug. Stone says we're going to wait, so we'll wait.

THREE

Another twenty minutes go by before we see movement behind those rocks. It only took Coop about ten minutes to go from the opening to that point on the way in, but it takes him almost half an hour on the way back. At first, I think that's because he is carrying something, but it's really because he can't quite maneuver his way out in the same way that he went in.

Stone tries to explain it to me, something about rock angles and protruding outcroppings, but I don't want to think about it. Although as she talks, I find myself remembering all the ruined wrecks I dived in space, and how sometimes going in one direction, avoiding all the pointy edges, was a lot easier than going in the opposite direction.

You can't always see the hazards, and you need to avoid them or you make things worse.

As Coop gets closer to the exit, his face stands out in sharp relief under the lights. Mikk has lowered his arms and turned down the lights somewhat so that they don't blind Coop as he emerges, but they still wash out his skin.

At least, I hope the lights have caused him to look paler than usual. I hate to think that he received even more bad news.

We move away from the opening as he comes through. He has scratches on one side of his face, a ripped sleeve on his environmental suit, and so much dust in his black hair that he looks like he has gone gray.

It takes me a moment—sometimes I can be slow—to realize that the reason his face is so pale isn't the light or his reaction to what he found, but that same dust, which coats him all over.

He comes out and gives me a small smile. Rossetti offers him a bottle of water, which he takes with relief. He sits on a boulder, downs most of the bottle, then wipes his arm over his mouth, smearing the gray dust.

"I was right," he says. "This base exploded."

Stone snorts. "You can't know that from eyeballing something. You're making a rookie science mistake. Just because you want to believe something doesn't make it so."

Coop finishes the rest of the water, puts a cap on the bottle, and hands it back to Rossetti. Then he tilts his head back and looks at Stone.

Anyone else would have used their height to an advantage, standing up and towering over Stone. But Coop doesn't need to. He has that intimidating withering gaze, and once again, he uses it on her.

"We have procedures," he says, "that are pretty straightforward—"

"And anyone could have tampered with them in five thousand years. I'm sorry, Captain, but you're being unrealistic."

Coop's eyes narrow.

"Shut up, Lucretia," I say. "You might know rocks and archeology and how time passes, but Coop knows more about these sector bases than we could ever know after decades of study. And I, for one, want to know what he found."

Stone's mouth thins as if she has to clamp her lips together so that she can't respond.

"Thanks," Coop says to me.

I nod and wait.

"Every sector base that's built underground has a standard lift that goes to the surface," Coop says. "One of the most important aspects of a sector base shutdown is to disable the lift. We do it in a prescribed way, so that the lift stabilizes, so that even if there's a groundquake or some kind of sinkhole, it never opens up the hole we dug for the lift. We don't want some unsuspecting local, five thousand years in the future, to step on our lift and fall hundreds of meters to his death."

Stone is motionless. He has her attention now.

He certainly has mine.

"The lift in each sector base is in the same place, near the living quarters," he says. "This base is no different."

"You found the lift," Yash says.

He nods.

"And it was never shut down," Yash says.

"Not only that," he says, "but part of the lift itself remains in pieces just like that platform over there, as if it was shaken off its moorings and descended rapidly from the top to the ground."

"That's your proof?" Stone says. "It means nothing. Someone could have forgotten to disable the lift before your people abandoned the sector base."

"You don't understand," Yash says. "Our shutdown procedures are exacting. No one forgets anything. These procedures get checked, rechecked, and checked again. The kind of error that Coop is talking about does not happen to a base that's decommissioned. Not ever. Our people might leave a few tools behind or forget an article of clothing. But anything that's dangerous, well, those things get checked so many times that it is absolutely impossible to overlook them."

Rossetti is nodding as well.

"You're making serious assumptions," Stone says.

I hold up my hand. "Was the lift in Sector Base V disabled?"

Coop nods. "Exactly in the prescribed way, and completely untouched."

"How did you open the door?" Yash asks.

I frown at her. "What door?"

"The door to the lift," she says. "It's keyed to our palm prints. Coop should be in the system, but it doesn't look like any of the technology has worked here in a long time."

Stone crosses her arms over her chest, as if this part of the discussion proves her point.

Coop holds up his hands. They're scraped and the fingertips are bleeding. "I opened it the old-fashioned way," he says to Yash with a grin.

She grins back, although I look away. "Old-fashioned" is, in part, a joke, considering how long they've been trapped here, in their future. They can't ever go back to their past. Their engineers and experts spent the first year here trying to figure out if they could replicate the series of events that got the *Ivoire* trapped here in the first place.

The engineers finally decided that they couldn't do it, not safely. They might trap the *Ivoire* in foldspace or in some other more inhospitable time.

They decided—as a crew—to stay in the future. But the pain of that decision shows up in words like "old-fashioned" and in Coop's haphazard grin.

I look at the rubble around me. I believe Coop, which makes me wonder how much of this damage has been caused by time, and how much caused by some kind of external force.

"What kind of explosion are we talking about?" I ask. "Something from above or something from within?"

I ask the question because we've learned that some malfunctioning stealth tech acts explosively. Usually, though—at least in a place like this—nanobits effect repairs as quickly as the damage happens. At least, underground. Above ground, sinkholes form and other damage happens as well.

We've already checked the area for malfunctioning stealth tech. The phrase isn't accurate: we're really looking for a malfunctioning *anacapa* drive. But we use the words anyway because it's a good way to delineate a working drive from one that has malfunctioned for so long that it's built up a dangerous field.

We had to check before we got here, because only the *Ivoire* crew, the Six, and myself could work here if there was still an active and malfunctioning *anacapa* on the premises. There isn't, which is why Mikk and Stone have joined us.

Even though we didn't find any malfunctioning stealth tech before we came down here doesn't mean that at some point in the past five thousand years the *anacapa* didn't malfunction and explode outward. The drive might have been completely destroyed, and the malfunctioning stealth field didn't happen.

So I look at Coop, then realize I should have asked the question of Yash. She's the one with the engineering background.

Coop is looking at Yash too. Stone is about to answer, but this time, it's Yash who gives Stone the withering look.

"Inside, outside, it's impossible to tell right now," Yash says. "We would have to examine the trajectory of the blast."

"If there's a single blast," Stone says. "I've dug bombed-out ruins. Sometimes those places were attacked from outside, and sometimes they were attacked from inside. A few times we knew that the places had been felled by a series of bombs exploding in unison. Rubble looks like rubble looks like rubble until you start taking it apart and examining the details."

She says that not because she's lording her knowledge over us but because she's giving valuable information. I have learned the differences in her tone.

I say, "I know you've worked many sites." In fact she's one of the best archeologists of her generation, and only her anger at the Empire has kept her with us. "I had no idea, however, that you'd worked bomb locations."

She smiles. "Not recent bomb locations, Boss. Ones that go back centuries. The history of the Empire is really a history of warfare. And some of that warfare is tiny and very personal—happening on a building-to-building, town-to-town level. You'd be surprised what I learn when I dig in small areas."

"You want to dig in here and figure out what happened, don't you?" asks Mikk. He has come to respect her as well. But as usual with Mikk, he's not asking this question so much because he's curious about Stone. He's asking it to guide me.

He just told me that *he* would like to dig in here and explore the area, particularly now that he knows that something interesting occurred here.

"I'm still stuck on inside versus outside," I say. "If the bombing was external, could it have brought down the mountain?"

"A series of targeted bombs from any point in the Empire's history could have brought down the mountain," Stone says. "Maybe from any time in human history. I know Old Earth had bombs that could bring down mountains long before it had anything resembling space travel."

Coop is watching her as if he's amused by all that she's saying. I hope she doesn't see his expression.

"But that lift," I say. "The way that Coop described it, and from what we see here with this platform—"

"It could all mean nothing, Boss," Stone says. "You really do have to factor in time."

I resist the urge to roll my eyes.

"Okay," I say, trying again. "Knowing what we know about the Fleet—"

And here I nod at Coop. He tilts his head toward me. Now I know he's amused. He probably thinks all of my questions are ridiculous. Sometimes we have interchanges like this, in which he can't believe the knowledge we lack. (Of course, sometimes I forget about the knowledge he lacks.)

"—if an air assault attacked the mountain, the Fleet probably had weaponry within the sector base to deal with it. Right?"

I look at Yash now.

"Generally, yes," she says. "Or they might have called in one of our ships."

"Exactly," I say. "The kind of serial bombing you're describing, Lucretia, doesn't seem likely, given what we know about the Fleet's defensive capability. The attack would have been stopped in its tracks."

"If the Fleet and its opponent were evenly matched," Stone says. "Superior technology always wins."

"Usually wins," Coop says softly. From my understanding, the ships that fired on the *Ivoire* had inferior technology, but the shot that crippled the *Ivoire* happened at just the right time.

"Usually wins, then," she says. "I'm sorry to say this, Captain—" and now she turns to Coop "—but while your Fleet has the best technology we've ever encountered, that doesn't mean that you were at the top of the food chain at the time."

Yash looks at him. He looks at her.

Rossetti, who notes the silent interchange, is the one who speaks up. "Sometimes we were evenly matched," she says. "But never, in my lifetime, did we come across a more powerful foe."

"In the history of the Fleet we did," Coop says. "But they weren't necessarily enemies. We didn't fight everyone. We were pretty well known for our diplomacy."

Again, he uses that wry tone.

"All I'm thinking," I say with some emphasis, because somehow the conversation has gotten away from me, "is that it strikes me that an external attack would have had to happen swiftly to completely destroy this base. Am I wrong about that?"

"Again," Stone says, "we have no way of knowing this. You're basing your conclusion on a series of faulty assumptions."

"For once, I agree with Dr. Stone," Coop says. "We don't know. But, for the record, we have weapons that could easily and quickly bring down a mountain. Most advanced cultures do."

"On the Dignity Vessel?" Mikk asks.

Coop gives him a sideways look. The crew of the *Ivoire* hates the term "Dignity Vessel." They haven't called their ships Dignity Vessels for centuries, but I can't break my people of the habit. Sometimes, I think, we use the term to stay in touch with the myth.

Something about Coop's look puts me on edge. "The Fleet carries all its weaponry with it," he says with more patience than I expected from that look.

Which is a long way to say "Of course."

"I haven't seen anything like that on the Dignity Vessels that we've found," I say.

The Lost Souls Corporation has five complete Dignity Vessels, although two are rebuilds. I know for a fact that the rebuilds do not have any such weaponry. But I feel odd, standing here in these ruins, discussing the weapons capability of ships I own, capability I didn't realize those ships have.

Coop stands up. He's not going to tell me if the ships have the capability or not. At least, he's not going to tell me in front of the others, and clearly, he hasn't told me since we've known each other. Apparently nothing is going to change right now.

"Here's what we know," he says, wiping his injured hands on his suit, then slapping them together as if he needs to get the dust off them. "We know that whatever happened here happened quickly."

"That still means there could have been a groundquake or something," Stone says stubbornly.

"We don't build sector bases near areas that have an active volcano or a recent volcanic history, meaning nothing has gone off in a thousand years or more. We also have the capability of finding fault lines." Yash is speaking both in present tense about the Fleet and with an undercurrent of anger. She's telling Stone that the Fleet—whatever Stone thinks—wasn't stupid when it came to the bases.

"So all of the evidence that we have at the moment argues for an external cause," Mikk says.

"Not outside necessarily," I say.

"No," he says. "I mean something man-made as opposed to natural forces."

Coop nods. He's rubbing his fingers. They must be sore.

"Whatever happened," Coop says, "it happened quickly. That lift argues for an attack of some kind."

"Why are you so set on believing that?" Stone asks.

He looks at her. "I'm not set on anything, Professor. I wanted this base to be intact, like Sector Base V. I wanted to be able to gain information from it and figure out roughly when my people left this place. The more I learn, the quicker I can track the Fleet's trajectory."

"Why does that matter?" Stone asks.

"Because if he can plot the trajectory," I say, "he can reunite with the Fleet."

"Not me, necessarily," he says. "But my ship, probably a few generations from now, can hook up with the Fleet."

I've told Stone this before. She thinks it's fantasy. But—again, making a lot of assumptions—*if* the Fleet still exists, *if* its mission hasn't changed, *if* it has followed the prescribed trajectory for another five thousand years, then the *Ivoire* can eventually find the Fleet. The *anacapa* cuts both time and distance of the search. Going through foldspace will put the *Ivoire* within range, provided all those other things (and probably a dozen more I don't know) actually line up.

Personally, I think this is as impossible as using the *anacapa* to send the *Ivoire* back to its own time, but I haven't said anything to Coop. He needs his own dream to follow, and I think that dream has kept him alive until now. I spoke to his first officer, Dix Pompiono, before Dix's suicide. Dix was quite clear on his belief that it was impossible for the *Ivoire* to hook up with the Fleet.

That didn't kill Dix, though. The loss of his world killed him. The loss of his friends and family and lover was something he expected, given his job. But the loss of everything familiar, and of the possibility of hooking up with the Fleet he had known—that upset him the most.

Coop seems to believe that the Fleet is the Fleet is the Fleet.

I keep thinking about the differences that five thousand years have brought to an existing language. I can't imagine the differences five thousand years would bring to a still-existing community of ships.

But I have learned that some arguments are futile. And if Coop believes he can get his grandchildren back to the Fleet and if that belief keeps him going, who am I to question it?

Stone, however, has none of those qualms.

"You do realize you're being ridiculous," she says to him.

"I also realize that your people thought my *anacapa* drive was a simple cloak," he says.

Her cheeks color. Unlike a lot of people on the receiving end of one of

Coop's sideways insults, Stone understood that he had just called her stupid without uttering the word.

"Tell me again why I'm helping you," she says.

"Because you're as curious as I am," he says.

She smiles just a little. Then she looks at the opening he just crawled through. "Boss, I think we need a team of about one hundred if we're going to do this dig right and get the information as quickly as the captain here wants it. I—"

"No," Coop says. But he's not speaking to her. He's speaking to me.

"No?" I say.

He nods. "I got the information I wanted. Something happened here. I want to go on to Sector Base Y."

"But we don't have any real answers," Stone says.

This time, he does look at her. "I have all the answers I need. Something horrible happened here. You figure out what that was if you want. I'm not looking for the details. I'm trying to track the Fleet, and this place won't help me."

"You know where Sector Base Y is?" I ask. It had taken him months to find Sector Base W, mostly on missions with a small team from his own ship.

"I do," he says. "I was hoping we could get our answers without going the extra distance."

"How far is that?" Mikk asks.

"It's about the same distance between sector bases," Yash says. "So as far as we are from Sector Base V."

Sector Base V is well inside the Enterran Empire. Mikk blanches. The distance is huge.

"We have an *anacapa* on *Nobody's Business Two*," Coop says. "We can do this."

Stone turns ostentatiously and looks at the destroyed base. "I think there's a lot to learn from this place, Boss."

"I agree," I say. "But this is Coop's mission. He asked us to run it, not decide where we're going. We can always come back here."

Stone sighs. "I hope you're right," she says.

THE ESCAPE

FOUR

"**G**o, go, go, *go!*" Squishy waved her arms, shouting as she did.

She stood in the mouth of the corridor and watched as scientist after scientist fled the research station, running directly toward the ships.

The corridors were narrow, the lights on bright, the environmental system on full. It would have been cold in the corridors if it wasn't for the panicked bodies hurrying past her. The sharp tang of fear rose off them, and she heard more than one person grunt.

"Go, go, go!" She continued shouting and waving her arms, but she had to struggle to be heard over the emergency sirens.

An automated voice, androgynous and much too calm, repeated the same instructions every thirty seconds: *Emergency evacuation under way. Proceed to your designated evac area. If that evac area is sealed off, proceed to your secondary evac area. Do not finish your work. Do not bring your work. Once life tags move out of an area, that area will seal off. If sealed inside, no one will rescue you. Do not double back. Go directly to your designated evac area. The station will shut down entirely in . . . fifteen . . . minutes.*

Only the remaining time changed. Squishy's heart was pounding. Her palms were damp, and she kept running her fingertips over them.

"Hurry!" she said, pushing one of the scientists forward, almost causing him to trip. "Get the hell out of here!"

Another ran by her, clutching a jar. She stopped him, took the jar, and set it down.

He reached for it. "My life's work—"

"Had better be backed up off site," she said, even though she knew it wasn't. The off-site backups were the first thing destroyed, nearly three hours before. "Get out of here. *Now!*"

He gave the jar one last look, then scurried away. She glanced at the jar too, saw it pulsating, hating it and wanting to kick it over. But she didn't.

She stood against the wall, moving the teams forward, getting them out. No one was going to die this day.

A woman clutched at her. "My family—"

"Will find you. They've been notified of the evac," Squishy said, even though she had no idea if that was true.

"Are they far enough away?" the woman asked, still clutching at Squishy.

What made these people so damn clingy? She didn't remember scientists being clingy before.

"They are," Squishy said, "but you're not."

She pushed at the woman, and the woman stumbled, then started to run, letting her panic take over. They'd had drills here: Squishy had made sure of that when she arrived, but apparently no one had thought about what the drills actually implied.

And this was no drill.

Her ears ached from the sirens. Then the stupid automated voice started up again.

Emergency evacuation under way. Proceed to your designated evac area. . . .

She tuned it out, counting the scientists as they passed. There was no way she could count a thousand people, not that all of them would run past her anyway. But she was keeping track. Numbers always helped her keep track.

Her heart raced, as if it were running along with everyone else.

Quint stumbled out of the side corridor, his face bloody, his shirt torn. He reached her and she flinched.

"We have to evacuate," he said, grabbing her.

"I'm going to go," she said. "I want to make sure everyone's out."

"They're out," he said. "Let's go."

She shook her head. "You go. I'll catch up."

"Rosealma, we're not doing this again," he said.

"Yes, we are," she said. "Get out *now*."

"I'm not leaving you," he said

"Oh, for God's sake," she said. "Get *out*."

And she shoved him. He lost his balance, his feet hitting the jar. It skittered across the floor, and she looked at it, wondering what would happen if the damn thing shattered.

He saw her. "Do we need that?"

"Aren't you listening?" she said. "You're supposed to leave everything behind."

"You didn't make the rules," he snapped.

She pointed up, even though she wasn't sure if the automated voice came from "up" or if it came from some other direction. It did rather feel like the Voice of God.

"Those aren't my rules," she said. "They're the station's. Now, hurry. I'll be right behind you."

"Promise me you won't do anything stupid, Rosealma," he said.

"When have I done anything stupid?" she asked, sounding calmer than she felt. Sometimes she thought that everything she had done was stupid. Hell, she knew that everything she had ever done was stupid. That was why she was here, to make up for the stupid, and it wasn't coming out so well.

"Rosealma—"

"*Go,*" she said.

He gave her an odd look and then hurried, half running, half walking down the corridor. Twice he glanced over his shoulder, as if he expected her to follow.

She didn't.

The corridor was emptying out. No one had run past in at least a minute. The damn sirens sounded even louder in the emptiness.

Emergency evacuation under way. Proceed to your designated evac area. . . .

"Shut up," she whispered, wishing she could shut the stupid voice down. But she didn't dare. She needed everyone off this station.

She needed everyone to live.

FIVE

*T*he mood on the skip was tense. The light was terrible. The tourist was lying next to the door, unconscious, blood covering his face. The three women running the dive stood near the control panel, looking down at him.

None of them wanted to help him. Rosealma knew that without consulting with the other two.

"He hasn't even gotten off the skip yet," Turtle said. She was thin and looked strange in her environmental suit. She hadn't put on the helmet, and without it, she really did look like a turtle.

She had gotten the nickname long before Rosealma met her, but Rosealma understood why the first time she'd seen Turtle in her environmental suit with her tiny head sticking out of it.

"Just because they have money doesn't mean they have brains," said the spacer-thin woman leading this little dive. She wouldn't tell anyone her name, insisting on being called Boss.

"Look," Rosealma said, squatting beside the stupid tourist. "I have some equipment. Let me see what I can do."

"We need to get him back." Boss ran a hand through her short cap of chestnut hair. "He needs a medic."

"I am a medic," Rosealma snapped.

Turtle looked at her in surprise. The two of them had been sleeping together for six months, and Rosealma hadn't told Turtle about her background. Or, rather, Rosealma hadn't told Turtle much about her background, including her medical training and her various scientific degrees.

"Then get to it," Boss said. "I don't think he'll appreciate getting an infection on top of losing the eye."

"He's not going to lose the eye." Rosealma grabbed the skip's medical kit from beside the control panel. Then she took her own tools from the bag she carried on every single trip.

"He's going to lose the eye," Boss said stubbornly, and she didn't sound sympathetic.

Rosealma wasn't sympathetic either. The guy really was an idiot. He had a tiny knife and he had been gesturing with it, explaining to Boss how he would cut just a small bit of the historic wreck as a souvenir, and how it wouldn't hurt the wreck at all.

Boss had gotten angry and told him that if he was going to cut up the wreck, then she wouldn't take him to it. He had leaned toward her, shaking that little knife, blade up, and said, *I'm paying you, honey, to take me to that wreck, and if you don't put me on it, then I'm not paying for anything.*

You already paid a deposit, Boss had said.

I'll take it back.

Just try, she had said, and smiled.

He had leaned toward her, waving that blade, and the skip had lurched just enough so that he had lost his footing. He had let out a little squeak and had fallen forward, the knife skittering out of his hand, leaving a tiny blood trail on the skip's floor.

Rosealma had glanced over her shoulder at the crucial moment. Turtle had been standing near the control panel, but she hadn't been touching it.

Or at least, she hadn't been touching it a moment after the skip lurched. What she'd been doing a second or two before the lurch no one would ever know.

"The idiot sliced through his own eyeball," Boss said.

"I don't know why you let him come on board with a weapon," Turtle said.

"I didn't," Boss said. "The thing was small enough for him to conceal."

"Doesn't matter," Rosealma said. "If you move away, I can help him."

"I almost wish you wouldn't," Boss said.

"Then you'll get sued," Rosealma said, although she didn't know if that was true.

She crouched over the stupid tourist, tilted his head back and cleaned the blood away from the eye. Then she used her handheld to magnify the eyeball.

Just like she thought. He had nicked it, making it bleed. Most of the blood came from the socket, not the eye itself.

She had an entire stash of lenses. Too many cases of laser blindness had made her cautious. The lenses would graft onto the eyeball and serve as a protection until the victim could get to a real medical facility.

Boss was watching. Turtle leaned over.

"Squishy," Turtle said.

"What?" Rosealma asked.

"It looks squishy. Is it?"

Boss uttered a shaky laugh and looked at Turtle. "For a minute, I thought you were calling her Squishy."

"Why not?" Rosealma muttered. "One name is the same as another."

She worked on the eye—and noted that it was a little squishy—but she didn't tell them that. Then she patched him up, but she didn't give him anything that would wake him. He needed to heal, and they didn't need to listen to his bluster. He wasn't going to get to dive his precious little historic wreck, and Rosealma doubted he would get his deposit back, no matter how hard he protested.

Boss turned the skip around and headed back to her larger ship, *Nobody's Business*. For the rest of the trip, Turtle called Rosealma "Squishy," and giggled.

The name stuck.

SIX

The corridor was empty. The sirens continued to wail, and the androgynous voice repeatedly informed Squishy that she had only five minutes to evacuate.

She reached down and grabbed that jar. It was warm. She wondered what the hell it actually was. She knew what it wasn't. It wasn't a functioning *anacapa* drive.

But it might have been a malfunctioning version of it, missing the various pieces that actually made the *anacapa* work.

She carried the jar to one of the side rooms and set it inside.

Then she took one last look around. It hadn't been a bad research station. The station had been well designed and well equipped, although all of the state-of-the-art protections, all of the one-of-a-kind technology couldn't help it now.

She tapped into the control panel on the wall, looking for heat signatures and individual life tags. Everyone who was supposed to be here was tagged, and should show up on the panel. Everyone who wasn't supposed to be here should show up as a heat signature.

She was the only heat signature and had the only tag. In a place that normally housed a thousand scientists, she was the only one who remained.

She let out a small sigh of relief.

The sirens sounded even louder than they had before, probably because the station was empty. All of the spaceships had left as well, except for her designated evacuation vessel. She opened its systems, checked to make sure it was empty, then shut it down.

Finally, she punched in an access code, opening previously sealed corridors, then sprinted out the door.

The androgynous voice accompanied her.

Emergency evacuation under way. Proceed to your designated evac area. . . .

She ran as fast as she could down the escape route she had set up more than a month before. She wasn't in the best shape any longer, even though she had made certain to exercise every day. It didn't matter. She couldn't run as fast as she used to.

She wondered if that would make a difference. Maybe she should have gone to her designated evac area.

As if to mock her, the androgynous voice was telling her:

. . . Do not double back. Go directly to your designated evac area. The station will shut down entirely in . . . five . . . minutes.

"Shut up," she whispered, using precious breath.

She skidded around the last corner, putting out a hand to catch herself, then headed to the last remaining ship.

It wasn't quite a single ship and it wasn't quite a skip. It was a modified cruiser, one she had designed herself and parked on the station when she first arrived months ago.

She reached into her pocket, clicked the ship's remote, and ordered it to start, hoping the station's systems did not prevent the remote access. She had set them up so that they wouldn't, but everything changed in an emergency.

. . . Do not finish your work. Do not bring your work. Once life tags move out of an area, that area will seal off. . . .

If she survived this, she would be hearing that stupid voice in her sleep. Small price, she supposed.

The doors were open to the docking area. The stupid voice was lying about everything being sealed off.

Well, not lying exactly. Unable to cope with directions Squishy had programmed long ago. She wanted *her* ship, not some designated evac vessel that she couldn't control. She hadn't even checked her dedicated evac vessel for supplies and provisions, although she made sure her cruiser was well stocked.

. . . The station will shut down entirely in . . . three . . . minutes.

She ran up the ramp. The door to the ship, which she had rechristened the *Dane* in a fit of whimsy, stood open. She hurried inside, slammed the lock, shot through the airlock and into the ship itself.

Only two meters to the command chair, and she crossed those faster than she had run through the corridors. She slammed her open palm on the controls, recited the Old Earth Standard nonsense poem she had learned in the last year, and the controls came on.

Then she hit the preprogrammed escape plan and the ship roared into life. It rose and headed toward the docking doors faster than they were opening.

She cursed and hoped there was some kind of failsafe for those doors, because she didn't want to slow down and she didn't want to hit them and she certainly didn't want to be here with the station about to blow.

At the last second, the doors slammed open (or, at least, she thought they slammed—they shook the wall as they hit it, which had to sound like slamming, although she couldn't hear it), and then she was free of the place.

The *Dane* zoomed away from the station as fast as the ship could safely go without hitting FTL. She turned the screens onto the station itself, imagined that snarky automated voice continuing its countdown to the now-empty station:

The station will shut down entirely in . . . five . . . four . . . three . . . two . . . one. . . .

She raised her head, expecting to see the station blow into a million pieces. Instead it remained intact, and she wondered if she had gotten her count wrong. She hadn't really been paying attention to the clock. She'd been running, not counting minutes.

Her heart was pounding and she was breathing hard. Her palm had left a damp print on the controls.

She stared at the screens and wondered, for the very first time, if she had gotten it all wrong.

SEVEN

NINETEEN AND A HALF YEARS EARLIER

*T*he woman sitting at the edge of the bar wasn't pretty. She was too thin, her head too small, her features not clearly defined. She wasn't even a woman—not quite, anyway. She was probably eighteen if she was a day, but she pretended to be older, and that had caught Rosealma's attention.

That, and the woman's brownish-blond hair. The hair was choppy, clearly cut by the woman herself. The woman's long fingers were wrapped around a mug of some kind of ale, and she looked lonely.

Maybe it was the loneliness that caught Rosealma. Or maybe it was the woman's sideways glances. Rosealma tried not to watch her, but there was something, something interesting, the first interesting thing Rosealma had seen since she left Vallevu.

The bar was old and seedy, the space station not much better. Rosealma had used the last of her hazard pay to get here, and really didn't want to leave. She had placed six months' rent on a berth that wasn't much more than a bed, an entertainment wall, and an unlimited supply of reading material from the station's rather eclectic (and ancient) library.

The woman glanced at her again, and Rosealma lifted her own mug of ale in a kind of toast. The woman smiled. She tilted her head sideways as she did so, as if she couldn't quite believe she had caught another person's attention. She might even have been blushing.

The bar owner, who was also the bartender, shouted at someone near the entrance, something about nonpayment of a bill. Rosealma didn't listen. Out here, everyone was short of money, and everyone wanted something for nothing.

She found it was easier to remain quiet about everything, to be ignored rather than draw attention to herself. She had come as close to disappearing as a human being could without actually losing her identity and starting all over.

The woman at the end of the bar glanced at Rosealma again, then looked at the seat next to her.

Rosealma's breath caught. She wasn't sure if she should walk over. If she had a flirtation with the woman, then she would be noticed, and everything would change.

Still, she hadn't had a real conversation in six months, and surprisingly, she missed talking. Not about trivial things like the quality of the ale or the best place to eat for the fewest credits, but about ideas and politics and science and the things that people talked about when they were laughing and relaxing with each other.

She missed interaction, and she had never thought she would.

She sighed, stood, and grabbed her mug of ale.

Then the lights flickered out, and her stomach fluttered. She recognized the moment as it happened: the gravity had changed. The lights came back on just as she floated upward, her ale floating with her, the glass emptying and beads of liquid dotting everything around her.

No one screamed like they would have had this been planetside, although a few people cursed as their beverages took on a life of their own. The chairs and tables were bolted down, but the mugs weren't, and neither was the ice or the bar snacks or the lemons, olives, and cherries.

She and everyone else in the bar were in the middle of a mess, which would only get worse when the gravity returned to normal.

Behind her, the bar owner shouted, "You son of a bitch!" and that was when she realized that the gravity change wasn't some kind of malfunction; it had been planned, probably to get money out of the bar owner.

She glanced at the woman and was startled to see how lovely she looked, her hair spiking upward, her long limbs gangly no longer. The woman looked at home in zero-g, as if floating was her preferred method of travel.

She used the tops of chairs to slowly propel herself toward Rosealma.

"It looks like there's trouble," the woman said, glancing toward the main entrance. The bar owner was shaking his fist, propelling himself backward as he did so, probably the only person in the entire bar who wasn't used to zero-g.

Rosealma couldn't tell which of the people floating around him had made him angry, and she really didn't want to find out. She smiled at the woman.

"I'm Rosealma."

The woman's eyebrows went up, giving her smile a wry cynicism. "Wow, that's a mouthful. You don't have a nickname?"

"Do I need one?" Rosealma asked.

"Everyone out here has a nickname. It's easier."

"Easier?"

"Yeah," the woman said. "That way we don't have to clarify which Rose or Alma we're talking about. We don't need last names or even first names. We're just too damn lazy anyway."

And then she laughed. The laugh was raspy and deep, and Rosealma realized that the woman hadn't been eighteen for a long time. She was at least in her mid-twenties, maybe older, and she had seen as much or more than Rosealma had.

"What's your nickname?" Rosealma asked.

"Turtle," the woman said. "You know what a turtle is?"

"Some kind of Earth creature."

"Earth hell," Turtle said. "The little ones are all the way out here. Some ships have them as mascots."

"You're someone's mascot?"

Turtle grinned at her. "Nah. I look like a turtle."

"You don't," Rosealma said, although she wasn't exactly sure what a turtle looked like. "You're the prettiest thing in this bar."

Turtle smiled and tilted her head again. Her cheeks did turn red. "You be careful," she said, "or I'll start thinking you're flirting with me."

"Maybe I am flirting," Rosealma said, startled at her own boldness.

Turtle's smile grew. "Then we should get out of this bar before the gravity changes. It's going to be a mess and I'll feel obligated to clean it up."

"I don't feel obligated to anything," Rosealma said. Which wasn't true, of course. She felt obligated for everything, and sorry for even more, and the weight of everything—from the regrets to the losses to the destruction of all of her dreams—threatened to crash her to the floor quicker than a gravity change.

"So you're running away," Turtle said. Her tone was businesslike, not curious. She wasn't asking a question, just stating a fact.

"No," Rosealma said. "You have to care to run away."

Turtle studied her for a moment, the smile gone. Then she nodded once. "Well, then, I need to run away from this bar." She extended her hand. "You want to come along?"

Rosealma looked at Turtle's hand, with its long fingers and visibly chewed cuticles. Rosealma took it almost before she realized she had made a decision.

"Let's go," she said, "and never look back."

Turtle raised their joined hands. "Deal," she said.

EIGHT

The station blew.

It started in the middle. A glow built, then expanded. The center disappeared in the light, and that's when Squishy realized it was imploding.

She stared at the screen in the *Dane* for just a moment. The silence in the cockpit was profound. She could hear her own breathing, and it sounded raspy. The *Dane* was cold—she had just gotten here, just started it up, just moved away from the station—

—and she hadn't moved far enough. In her desire to see the station explode, she had put herself at risk. God knows what would happen when that place went, with all the malfunctioning stealth tech on board. How many interdimensional rifts would open? How many pulses would plume along with the debris?

She slammed her palm on the control panel, her fingers grasping for the FTL command. It took four movements to launch FTL, and her shaking hand made all four hard. It felt like the movements took forever, even though it probably only took a few seconds. Still, she had to get out of here.

The *Dane* winked out, the images vanishing from the screen, and as they did, she collapsed in the command chair, hands to her face. Her heart was pounding, and she was feeling just a little queasy.

She had pulled it off, and no one died.

"You want to explain to me what the fuck just happened?"

The male voice made her jump. She had thought she was alone. She had *assumed* she was alone. She hadn't even checked to see if anyone had gotten into the *Dane*. The *Dane* would have masked a heat signature from the station's control board. She would have had to ask the *Dane* as she got into the airlock, and she had been in such a hurry, she hadn't thought of it.

She was such an idiot.

She dropped her hands slowly, making herself breathe as she did so. She wanted to seem calmer than she was, even though he had seen her jump.

She recognized the voice—how could she not? She had lived with it for years, and when she heard it again, even after the loss of decades, it was as if she had never been away from him.

Quint.

She turned her chair toward him.

He leaned against the entrance to the cockpit, arms crossed. He had probably explored the entire ship, not that there was much to see. Two cabins, a full galley, some storage, and of course, the area she called the mechanicals, where most of the things that ran the cruiser or helped its passengers survive lived.

She hadn't checked any of it. She had assumed that her locks would hold, that no one would access this ship. She certainly hadn't expected anyone to get on it in the middle of a crisis.

Her mistake.

She felt it in the small cockpit. Even though he stood at the entrance, he wasn't that far away from her. He had seen her stare at the screens, heard her raspy breathing, saw her momentary panic.

And he knew her well enough to know what all of it meant.

She knew him well too, and she had never quite seen him like this. Blood had dried on his face, black and crusty, outlining the wrinkles he had allowed to appear on his skin over the decades. He had managed—in his escape from the station—to find his uniform jacket. It covered the ripped shirt, although she could still see bits of fabric folded strangely across his chest.

He probably hadn't looked at his reflection. He probably didn't realize the blood was still on his face, if he had even known it was on his face in the first place.

The fact that he was on her ship surprised her. Not because he had figured out it was hers, but because it took some stones to avoid the evac ships and wait for her, stones she hadn't realized he had.

She hadn't answered his question. He raised his eyebrows, silently asking it again.

"The station blew up," she said. "Or it was blowing up, just like we knew it would. I just hit the FTL. The last thing we want is to be near that part of space. There's a good chance that explosion could open an interdimensional rift."

He frowned. "A what?"

She almost smiled, but she didn't. She had distracted him. He hadn't really been asking about the station before.

"An interdimensional rift." She swallowed. "The stealth tech was unstable."

"It's always been unstable," he snapped. "You know that better than most."

She nodded. She did know it better than most. That was why she had come here in the first place. But she wasn't going to tell him that. At least, not yet.

"Yes, I do know that," she said. "But this time, the entire research station paid the price instead of a few volunteers."

"A few . . ." His face turned red. She had forgotten about that reaction he had until just now. She had made him angry. It was amazing that she still knew what buttons to push after decades apart. He finally managed, "It wasn't a few."

She knew that. It had been hundreds of people, most of whom hadn't volunteered at all, unless their induction into the Enterran military counted as volunteering.

They had fought about this before, the two of them. She still remembered every word of those fights.

"This time no one died in the unstable stealth tech," she said.

"That you know of," he said.

"No," she said. "I know this for a fact. No one died."

He glared at her. He didn't believe her.

He never had.

NINE

Warning sirens whooped. Rosealma recognized the sound from the drills. Something had gone wrong in the science lab.

Her lab.

She raced across campus, across the sidewalks, and through the gathering crowd in front of the Ancient and Lost Technology Building. Somehow she had grabbed her identification out of her pocket while she ran and clutched it in her left hand.

Guards stood in front of her holding laser rifles.

She had never seen weapons on campus before, and they frightened her more than the alarms did.

The day was sunny and bright, the grass bright blue just like it was supposed to be. The weather warm, the air fresh. Only the sirens marred the perfection.

She held up her identification. It was supposed to get her into any lab connected with Ancient Technologies, and it should definitely get her into this lab. This was her lab. She was one of the research assistants.

"I work in that building," she said, trying to sound brave. "What's going on?"

The guards didn't answer her, at least not directly. They glared at her. She had never seen people look so fierce. They held their laser rifles sideways, blocking her passage. Other graduate students arrived, running from all parts of campus, just like Rosealma had.

"What the hell?" someone asked behind her, but no one answered.

The building looked normal. Its windowless black façade reflected the other buildings around it, just like it always had. She expected to see some kind of cataclysm through the blackness, something that would indicate what kind of problem she faced.

If she knew what the problem was, she could solve it.

Or she could try.

Guards couldn't try. Guards had no idea how to solve problems. She had learned that on the *Bounty*, the cargo ship she had grown up on. Guards were just there to protect things or to prevent something, not to solve anything.

"Please," she said, stepping closer. "Let me in. I can help."

She couldn't quite understand what had gone wrong here. There were several such laboratory buildings on campus. Ancient and Lost Technologies was not the most dangerous lab on campus. Not even close. In fact, the most dangerous labs weren't on campus at all, but in a small industrial park several kilometers away, covered with protective domes and barriers in case anything bad happened.

Nothing encased the Ancient and Lost Technologies Lab Building. There was no need. Everything they did here was in the name of history more than in the name of science. The experiments that occurred here were hopeful experiments designed to recover lost knowledge, without any real chance of that happening.

Or so she had been led to believe. That was part of the speech she had heard when she accepted the post-doc to work in stealth tech. She was told they might discover something that could aid ships in the region in their cloaking, but probably not. Not unless they actually found some kind of schematic from a Dignity Vessel or from the technology the vessels left behind.

And no matter how hard scholars like Professor Dane searched, they hadn't found anything like that.

"Seriously," Rosealma said to the guards. "Let me in. I work here."

Then Quint showed up. He was breathing hard, and his handsome face was red. His cropped black hair glistened with sweat. He had been running from a long distance away. He had a class clear on the other side of campus. She had teased him about it when they left his dorm room that morning.

He didn't say anything. Instead, he put his gigantic arm around her shoulder, pulling her close, pulling her away from the weapons. He smelled so sharply of fear that she turned her head.

"Let it go," Quint said softly. "It's not our business."

"But it *is*," Rosealma said. "Something's wrong in there."

He pulled her back farther. She stumbled against him, struggling as he moved her. She didn't want to go backward. She wanted inside. She wanted to make sure everything was all right.

His hand clamped hard on the soft skin of her upper arm. "Stop fighting me."

She wasn't fighting him. She just didn't want to move.

"We shouldn't be going away," she said. "We should help."

He stopped and held her beside him. He looked more serious than she had ever seen him. The expression on his face held her in place more than his hands did.

"Look at those guards," he said. "They're not campus security."

"The hell they aren't," she said. "They're in the building all the time. Of course they're campus police."

"God," he said, his voice lowered to a whisper, almost as if he was talking to himself. "Sometimes I forget how sheltered you were."

"Sheltered?" She raised her voice. If anyone had been sheltered, it had been him. She had been all over the sector before her fifth birthday. She knew more about the sector than anyone at the school, more than her professors, more than her fellow students. If someone mentioned some place in class, chances were Rosealma had been there, and no one else had. "I'm not sheltered."

"Wrong word, then," he said in a tone that told her he didn't believe that. He was just placating her. "Sometimes I forget you don't know a lot about the Empire."

She was going to argue—she would have argued vociferously (she loved arguing with him), if it wasn't for the sirens. She had never heard them outside of a drill in any place planetside. On a ship, they meant the worst kind of disaster.

Here, she had no idea. So he was right about that, at least.

"What do you mean?" she asked.

"The guards are not campus security," he said. "They're military. Don't you recognize the uniforms?"

Her people avoided uniforms. They avoided the Empire as much as they could, even though they worked within it. They followed the regulations, of course, because that enabled them to travel long distances on their cargo ship without interference. The Empire was an annoyance, like the small governments that made up the Empire were annoyances. Regulations that changed from port to port, type of cargo to type of cargo, docking regulation to docking regulation, inspection to inspection. Nothing more.

"No," she said softly. "I don't recognize the uniforms."

He cursed under his breath, then shook his head. "You've been working on a project for the Empire's military wing and you had no idea that's who funded you?"

Her stomach clenched. The sirens continued. More and more people were arriving, crowding them. More guards came out of the building.

She stared at their uniforms. Green and gold, with piping along the sleeves. Laser rifles so new they had a shine. Men and women her age, no older, muscular in the way of the planet bound, their expressions flat and serious.

The imperial military? She had heard horror stories about them, about the way they could just take over a ship, even a ship as large as the one she had been raised on, but she had never seen them before.

Or, to be more accurate, she had never realized that she had seen them before. She had seen them in various places all over the sector, hanging back, holding weapons.

She remembered asking her father as he tightly held her hand in a docking bay who those uniformed people were near the door into some starbase whose name she had long forgotten.

Baby, he had said in that tone of his, the one that meant "ask me later," *they're just guards.*

He had been right; technically he had been right. They had been guards. Just not the kind she thought. And she had never asked him about them again—or maybe she had in the same kind of circumstance and he had given the same kind of answer.

She had been so young then, and there was so much she hadn't questioned. Things happened, and that was just the way life was. The way *her* life was.

So when she saw them here, she had made an assumption, based on long-ago information.

Baby, they're just guards.

Yes, they were, but not harmless campus security guards.

Members of the Enterran Empire Military, the fearsome military that shut down entire cargo routes without warning, and fired on ships that didn't follow the proper protocol.

"They don't fund me," she said to Quint, only because arguing was her default mode, and she needed time to think. "They fund my professors."

She was looking at the guards. They seemed different now, now that she understood who they were. She was having trouble catching her breath.

She had worked for the military? Really? And no one had told her?

"Who do you think wants stealth tech?" Quint asked softly.

She looked at him. She didn't answer him, because she couldn't. She had been doing it for the *Bounty*, for all of the cargo monkeys. But they wouldn't be able to have stealth tech, not if the tech was owned by the military. They wouldn't want any commercial ship, any nonmilitary vessel to have a tool like that.

She leaned her head forward and rested it on Quint's shoulder. She felt stupid, something that she hadn't felt since she arrived here all those years ago.

He put both of his arms around her and held her close. He probably had no idea what she was feeling, probably thought she was upset about the sirens and not getting into the building, and she *was*, but the fact that she had missed the implications of everything, that disturbed her even more.

Then the sirens shut off.

She lifted her head. Her ears rang, and for a moment, she seemed to be hearing an echo of the sirens, as if sound could linger in the air long after the source shut off.

Her heart continued to race.

She turned. She and Quint were in a crowd of maybe two hundred people now. All of them had gathered because of the noise, and now fidgeted because the noise had stopped.

A woman came out of the building and stood on the steps. Rosealma had seen her before too. She was the director of the Experimental Lost Technologies Unit. She was squat and blond, her hair frizzed as if she had forgotten to comb it. She was much older than Rosealma, in that middle-age range where Rosealma couldn't even guess a decade. Not elderly, but old. Mature. Adult.

The director held up her hands for calm. It took a moment, but the entire crowd turned toward her and became completely silent.

Quint's arm tightened around Rosealma, but she didn't lean into him or put her arm around him. Instead she stood stiffly beside him.

"We've had a situation here," the director said, her voice hoarse. "I can't yet explain it. I'm not sure I understand it. We do need scientists, doctoral candidates and post-docs to come inside. If you've been working in this building, please show your pass. Only the people involved in this particular experiment will get through. We will answer everyone else's questions as soon as we know what's going on."

"Is everyone inside all right?" someone shouted from the back.

The director looked even more tired than she had a moment ago. "I am not taking questions at this moment."

Rosealma's breath caught. The director deliberately did not answer the question that could have soothed the crowd. Which meant something had happened, something serious.

But why not answer that question? Either everyone was fine or someone wasn't. People were wounded, people were grievously injured, or people were dead.

There was no in-between.

Yet a feeling prickled against the back of her neck, a sense of foreboding that she couldn't quite will away.

The crowd was separating. Those who didn't have a pass to the building were stepping back. The others were queuing up. The guards were scanning the passes, letting in only a few people.

The director had gone back inside the building.

"Come on," Rosealma said to Quint.

He didn't move for a long moment. "I don't like this," he said.

"Me, either," she said, "but I think they need all the help they can get."

"If they don't know what's going on, then how do they know it's safe?" he asked.

She gave him a sideways glance. He wasn't looking at her. He was staring at the building as if it could give him answers.

"Don't you want to know what's going on?" she asked.

"Not at the risk of our lives," he said.

She turned inside his arm so that she could face him. "What does that mean?"

"It means that we're just lowly post-docs, working on something that isn't even ours. We don't need to risk our lives because someone says we must."

She tilted her head as if she had never seen him before.

"I'm going in," she said, and slipped out of his embrace.

TEN

Squishy's heart was pounding, and she had trouble catching her breath. The physical reaction made sense. She had just fled a research station, run to her ship, and gotten it out of the area as the station blew. She should have been shaking with the release of adrenaline, but Quint's presence prevented that.

She'd had an adrenaline surge just a few minutes ago when she saw him standing in the door of the cockpit. She still hadn't gotten used to him, even though she had been working near him for six months.

He hadn't moved, except to glare at her.

She felt defensive. He always made her feel defensive. It was all she could do not to move in front of the control panel, blocking him from it. She had to do her best to keep up the pretense of calm.

She had already pushed one of his buttons; he could just as easily push one of hers. And maybe he was.

"I know for a fact that no one died when that station blew," she said. "That's why I left last. I made the computer system check for anyone else."

"And if someone else was on that station, what would you have done?" he asked.

She stared at him. She had worried about that. As she had been scanning for heat signatures and identification tags, she had worried about that. Scientists didn't always listen to instructions, but apparently these had.

At least about the evacuation.

He crossed his arms. "Tell me, Rosealma. You only had five minutes left. What would you have done?"

He would keep pressing her until she answered him. He had always done that, and she had always hated it.

"Something," she said, knowing her answer was inadequate, knowing that it was probably wrong. What would she have done? What could she have done?

At that point, nothing. Maybe opened a few corridors, prayed that whom-ever was trapped had gotten out on their own. Could have gotten out on their own.

He rolled his eyes. "'Something.'" That word had more sarcasm in it than any he'd uttered so far. And Quint was good at sarcasm. "Don't lie to me, Rosealma. You wouldn't have done anything. You couldn't. There wouldn't have been time. You would have run to your little escape route and hoped for the best."

It was her turn to flush. She made herself breathe so that he couldn't see any other anger response from her. She was as angry at him as she had been the day she left.

And if someone had asked her just two days before if the anger against him had faded, she would have said yes.

Amazing how all of the old patterns came back as if time hadn't passed at all. Time was such a strange thing—fluid and rigid all at once, existing in different dimensions at different speeds, and yet happening right now, this instant, moving forward, never backward.

"How come you didn't go to your evac ship?" she asked, then felt a moment of panic. His ship hadn't waited for him. Had it?

She made herself take another deep breath. It hadn't. She had checked, made certain that all of the evac ships had left before she had.

She wondered if he saw the thought flicker across her face. It had been decades, but he still knew her too. And it was taking him a long time to respond to her question.

"I wanted to make sure you got out," he said.

"Don't lie to me, Quint," she said in the exact same tone he had used.

He tilted his head. The expression used to be attractive on his unlined, youthful face. On his older, blood-covered face, it was a bit ghoulish.

"I'm not lying to you, Rose. If you'll remember, I tried to get you out earlier."

"I do remember," she snapped, "and I told you to leave. You did. But you didn't go to your evac ship, and now I want to know why."

His face was expressionless. He did that when he had an emotional reac-tion that he didn't want anyone to know about.

"What if I hadn't come to this ship?" she asked. "You would have died. This ship is tied to me. You couldn't have gotten it out of the station."

"But you did come," he said softly.

And he had known she would. She had asked the wrong question. The answer to her initial question was simple: he had come here because of her. What she should have asked was this: How had he known she would be here?

She stared at him, feeling a tug. She wanted to continue the fight—it was familiar, it was comfortable, it was how they related—but she also wanted to get him the hell off of this ship. She had no idea who he really was now. She had changed a lot in two-plus decades. He probably had too.

"The ship is registered to you, Rose," he said after a moment.

She felt her breath catch. She hadn't expected him to answer her.

"You still use my name," he said.

She shrugged a single shoulder. He found her use of his last name significant. It wasn't. She used his last name because it was her last name, at least in the Empire. Quintana. Young and naïve and supposedly in love, she had taken his name and had become the wife of Edward Quintana, better known as Quint. He had had a nickname then. She hadn't.

She swiveled her chair away from him and looked at the control panel. She tapped the coordinates, altering them. She couldn't go to the rendezvous point, nor could she go back to the Nine Planets Alliance, not with him on board.

Fortunately, she hadn't been in touch with any of the others since she started her work at the research station.

She hoped they had gotten their jobs done. Some of it she knew they had completed—the off-site backup site had gone down on time—and some of it she wouldn't know if anything changed, not if she didn't get in touch with them.

It was hard to destroy all of the modern research on stealth tech. She knew she would miss a lot of it. But that was why she had decided to blow the facility, why she figured it had to be destroyed from the inside out.

Before she had planted the explosives, she had planted information that showed how flawed stealth tech was, and would lead anyone who investigated to believe that the tech itself caused the explosions.

Which, technically, it had.

She wasn't quite sure where to go, so she programmed in a space station at the edge of Enterran space.

"You changing our course, Rose?"

"Just making sure it's correct," she said, feeling a bit breathless. It was hard to lie to him, just like it had always been. Her cheeks warmed. Somewhere inside her was that young girl who thought she had fallen in love.

"Tell me what really happened on the research station," he said.

"I don't know," she said, not facing him. If she faced him, he would see the lie. "Some kind of chain reaction is my guess. There should have been better protections for working with stealth tech."

"Scientists have worked on stealth tech for years," he said. "No research station has ever blown up."

Not the entire station. But parts of a previous station had blown apart. He had conveniently forgotten that.

"Scientists had never had a dedicated site to work on stealth tech before," she said. "I suspect that was the mistake."

"Why?" There was something in his voice, something new. He didn't trust her.

Of course he didn't trust her. She had left him, then divorced him. She had never given him the courtesy of an explanation. She always figured he knew.

Only when she got older, and her relationship with Turtle decayed, did she realize that each person experienced the relationship differently. He probably hadn't understood what happened, any more than Squishy could explain why her relationship with Turtle died on a disastrous dive with Boss ten years ago.

"Why would that be a mistake, Rosealma?" His voice sounded strangled, as if he were trying to pull the emotion from it.

"I believe stealth tech builds on itself." Or at least, the kind of stealth tech the Empire was developing. They were only working on one small part of what turned out to be a powerful drive used by the Dignity Vessels. The *anacapa* drive was dangerous in experienced hands. In inexperienced hands, it was deadly.

As she had learned repeatedly over the years.

"And your belief is based on what, exactly?" Quint asked.

She swallowed hard. She didn't want to answer that honestly.

"I came back to stealth-tech research a few years ago," she said.

"When you left Vallevu?" he asked.

She turned, surprised. He hadn't moved, arms still crossed, head still slightly tilted.

"I still have friends there too, you know," he said.

She hadn't even thought of that. She could have kept up on him in the two years she lived there without him, but she hadn't even tried. He wasn't someone she thought about. She didn't want to think about him, even with him standing right there.

"Yes," she said tightly. "After I left Vallevu."

"I couldn't find you anywhere after that," he said.

"I didn't realize you were looking," she said, refusing to be relieved. She didn't want him to know she had gone to the Nine Planets Alliance. She didn't want to tell him anything.

He shrugged. "The Empire had no record of your work after you got discharged."

"You checked," she said, feeling cold.

"When you got here," he said, "you better believe I checked. You'd taken up a medical practice on Vallevu. I had no idea why you were back in stealth tech. I'm still not sure I believe it, not after so long an absence."

"Sometimes the Empire doesn't keep records about its researchers," she said.

"I can access most records," he said. "Even the ones they don't keep."

She felt cold. "You can't follow everything."

"I can try," he said.

Her heart was racing. He wasn't threatening her, was he? Was he here because he knew what she'd been doing, because he understood that her purpose on the station hadn't been benign?

For the first time, she wasn't exactly sure how to handle him.

She had to give him something. She wasn't sure why; she just knew that she did.

"I worked salvage for a while. I gave the Empire a mostly intact Dignity Vessel back then. If you check the records, you'll find it."

He continued to watch her, as if he didn't entirely believe her. If he mentioned that the same Dignity Vessel had exploded about two years later, then she would know she was in real trouble.

Instead, he sighed and let his arms fall to his side. "Salvage, Rose?"

It was her turn to shrug. "Once a cargo monkey, always a cargo monkey," she said with less levity than she had planned.

"Still," he said, "someone as brilliant as you shouldn't work salvage."

"I needed time off from being brilliant," she said. "Being brilliant kills people."

"And working salvage doesn't?"

She thought back to the dive that had caused her to break up with Turtle, the dive that had cost the lives of two other divers because Boss hadn't believed that Squishy had known what she was talking about. Squishy had known that the Dignity Vessel they had found was dangerous, and Boss wouldn't listen. The deaths weren't the worst of it. The deaths had simply been a symptom of the way that stealth tech—imperial stealth tech—seemed to drive everyone insane.

"Do you ever hate your life, Quint?" Squishy asked.

He studied her for a few minutes. She could see him trying out and discarding several answers, including the first one—the truthful one, whatever that may have been.

"No, I don't hate my life," he said. "Why?"

Because, if he regretted all he had done, they could talk.

But he didn't, and she knew that meant trouble.

"How come you didn't evacuate with everyone else, Rosealma?" Quint asked.

"I did evacuate," she said. "I'm alive, just like you are."

He shook his head. "You had an escape route planned. You came to this ship, not to your evac ship."

"So did you," she said.

"You know what I mean," he said.

She ran her hand along the edge of the control panel. This cruiser felt small with two people in it. She really wanted to get rid of him, but she didn't know how. Drop him off somewhere? Dump him into one of the escape pods? Ask him politely to leave?

"What are you implying?" she asked, tired of the dance. "Are you implying that I was behind what happened?"

"Were you?" he asked.

The question hurt, even though it was logical. Even though she had been behind it.

"How dare you ask me that?" she said softly. "How dare you? After all we've been through, why wouldn't I have my own escape planned? Why wouldn't I plan for disaster? I figured I'd be running out of that facility at top speed at one point or another, and in no way was I going to trust a ship attached to the research station, under computer control of that station. I figured I'd only get one chance to save myself, and I was going to do it my way."

Quint stopped leaning on the doorway. He ran a hand over his face, his fingers stopping as they hit the dried blood. He seemed startled by it, then took a shaky breath.

"If that's how you felt, why did you come back?" he asked.

"Because I couldn't stay away," she said. "I know more than most people. And I couldn't let other scientists stumble around in the dark."

"Yet the results were worse than before," he said.

She shook her head and said again, "No one died this time."

"You could argue that no one died before," he said.

"You could argue it," she said. "But you would be wrong."

ELEVEN

*T*he research station was a marvel. Squishy hadn't seen anything that big or that well constructed before. It extended as far as the eye could see. When she brought the *Dane* into the station, she had watched through the portholes, amazed that this gigantic thing before her was man-made. Huge, black, extending in all directions, the station looked like a maze designed to confuse children, with rings around various levels, and labs isolated in wings so far from the main part of the station that there was only one way to access them.

At that moment, she thought her task impossible. Later, as she got used to the place, she realized it wasn't.

But that moment of entry, that moment when she walked into the station alone, she wondered if she was strong enough.

That feeling remained until she realized that even the largest, most well-built thing could be brought down, usually by its own flaws.

The first flaw? The Empire's belief in credentials. Hers were still valid, still respected, despite the twenty years since her discharge from the imperial military. She was considered one of the pioneers of stealth tech, and as such, the researchers were happy to have her back into the fold. They were pleased that she had returned and saw it as a happy accident, one that would enable them to make the breakthrough they had always strived for.

Her time in Vallevu had served her well. After Squishy had left Boss's team the first time, she had come home—or what she thought of as home—to the former military base where she had first been stationed. Back then, the families lived on the planet below for safety's sake, and that part had worked.

No one in the families had died. But they all got scarred so badly that the Empire actually took pity on them, decommissioned the base, sold them the land, and gave them enough money to fund the community, so long as they never talked to anyone about what happened. It made the small community of Vallevu wary of outsiders, but Squishy hadn't been an outsider. Not when she limped home, defeated and ruined, her second attempt at a career ending in death just like the first.

Her years in Vallevu, both times—before and after—allowed the Empire to track her life. Or to track it enough to believe it understood her. It thought she had gone into space to clear her head, then returned to her work. Her second time in Vallevu had been as a doctor, not a stealth scientist, but she had done some research into the effects of loss on communities, and she had published her work.

That loss study, done with the permission of the people she lived with, had focused on Vallevu, the loss she dealt with, the loss of stealth-tech researchers.

Squishy's entire life had been tied to stealth tech, more than the Empire realized.

And she hated stealth tech, more than the Empire realized.

If they had known that, they never would have allowed her within a thousand light-years of this place. Instead, they invited her on board, claimed to be happy to have her, and gave her one of the best offices in the entire place.

First she got assigned a division to help her get up to speed on the current thinking in stealth tech. She had to restrain herself. Stealth-tech researchers in the Empire were going in the wrong direction. They thought stealth tech was merely a cloak, something that would take a ship out of time for a second and then bring it back. Or maybe even take the ship out of phase just enough that it could still see the area around it without interacting with that area.

They had no idea that the cloaking aspects of stealth tech were a side effect of a much more powerful technology, one that flew Dignity Vessels for thousands of years, one that enabled them to travel over distances that the Empire simply couldn't imagine in time that seemed almost miraculous.

She couldn't tell anyone here that, and she didn't want to.

Not even when she realized Quint worked here.

She hadn't checked the employee manifest at the station before she arrived, partly because she was afraid if she saw the names of old colleagues, she would abort the mission.

She couldn't abort. Too many others had taken a leave of absence from Lost Souls to run important aspects of the mission—dangerous aspects—in other parts of the Empire.

If she failed her job, their risks would have been for nothing.

And when she saw them at the rendezvous point, she would have to face them, telling them why she had failed.

She didn't want to fail. This was her idea, after all.

Although two days into her mission, she wondered if she was crazy, when she sat in the spectacular office the station had given her. The office was in the very center of the administrative wing, with a 360-degree view of the interior of the station itself. If she looked out the clear panels, she could see scientists at work in their offices or in their labs. Only the top secret areas were blocked off.

If she wanted to, she could open the privacy tiles on her ceiling, so that she could see the labs and rings above her. The idea of others looking down on her unnerved her, so she kept the ceiling privacy tiles closed, even though she didn't plan to keep her work hidden from anyone here.

Her mission was twofold: she had to gain everyone's trust, and she had to destroy the station. The whole station, not a part of it, not a wing. Everything had to be obliterated.

And she had to do it by herself, without losing a single life.

Sometimes that felt impossible, and sometimes she thought she was the only person in the entire universe who could pull it off.

She was thinking it was all impossible on her second day, as she unpacked what meager belongings she had brought with her—mostly her medical tchotchkes and some artwork she had kept from the children in Vallevu. She initially put the art out, but it made her sad, so she was in the process of repacking it when a man ducked his head into her office.

"Bet you never expected to see me again."

She turned, and her breath caught. Quint. She hadn't seen him in twenty years. Those years had aged him. He had thickened. His face had worry lines that accented his cheekbones and made him traditionally handsome. His hair remained black, and his eyes, while tired, were still just as dark and just as mysterious.

She hadn't expected to see him again. She didn't want to ever see him again. And apparently he knew that, or he wouldn't have made that statement.

Still, she wasn't going to take the bait. He wanted her off balance, scared or angry. She was off balance, but she had been off balance before he arrived.

She wasn't scared or angry. She had bested Quint more than once. She could do it again.

"If I had expected to see you again, it wouldn't have been here," she said.

"I hadn't expected to see you here either," he said, then stepped farther into the room.

She wanted to remind him that she hadn't invited him in, and then tell him that he wasn't welcome. But she didn't do that.

Instead she quietly watched him as he made his way around the room, glancing at the other chairs, the view, and the personal items she had just started to put out.

He used to hate silence. She wondered if he still did.

After a moment, she got her answer. He returned to his spot near the door. He pushed it so that it closed most of the way. Anyone who passed in the hall would understand that they were having a semi-private conversation and wouldn't listen in.

Since all of the chairs had something on them, he crossed his arms and leaned against the wall.

"So," he said, "how do we play this? As the friendly exes who occasionally share a beer or as the exes who can't stand the sight of each other and avoid each other at all costs?"

She let her gaze sweep over him as she assessed him. Even though he had thickened up, he hadn't let himself get out of shape. If anything, he looked more muscular than he ever had. He also looked like he had lost his sense of humor somewhere and hadn't bothered to retrieve it. His words could have been construed as light and flirtatious if his tone had matched.

It hadn't.

He meant the question, and he wanted to hear her answer.

"Is there something between beer and hatred?" she asked.

He leaned his head back so that his skull brushed the wall. He was leaning against the last privacy panel before the wall opened into her spectacular view. The clear panels reflected him over and over again, see-through versions of Quint lining one side of the room.

"You don't hate me, then?" Somehow he didn't sound vulnerable when he asked the question. "The last time we saw each other, I got the impression that you did."

"We last saw each other twenty years ago, Quint," she said. "I don't know you anymore. I have no idea who you are now."

"Really?" he asked. "Do you think people can change so much they're unrecognizable to each other?"

She studied him for a long moment. He still had no clue what had happened between them, and she didn't feel like enlightening him.

"Twenty years is a long time, Quint," she said. "I have no idea what you've done during that time. I didn't even know you would be here."

"Really?" he asked. "You didn't check the station manifest before you arrived?"

"Should I have done that?" she asked. "What would it have gained me, besides learning that you were here?"

He didn't respond for the longest time. Instead, he watched her. She wasn't sure what he was studying her for. Was he comparing the old her to the new her? Or was he trying to unnerve her?

Or both?

Then she realized he had unnerved her. She had been thinking about the past, and not the present.

"What are you doing in my office anyway?" she asked. "There are a lot of people on this station. How did you even know I was here?"

"I always check in the new arrivals," he said.

"What kind of job is that, checking in new arrivals?" she asked.

"Security," he said.

He had been a promising scientist when she met him. But he had gone farther and farther away from science when they were together. She hadn't expected him to abandon it altogether.

"I was surprised to see your name on the arrivals list," he said.

"I'll bet," she said. "You didn't check me in."

"That's what I'm doing now," he said. "You need a tour of the facility? An introduction to the other staff?"

"That was already taken care of," she said.

"Because you're a VIP," he said, and she couldn't tell if he was being sarcastic or not.

"They seem to think I'm the godmother of stealth tech," she said, trying to make a joke. Instead her eyes filled with tears. She didn't want him to see that, so she turned away.

"Yeah," he said, "we never really know who we're going to become, do we?"

"Or who others think we should be," she said. "Whether we want to be that person or not."

TWELVE

"**W**here are we going, Rosealma?" Quint asked. He rubbed on his face, trying to remove the caked blood.

She sighed, stood up, and got out her medical kit. Time to see how injured he really was.

"I don't know where we're going," she said as she tugged the small kit out of the storage area near the door. She set the kit on her chair.

"You changed course a while ago," he said.

She opened the kit, slipped on some gloves, and removed some cleansing strips. "Yeah, I did."

The less she lied to him, the better.

"From where to where?" he asked.

She cupped the cleansing strips in her right hand and walked over to him. "I have no fucking idea. Now hold still."

"What about the rendezvous point?" he asked as she grabbed his chin with her left hand, and it took all of her control not to start in surprise.

How did he know about her rendezvous with the others? And then she realized that he didn't. The scientists and researchers were supposed to gather at some point if there was any threat to the station.

She tightened her hold on his chin. Her fingers were probably causing bruises, and she didn't care. She wrapped the cleansing strip around her index and middle finger and began to wipe off the blood. "Scrape it off" was a better way to put it.

"I'm not going back to join anyone from the station," she said. "I was stupid to go back in the first place. It's as if every time someone messes with stealth tech the accidents get worse. I can't keep involving myself in that."

"Yet you can't stay away, can you?" he asked, the words somewhat mangled from the force of her fingers on his cheeks.

She didn't answer him. As the blood came off, she found a series of small cuts, some of which still had debris embedded in them.

"What happened to you?" she asked him. "I thought there weren't any explosions on the station until that big one."

"Cloris Kashion saw something embedded on one of the stealth-tech tubes," he said. "She decided to remove it."

Squishy's heart started to pound. She wondered if he could feel it through her fingertips. She forced herself to concentrate on cleaning the wounds.

The stealth-tech tubes weren't really tubes at all. They were jars filled with just enough material to start a stealth-tech reaction. Only the material didn't have the right composition. So much was missing, so many details she had only just started to learn when she started working with a real, active Dignity Vessel's *anacapa* drive. The pieces that the Empire had of what it called stealth tech were so dangerous that they could make entire regions of space impossible to pass through.

She had attached the explosive devices to the various tubes. It had taken her two days. The devices were tiny and almost impossible to see. They slipped into the tube, and once turned on, interacted with the tech, destroying it.

She had initially developed the weapon years ago, but she had since modified it with the help of the Dignity Vessel's engineers, so that it wouldn't open the interdimensional rift she had mentioned to Quint.

"There was just a flash of something as her hand went around the tube," he said. "I can't tell you what it was, only that I had seen it before somewhere, and I knew—"

He shook his head or tried to. Squishy's fingers were still clutching his chin. His gaze met hers, and so far as she could tell, she was seeing deep inside him. He was vulnerable, and at this moment—or maybe at the moment he remembered—he was scared.

"I just shoved everyone out and tried to grab her, but she had pulled on that thing, and the tube exploded, sending me backward through the door. We got it closed, but just barely. That was when I came looking for you."

"And you got her out, right?" Squishy asked.

His look changed. Subtly. It went from open to closed, from frightened to shut off, in the space of a second.

"You could argue that no one died," he said.

She closed her eyes. "And you would be wrong."

THIRTEEN

*T*he inside of the Ancient and Lost Technologies Laboratory building smelled the same as it always had. A bit dusty, a bit sterile, not because of chemicals used, but because it got cleaned every single day, which wiped out the bulk of the odors.

As she stepped inside, out of the pale sun, away from the still-confused crowd, the fact that the building smelled the same surprised her. She had expected something sharp, like blood or urine or the tang that certain laser weapons give off.

The lifts were shut down, which was her first indication that something was wrong. Her lab was on the tenth floor, and she climbed the black reflective steps, which were made of the same material as the building's exterior.

Red warning lights started flashing on the ninth floor, warning unauthorized personnel to stay away. The audio announcement was off, however, probably because it was usually accompanied by sirens. It seemed to take forever to reach the tenth floor.

The lab was shut off by a triple entry system. First, she had to press her palm against a door at the top of the stairs. Before the door unlocked, it displayed a warning:

Possible Hazard Inside. Proceed With Caution.

That flashed twice, followed by:

Only Authorized Personnel. Authorization Subject To Revocation Without Cause.

And then the hazard warning appeared again.

Finally, the door unlocked, slid open just wide enough to admit Rosealma, and closed behind her.

That had never happened to her before, at least not here. She had gone through airlocks all of her life on ships and in ports, but never inside a planet-side building, and never on campus. The campus prided itself on being open. Even the restricted areas could be opened to unauthorized personnel if someone simply queried an administrator.

Although probably not today.

She stood in the airlock, feeling odd. It was simply a building space between doors. She could see light around both doors, which meant that air and contaminants leaked through.

The door in front of her had never been closed before. She touched it with her palm, and the same warnings ran along the door's message board.

Then the door clicked open, letting her into what she had always thought of as the real airlock.

The front of the lab was sealed in the same way that spaceships sealed their exteriors. She couldn't peer in, she couldn't breathe any of its air, and she couldn't hear anything from the interior. Her heart pounded.

She touched her palm to the entry panel, and the door opened, revealing chaos.

But not the kind of chaos that she expected.

She had expected smoke and still-flaring fires, people dead on the floor, destroyed workstations, and gigantic holes in the wall.

Instead, she found people running back and forth or clustering in groups. Half of the staff wore the silly white lab coats that the professors in Ancient and Lost Technologies insisted upon, and the rest were in civilian garb, just like she was.

But they were consulting, talking over each other, looking at readouts— and not looking in the direction of the experiment booth at all. The silence, the decorum, the protocol was gone, replaced by a visible sense of panic.

Visible and pungent. That stench of fear she had expected below dominated here.

She stepped away from the door, and it closed behind her. No one noticed Rosealma's arrival. They just kept talking and comparing notes. She could make out individual words but not their context, so she tuned it out.

She walked forward. The experimental lab was divided into sections that were walled off from each other, each with its own environment.

Three of the sections were shut off, dark, just like they always were. They were unassigned and not in use at the moment. No one had been conducting experiments in them.

The other seven sections seemed to be in some stage of usage. Lights were down in three of those, but the dim lights still showed experiments in progress. Two of the remaining four sections had scientists inside, consulting just like the scientists outside the labs were doing. No one seemed to be doing actual hands-on work.

One section had lights on full and several containers on several tables. She couldn't tell if activity in that room had been interrupted or if someone had just turned on the lights to see what was happening.

The remaining section was the one that caught her eye. That section, directly in front of her, was the one she went into the most often, where the stealth-tech experiment that she had been working on was conducted.

Or had been conducted.

That section was completely empty.

Nothing remained—not a table, not a chair, not a computer. Even the lights seemed odd, and it took her a moment to figure out why. The lights weren't on inside the section. Spotlights from the airlock area were shining into the section, as well as lights above the containment equipment.

"What's going on in section 14B?" she asked the next person who scurried past her.

"That's what we'd like to know," he said as he hurried by.

She hadn't expected that response. She wanted someone to tell her the section had been cleared out because of the emergency, that the area was no longer in use. But not *that's what we'd like to know*.

She looked at the cluster of scientists nearest her. She recognized several of them, but none of them were Professor Erasmus Dane, who ran the experiments that Rosealma worked on. Professor Dane was in charge of this entire lab; he should have been there, directing everyone.

Rosealma walked over to the scientists. Three vids were playing on three screens, but no one watched them. The vids were real-time recordings of the experiments, and from the time stamp, they were from earlier in the day.

"Where's Professor Dane?" she asked the group.

They started guiltily. Four people didn't even look up. Two looked away. Only one person faced her. Assistant Professor Herman Gill.

He wasn't much older than she was. He had been the whiz kid of his class, fast-tracked through school, through his post-doc, through everything, given tenure over and above a lot of other more established professors because of the quality of his research. Every school, every major organization in the sector wanted him. He wanted to stay in academia, and he had his choice of places to go. Mehkeydo University had offered him terms so amazing that Rosealma had even heard about it.

The only concession he had had to make was an assistant professorship to start. He didn't mind, so long as he had time to do his experiments.

His round cheeks were red, his blue eyes wild. Beads of sweat dotted his forehead. His brown hair stood up in spiky streaks, not because it was supposed to but because he'd been running his fingers through it or he had forgotten to comb it when he got out of bed.

He didn't look like a whiz kid now. He looked terrified.

"You're Professor Dane's assistant, aren't you?" he said in a voice calmer than she had expected, given his appearance.

There was no good answer to that. Rosealma was more than Professor Dane's assistant, less than Professor Dane's partner.

"I want to know where Professor Dane is," Rosealma said. "He should be here."

"Do you work with him or not?" Gill snapped.

"Yes," Rosealma said.

"Then maybe you can figure this out."

He tapped the screen in front of him. It showed 14B in speeded-up time. As Rosealma watched, things disappeared. First an apple sitting on the table, then a pen, then the table itself crumbled and disappeared. As it did, one of the assistants, an idiot named Russell Fowler, blundered into 14B.

The moment he entered, he stopped. He seemed to blur a little. Then he looked up. Or, to be more accurate, his head changed positions, but Rosealma didn't see how exactly. It wasn't a smooth movement. At one point his head was down; at another, it was up.

The chair vanished, and when Rosealma was looking at it, Fowler crumpled, and a moment later, he was gone as well.

"What the hell?" Rosealma asked. "Who made this recording? It's clearly been doctored."

"It's not doctored," Gill said.

That was when Rosealma realized the lighting had changed. She stared at the emptiness for what seemed like a long time.

Then Professor Dane appeared in the frame. Professor Dane was a formidable man, tall and broad, given to wearing vintage suits and capes when he went outside. He had on a cape in the vid.

He was gesturing; then he waited, nodded, and pulled open the door. He stepped inside and vanished.

Just vanished.

Gill stopped the vid. "That's all we have. No one has gone in since."

Rosealma studied him. He wasn't lying to her, that she could tell anyway. But she didn't trust the vid. She didn't trust any of this.

"Show me all of the vids from all the angles in real time."

"It'll take three hours," he said.

"That took place over three hours?" She turned toward the frozen screen, whose image was no different than the image she saw when she looked at 14B itself.

"Three hours, from the moment that things started vanishing to the moment we lost Professor Dane," Gill said.

"Russell was working here by himself?" Rosealma asked.

"Others were working on different experiments," Gill said.

"Were you here?" she asked.

He shook his head. "I got here just before Professor Dane."

"How long had Professor Dane been here before he went inside 14B?"

"An hour."

"But he still had his cloak on."

"He didn't take it off. He started working immediately." Gill crossed his arms. "What are you people messing with?"

Rosealma stood back and looked at everyone in the room. She was the only one who had worked directly with Professor Dane. No one else was involved with 14B.

"Where's the rest of the team?" she asked.

"We had a death," he said. "We couldn't call in a team directly. You know protocol."

She didn't know protocol. At least, not on a death. There had never been one in the lab while she worked here, while she had gone to school here. At least not a death that she knew of.

"How do you know you had a death?" she asked. "I don't see a death here."

"God," Gill said, "you sound just like Professor Dane."

Rosealma's cheeks got hot, but she didn't back down. Something was off here—something besides the strangeness in 14B.

"When did the sirens go off?" she asked.

"I hit them," he said, "shortly after Professor Dane got here."

Whiz kid my ass, Rosealma thought. *Control freak who thought he knew more than everyone else, more likely.*

"So you deliberately prevented Professor Dane from summoning his team," she said.

Gill gave her a startled look. "We had a death—"

"You had a disappearance," she said. "And it might be harmless. Do you know what stealth tech is? It's a cloak."

A bead of sweat ran down Gill's face. "If it's a cloak, then how come Professor Dane hasn't returned yet?"

"Maybe because it's still on," she said.

"Maybe?" Gill asked.

"It's an *experiment*," she said. "I can't be precise. I don't even know what Fowler was doing in there. We have strict orders not to go inside that room when an experiment is running."

"Yet Fowler and your Professor Dane did just that."

"Maybe Professor Dane had a reason," she said. "Did you show him the vid?"

"Yes," Gill said.

"In real time?" she asked.

"There's no time to view it in real time," he said.

"Idiot," she breathed.

"What?"

"I just called you an idiot," she said. "If it's a cloak, then no one is harmed, no one is dead, you just made some stupid assumptions. I want Professor Dane's team here. I want to find out what happened."

"We all do," Gill said. "But the professor should have been able to break a cloak."

"From inside a room? Without any controls?" She had raised her voice so loudly that everyone in the lab was watching them now. "How would you expect him to do that?"

"He went in there. He had to have known that something would happen."

"He probably went in there to pull Fowler out," she said.

"And that didn't work," Gill said.

"Because the cloak might have malfunctioned," she said. She shoved him aside. "I hope to God that the malfunction is something we can reverse. Because if they died in there while you were screwing around, then it's on you."

"So you think they're dead too," Gill said, and she finally understood what was in his voice. He was scared—scared not just that they were dead, but that his career was going to follow. Maybe he had never failed before. Maybe he had never lost this kind of control before.

She hadn't either. She had no idea what she was doing, although she had more of an idea than Gill did.

"I don't know what they are," she said, "and I won't know if you don't get the hell out of my way."

He took a step back, startled. No one talked to the whiz kid like that.

"Someone get the rest of the team," she said. "I'm going to need help here."

"Do you think you can get Professor Dane back?" a woman asked.

"I'm not sure Professor Dane has gone anywhere," Rosealma said. "But I sure as hell am going to do my best to find out."

FOURTEEN

*Q*uint actually needed some minor surgery on some of the cuts. They were deep and too wide, and filled with all kinds of debris. Squishy convinced him to go to the nearest cabin, the one with the biggest bed. Before she had him lie down on it, she pulled the bedding.

She had no idea what had lodged in his face, but she didn't want it on anything important. She used a disposable liner and had him lie on that.

He eased himself onto the bed, watching her the entire time. Some movements of his were so familiar. That one was. He used to lie down and pat the bed beside him, half smiling at her in a way he thought enticing.

It had been enticing in the beginning. And then it became uncomfortable. And finally, embarrassing.

Not for her. But for him.

She hoped he didn't remember that.

He eased onto his back, folded his hands across his chest, and closed his eyes, but only for a moment. He opened them quickly, as if he remembered he couldn't trust her.

Although opening himself up like this was a kind of trust. He let her use a topical anesthetic to numb his face, and then he watched her work, her hands against his warm skin, her fingers working with the small, sensitive tweezers. They did 90 percent of the work, examining the cut and its edges so that she knew if she had removed all of the debris. But she still used her fingers to probe the edges of the wounds, a holdover from her medic days on Boss's diving runs.

Quint had been through medical procedures before. He knew better than to move. She got into a rhythm, working the cuts, removing the debris, operating almost by rote.

Her fingers knew what to do. The work was familiar—too familiar. It gave her time to mull what Quint had said.

Squishy hadn't compared the number of people who escaped to the number of people who had been in the station that day. And if Quint was right, then a few people—not just Cloris—could have died, and it wouldn't have shown up on Squishy's scans. At least, it wouldn't have shown up with the scans she had done.

Maybe if she had done some others . . .

She forced herself to concentrate on the microsurgery she was doing. She had to clean out those wounds carefully. She couldn't leave even the smallest bit of debris in them. She had no idea if whatever had embedded itself in Quint's skin had been from the particular stealth-tech experiment that Cloris had destroyed. It might have been from Squishy's bomb, or it might have been from the room itself. Or something from a rift—she had no idea.

But Cloris had vanished. Quint had told Squishy that much by repeating her own words to her. Cloris had vanished in that bright light, and because the imperial military's science branch had yet to rule on what that meant in connection to stealth tech, Cloris was still technically alive.

Squishy had failed. She had planned to pull off this particular job without killing anyone.

Quint's gaze kept moving as her hands moved. It must have seemed odd, her gloved fingers touching him so close to his eyes. But he didn't flinch, and he didn't say anything, and that bothered her almost as much as his steady stare. She felt like he could see through her, and that bothered her too. She had loved that about him when she was younger, but she had become extremely private over the years. She valued that privacy. It was part of her. She didn't want to change it now.

When she finished, she rubbed an additional numbing agent across his skin. He would be sore for days because of what she had done. Field medicine wasn't nearly as good as medicine at any starbase.

"You're going to need to see a real surgeon," she said as she removed her gloves and dropped them into the bin she'd built into the cruiser. "You'll need a double-check on my work."

"Your work is fine," Quint said, his words slightly mangled because the numbing agent made it hard for him to move the muscles in his cheek.

"No, it's not," Squishy said. "You'll have terrible scars if you don't see someone soon. I don't have the equipment to properly fix the skin. I'm going to do a scan for somewhere nearby that has good medical facilities. I'll change our course and drop you there."

He sat up, put his hand up as if he was going to touch his face, and then clearly changed his mind. "Then what will happen to you?"

"I'll stay until your surgery is over," she lied.

He smiled—or tried to. It looked a bit lopsided because of the numbing agent. "No you won't, Rosealma. You'll leave the minute they take me into the facility, not that it matters. The Empire is looking for you and they will find you."

She went cold. "What do you mean?"

"I mean that before we left, I let the authorities know that you were the one who blew the station. I gave them the identification information for this ship. They'll track you, find you, and put you in prison, Rose."

She rubbed her hands together. Her palms were wet. She had gone from cold to a cold sweat in the space of a few seconds. "Why would you do that?"

"You killed Cloris," Quint said.

"Not according to imperial law, I didn't," Squishy said, then realized she was admitting to the explosions. "Besides, there's no proof I did anything wrong."

"There wouldn't have been," he said, "if you had gone directly to your evac ship, Rose. But you didn't. You came here."

"I explained that," she said.

"Yeah," he said quietly. "You did."

Squishy used cleaning solution on her hands, then cleaned her surgical instruments. She didn't put them away, however. She still needed to run them through the sonic cleaner. But she didn't want to leave Quint alone.

He was sitting up. His skin looked raw. The cuts dotted his face.

"You came here too," she said. "It would have been easier for you to evacuate. You had already given the authorities my information. There was no reason for you to join me."

He gave her a hurt look. "You need me."

He had said that in the past, and it never failed to provoke her. It angered her now. She didn't need him. She had never needed him.

She had no idea why he thought she did.

"Why do I need you?" she asked, unable to keep the sarcasm out of her voice.

"Because I'm the only person who can prevent you from disappearing into the bowels of the Empire's prison system."

"You sound like I've already been tried and convicted," she said.

He shrugged. "Times are different now. You destroyed government property. Military property. That was classified as a weapons research site, Rose. They don't need to try you. They just need to show a few select judges that you're guilty."

Her eyes narrowed. "You think they'd charge me with murder?"

"Probably not," he said. "They'll probably charge you with treason. Which is worse."

She swallowed in spite of herself. "Murder can carry a death penalty. How is treason worse?"

He looked down at his hands. "There are some things, Rose, that you don't want to live through."

She cleared her throat, set her surgical instruments down, then let her hands hover over them as if she was going to use them as weapons. She didn't want to think about all of the implications of this conversation. But she couldn't put off thinking about it any longer.

"How do you know that there are some things I don't want to live through?" she asked Quint.

Quint sighed. "I work in Imperial Intelligence, Rose."

She frowned, suddenly feeling confused. "You used to work in military intelligence. Then you moved on. On the station, you were head of security. You told me that not six months ago."

He shook his head ever so slightly. "I didn't tell you that. I implied it. You didn't really care enough to investigate."

He was right: she hadn't cared. She had been more concerned with keeping him away from her than she had been with the intricacies of his job.

"What does that mean, Imperial Intelligence?" she asked. "And how is that different from military intelligence?"

He let out a small sigh. "It's different in degree, Rose. Military intelligence is child's play compared to what I do. I was promoted after you left. I run an entire intelligence division now. I have more information at my fingertips than you could ever imagine."

Her stomach turned, although she wasn't sure why. Something about what he was saying disturbed her, and disturbed her so deeply that she didn't want to look at it closely.

"So what are you doing here with me?" she asked. "How come you're not on one of those ships or contacting the Empire or something?"

"You're my Achilles' heel, Rose. You know that reference? It's not from Professor Dane's class, but it's from the same department. Lost cultures. Cultures so old we only have stories about them."

"I know what the phrase means," she said.

And it frightened her. How could she be his weakness? They hadn't seen each other in decades.

"I should have reported you," he said softly. "I should have reported you the moment the *Dane* crossed into Enterran territory."

It felt like her heart stopped. Then she realized she had forgotten to take a breath. "What do you mean?"

"Squishy," he said, standing up. He started to come toward her, then seemed to think better of it and stopped. "How can you let them call you Squishy? You have a beautiful name. You're a beautiful woman, Rose."

He knew she had lived outside the Enterran Empire. He knew her nickname. He knew much more about her than she had ever known about him.

"For the first time in your life," he said, "when you left Vallevu, you didn't leave it entirely. You stayed in touch. You let some people know how you were doing. You didn't say much in the messages, but the messages came from the Nine Planets Alliance."

Her fists were clenched so tightly that her hands ached. Had she made a mistake coming to the Empire? Not for herself, but for all the others? For the work she had been doing back at the Nine Planets? Had she let the Empire in when Boss and the team had worked so hard to keep the Empire out?

"Don't worry," he said. "I couldn't track you inside the Alliance. They have good protections in place."

Her heart started pounding. She had forgotten that he used to do that, answer her questions even when she hadn't spoken them.

"But I have a hunch I know what got you out to the Nine Planets," he said. "There've been credible rumors that the Nine Planets has made breakthroughs in stealth tech. I know enough about stealth tech to know that the person who understands it best is you."

She almost denied it. She didn't understand it best, not anymore. Now there was an entire department of people who worked with the *anacapa* drive, who had worked on it all of their lives, working with knowledge passed down from generations. Now she was behind in her understanding of the technology.

Although not in her understanding of the technology that the Empire was developing. Imperial stealth tech consistently malfunctioned and killed because imperial stealth tech tried to harness a burning log with a rope. Sometimes the rope held for just a moment, but eventually it would get burned as well. Everyone who worked in imperial stealth tech believed that the log was the technology. They didn't even see or understand the fire.

"I wanted you back here," he said, extending his hands. She looked at his hands, then looked at him, keeping her gaze level, showing as little emotion as she possibly could. He was scaring her. He probably knew how much he was scaring her, and by extending his hands, he tried to calm her.

Slowly, he let his hands drop.

"I wanted you working for us again," he said. "You know so much, and things have gone so wrong."

"You're the one who leaked that information about the stealth-tech research," she said. Anger she hadn't even realized she was feeling made her voice tremble. "You're the one."

He nodded. "I figured it would bring you back. And it did."

FIFTEEN

Squishy stood in front of the schematics for the small *anacapa* drive displayed on the table before her. She had her hands clasped behind her back. Six people crowded around her. The room was long and narrow, adjacent to her office, an office she rarely used. Mostly, she was in the various labs, working on a dozen projects.

Once upon a time, she supervised all of the work on the space station, but she couldn't any longer. Too much was being done. So much, in fact, that Boss—or to be more accurate, the Lost Souls Corporation—had recently purchased another space station for different kinds of work. Squishy didn't know what happened at the new place except in theory. Most of the work there was dedicated to historical and anthropological research, as well as ground sciences like geology—things that held no interest for her.

What interested her—what had always interested her—was this technology. More than biology, more than all of the medicine she studied, she wanted to know about *anacapa* drives.

She stood back from the schematics, then ordered up a holographic version. It rose and floated above her. She tapped the screen so that she got a three-dimensional model of the drive. It floated next to the schematics, about the size of her fist, encased in black. She ordered the casing removed and studied the drive.

It looked wrong to her, but she wasn't the expert. The people beside her were, but the person whose opinion mattered was Bradley Taylor.

Taylor had come from the *Ivoire*, the working Dignity Vessel that Boss had found four years before. He was young, and when he first came to the Nine Planets, he hadn't been old enough to get work in the *Ivoire*'s engineering department. But he had a knack for *anacapa* drives. He loved them as much as Squishy did, and once here, he had become her de facto right-hand man.

"It doesn't look complete to me," Squishy said, directing her comments to Taylor. The others listened.

"It does seem small," he said, "but I can assure you that it works."

She programmed both holographs so that they revolved. Then they turned upside down, moving in all three dimensions. She watched, but that discomfort remained.

She shook her head. "Something's wrong. I just can't tell what it is."

Taylor didn't seem upset. Instead, he leaned into the images and watched them move as if they held the answers.

"I wish we could run some tests," he said.

"No tests until I have some idea that this will work," she said. Too many people had died in "tests."

No one from the *Ivoire* objected either. The only reason they were at the base was because their *anacapa* drive had malfunctioned a long, long time ago.

"We know that the *anacapa* part will work," said Sadie Juarez. She was thin and intense. She had come from one of the top universities in the Nine Planets. She was a brilliant theorist, but she still hadn't grasped the dangers of the research. "Maybe there's some kind of way we can isolate the experiment . . ."

She let her voice trail off so that everyone knew what she was saying, even though she hadn't finished the thought.

"We're not the Empire," said Ward Zauft. He had helped Squishy since she started her research at Lost Souls. He was wiry, had too much energy, and was always keeping an eye out for problems in experiments. She liked that the most about him. "We don't let eighty-five people die just because we hope the experiment will work."

Squishy nodded, then frowned. Eighty-five was a specific number, and it was too small to encompass all of the people who had died in the last few decades.

She turned toward him. "Eighty-five?"

"Haven't you heard? That's the latest loss. Eighty-five people because some stealth-tech experiment went awry." He wasn't even looking at her. He was clearly thinking about the drive in front of him, not the news he was passing on.

"Where did you see that?" she asked.

Something in her tone seemed to catch his attention. He looked away from the rotating drives, his gaze meeting hers. A slight frown creased his forehead.

"It got leaked and made some of the science news sites just this week," he said. "They said the eighty-five people who died were the latest tragic accident in a program plagued by them."

"I heard it, too," Juarez said. "The story said that the numbers couldn't be confirmed but that maybe as many as eight hundred people have died in stealth-tech-related experiments in the past twenty years."

Squishy was shaking. She knew of the first two hundred of the dead. She had a hunch that eight hundred figure was too small.

"So they're warning people away?" she asked. "Telling them not to work for the imperial science programs?"

"It wasn't that kind of news," Juarez said. "It was my impression that they were just interested in the statistics, nothing more."

Statistics. Squishy let out a small breath. "I don't want anyone running an experiment on this until someone who has worked with *anacapa* drives for a decade or more looks at this."

Then she excused herself and went to her office. She felt lightheaded and off balance.

The Empire was still experimenting with stealth tech, even after she and Boss had tried to shut them down. And people were still dying in the experiments. Over and over again, people were dying.

What would it take to convince the Empire that stealth tech was too dangerous to pursue? Or could it be persuaded?

Maybe she and Boss had been on the right track six years before. Maybe they should do everything they could to destroy the research. All of the research.

She didn't like the way her thoughts were going, but she recognized the feeling. She couldn't keep working here while people were dying back there. Particularly if they were following protocols she had developed decades before.

The scientists with the Empire's program were following faulty assumptions with old information, and that wasn't just dangerous to them. It was dangerous to the entire sector.

Something had to be done.

And she knew only one person she trusted to do it.

SIXTEEN

*Q*uint ran his hand through his hair, making it stand on end. He walked toward her. There wasn't a lot of room in this cabin. It took all of Squishy's strength not to back away.

"When the *Dane* entered imperial space," he said, "I was actually hopeful. I thought you had come back to help us."

"I did," she said softly.

"No, you didn't," he said. "You came back here to destroy us."

Quint's words offended her. Squishy stood perfectly still, trying to control the anger.

"I did not come to destroy you," she said. "People who destroy things kill people."

"You killed Cloris," he said.

Her cheeks heated. She made herself breathe before she spoke. Even then, her words were clipped.

"I didn't come to destroy you," she said again. "I came to help you."

His face flushed. The wounds disappeared in the redness. He took a step away from her, moving his head at the same time so she couldn't see his eyes.

"That's what I wanted to believe, Rose," he said, clasping his hands behind his back. The posture looked terribly familiar. She did it all the time, and she realized, with a sinking feeling, she had learned it from him. "I wanted to believe that you could stop all of the deaths. Didn't you ever wonder how you got in so easily? Why no one cared that you'd been gone for so many years?"

She had wondered, then chalked it up to the Empire's incompetence. She figured people were watching her, but it didn't matter. She had an entire team, she had a way to contact them if she needed to, and she had no actual work to do until she destroyed the research station. For six months, her work had been blameless, although she made a point of stopping those experiments, the ones that would have resulted in someone's death.

He tilted his head back. "I *believed* in you, Rosealma. You're brilliant. I honestly thought you could fix it all."

Her breath caught in her throat. It all fit: how she got in, why he kept showing up, asking the occasional question, keeping an eye on her, telling her she was doing well.

She shook her head. "I did fix things, just not the way you wanted."

"You just set them back some, Rosealma. You didn't fix anything at all," he said.

She almost, almost told him about destroying the backup research, but she didn't. The only thing her people hadn't destroyed was the scientists themselves. Someone destructive would have destroyed them too. But she wasn't destructive. It would take the scientists years to reconstruct their work, and maybe by then, someone new would come in, someone to tell them about the folly of their ways.

She could send them that researcher. She could send in moles who would direct them away from their own destruction and onto a path that would lead nowhere.

If she ever got out of this.

He was frowning. She couldn't trust him. Not even when he said he could keep her from the worst punishments. Maybe he could. But he wouldn't save her from interrogations. And the last thing she wanted to do was betray her friends.

She didn't dare trust him. He always tricked her.

And then she got cold. He was tricking her now, forcing her into conversation while the military closed in on her ship. She wasn't leaving the area—

—because of him.

She had to get away from him. Or at least, she had to try.

She made her expression change. She frowned with—she hoped—concern.

"Oh, dear," she said, keeping her voice calm. "You're bleeding again."

He raised a hand toward his face.

"Don't touch it," she said. "I don't know what got in those wounds. But something's keeping them from healing. I don't want you to spread it. Sit back on the bed."

He looked alarmed. He sat down.

She grabbed her kit and brought it over. Then she picked up the numbing agent. "Lean back. Close your eyes for just a minute."

He did. She grabbed one of the anesthetics, hoped the dosage wouldn't be too much for him, and as she wiped the numbing agent along his clean cheek, she inserted the anesthetic into his neck.

"Hey!" he said, opening his eyes. He tried to sit up. But she held him down with one hand, knowing the anesthetic would work quickly.

He fumbled, reached, and fell backward.

"Hey," he repeated softly. And then he closed his eyes.

She stepped back, counting for a full minute. No one, no matter how strong they were, could stay awake with that stuff flowing through them. She checked his vital signs. They were good.

She hadn't really thought this through. But she had only a few minutes to execute the plan, however haphazard it was.

Her heart was beating harder than his was. She hurried to the main cabin to check its escape pod. If that pod wasn't set up, she'd have to take things from one of the other pods.

But this one had food and water for a week, more if he rationed. Her hand floated over the pod's communications equipment. If she took the communications system out of the pod, she would buy more time. He couldn't contact anyone. She could leave the emergency beacon.

But he might die before anyone found him.

Then she shook her head. One person too many had already died on this mission. She wasn't going to kill Quint too.

She left the pod's door open. Then she went to the bed. It had been a long time since she lifted someone heavier than she was. She eyeballed him. She thought she could do it without reducing the gravity in the ship.

She slid under him and pulled him over her shoulder, wobbling a bit under his weight. She lurched like a drunk as she carried him to the pod, glad that the ship was relatively empty, so she didn't hit much. She crouched, her knees screaming in protest, then let him fall to the floor.

He didn't wake up.

She shoved him into the pod, checked his vitals one last time, and let out a small sigh of relief. He was fine. He would be fine.

Weirdly, she felt the urge to apologize. She was leaving him yet again without any explanation—or, at least, without an explanation he could understand.

But she didn't say anything. Instead, she closed the pod door, and then she went to the cockpit. She needed to check one thing.

She hurried to the control panel, and noted the coordinates, and made sure the pod's emergency beacon showed on her communications readout.

Then she went back to the cabin, saw her supplies on the nearby table, the scrunched pad where Quint had been just a moment before. The pod glistened in its bay, the door still closed.

She couldn't help herself: she had to open it to make sure he was still inside.

He was. And he was still unconscious. He hadn't moved at all.

She closed the door and hit the in-room command, jettisoning the pod.

The panel doors closed, then the wall vibrated as the pod disconnected itself from the ship.

"Get out," she whispered. She never wanted to see him again, and she was afraid she would.

She hurried back to the cockpit and looked at the screens, watching as the pod tumbled away from the *Dane*. She needed to get out of this sector. This cruiser couldn't escape Enterran space fast enough to get her to the Nine Planets before Quint was found. Plus she had believed him when he said that he had already released information about the ship.

Everyone would be looking for her.

For that reason alone, she couldn't go back to the rendezvous, nor could she contact the others. She hoped they would follow instructions and leave after the designated period of time.

Not that anyone would be looking for them. As far as the Empire knew, as far as Quint knew, she had been working alone.

The pod got smaller and smaller until it was just a dot on her screen. She should just leave him to his fate. After all, one death in the service of a cause didn't matter. That was his philosophy, anyway.

But it wasn't hers.

She went to the control panel, scanned for the nearest starbase, and sent a coded message, warning of a ship in trouble, and escape pods at these coordinates.

It was the least she could do to salve her own conscience, even though doing so might cause her capture.

She had no idea if she would get out of this alive, but she was going to try. And she was going to try to do it alone.

SECTOR BASE Y

SEVENTEEN

*T*he *anacapa* drive, when it's working properly, operates quickly and efficiently. It moves a ship from one part of space to another in a blink. But it can also move a ship forward from one time to another without moving it in space at all. And the *anacapa* drive can move a ship in both time and space, but less efficiently and using a lot more energy.

I never want to be on a ship that uses its *anacapa* drive to move in time. Maybe I'm superstitious. Maybe I'm practical. Or maybe I'm simply wary. The *anacapa*'s move through time is what brought the *Ivoire* here. The movement through space itself seemed to have worked fine.

Coop, Yash, Mikk, and I are in the cockpit of *Nobody's Business Two*. This ship is much bigger than the original *Business*, and I used to think that ship huge.

The cockpit alone here has the capacity to hold a dozen people. I could staff it with a real crew if I wanted to. I don't want to. I have never overcome my aversion to crowds of people, and now I doubt I ever will. It seems to be an integral part of me, one that makes me even more unsuited to running Lost Souls.

Right now, Ilona Blake is actually running Lost Souls. She did so for most of the previous year, with my supervision. She made no mistakes that I could find. She's efficient, organized, and friendly. She knows how to make people do whatever she wants when she wants them to. And she understands Lost Souls' mission. Better yet, she believes in it down to her very core.

If all goes well, I'm going to promote her to chief operating officer when I get back. The less I'm involved in the day-to-day workings of the corporation, the happier I'll be.

I am weirdly happy right now. I sit in the pilot's chair of the *Two* and look at the strange foldspace star map on the screen in front of me. Mikk stands near the door, massive arms crossed as if he's standing guard. He's ready to jump in should something go wrong, which is just his nature. Right now, he's the unnecessary person on the bridge, but I want him here so that I don't feel outnumbered by *Ivoire* crew, even if there are only two of them.

Coop sits to my right, my nominal copilot, and Yash sits to my left. Yash is the most important one in this cockpit right now. She's the one who operates the *anacapa* drive. I can do what any pilot can do—I can turn it on and off. I can actually do a few other things, because learning the capabilities of the *anacapa* has been one of my priorities.

But should something go wrong—and most of my experiences with *anacapa* drives, particularly before I knew what they were, were with drives that had gone horribly wrong—I want someone in front of those drive controls who can design an *anacapa* drive from a hair follicle and chipped tooth.

Even though the *Ivoire* had an entire team of engineers in charge of various aspects of the *anacapa* drive, no one on that ship knew more about it than Yash. Therefore, she's the one I want to operate this brand new *anacapa* drive built especially for the *Two*.

The journey to Sector Base Y is the farthest I will have ever traveled in foldspace. Before that, it was the journey to Sector Base W from the Lost Souls' space station. This is probably—and I'm guessing because I didn't put in the coordinates—five times the distance.

I am nervous, but not like Mikk is. Mikk is nervous because he doesn't want to get trapped. Neither do I. But I'm nervous because our *anacapa* is new, built by Yash and her engineers specifically for the smaller vessels owned by the Lost Souls.

Yash says that the principle is the same, and the size of the *anacapa* doesn't matter. I don't know enough about the science to know if she's right, and it's not like we can verify with an outside engineer. I'm all about verification. When Ilona first ran the corporation for me, I had outside auditors double-check her financial work (without her knowledge, of course). I use a variety of outside experts from the Nine Planets to verify different aspects of our research—although never the totality of our research on a particular topic because I don't want the scientists to know exactly what we're doing.

We're also selling trademarks and patents on bits of technology from the Dignity Vessels—tech unrelated to the *anacapa* or the weaponry, of course. And we're not discussing where that tech comes from.

I am paranoid but, Coop says, in a good and healthy way, considering the power of the Empire.

The only way I could even partially double-check Yash's claims for the new *anacapa* before taking it into the field for the first time two years ago was to have Squishy look it over. Squishy heads our part of the *anacapa* division, or as she insists on calling it, the stealth-tech division.

She says she uses the name to remind her of past sins.

I think she's just being as stubborn about the wording as the rest of us.

I wanted Squishy on this trip, but she took a prolonged leave of absence several months ago, claiming burnout. Since she hasn't taken time off in almost seven years, I let her go. But I miss her.

And even more than that, I miss her cranky—honest—expertise.

I lean back in the somewhat ostentatious pilot's chair and frown at foldspace. It's still a relatively strange concept for me to contemplate. Coop gave me the layman's explanation shortly after I met him, and it's still the one I default to.

The *anacapa* drive creates an actual fold in space, the way that a person would create a fold in a blanket. The *anacapa* user knows where she is and where she's going. She gives the *anacapa* those two coordinates, and the *anacapa* gets the ship from here to there as if it has taken a shortcut—which, I suppose, it has.

That shortcut can have an impact on time as well, and I don't understand that mechanism as well as I understand the distance mechanism. In fact, I don't even try anymore. I know that the *anacapa* works, and when it works well, it's a godsend for long-distance space travel.

When it works poorly, it can cost lives, or worse. It can destroy communities, or send ships forward five thousand years.

I try not to think about that when we're in foldspace, but I find myself dwelling on it each and every time. I guess foldspace makes me a lot more nervous than I want to admit.

Suddenly the ship does a little dance that I have come to recognize as a shift out of foldspace. Everything skitters—vision, hearing, even that sense of motion. The first time I experienced it, I thought it felt like the entire ship's crew tripped over the same spot in a rug at the very same time. It is as if we've hit some kind of mutual bump and we go over it together.

Then we're level, on the other side of foldspace, and the *anacapa* automatically disengages.

Still, Yash watches both it and the coordinates at our arrival point. She can reengage within seconds if we need her to.

"This it?" Yash asks Coop.

"It should be," he says.

We've stopped near a planet named Treffet. It's inside the habitable zone around its sun, but is uncomfortably close to that sun—at least for me. It's in roughly the same area in relation to its sun that Wyr was. Wyr is where Sector Base V is, and is one of the hottest places I've ever had the misfortune to go to.

But the weather will be the least of our problems. We're far from home in more ways than one. Treffet doesn't belong to the Nine Planets Alliance, nor is it a part of the Enterran Empire. Treffet, so far as I can tell, is filled with nonaligned cultures, not that I've done a tremendous amount of research.

I had planned to do that research if and when Coop decided we would go to Sector Base Y. I figured I had months, maybe years, given the amount of work we would have to do at Sector Base W. When we got here, we would be prepared to deal with Treffet's ruling bodies, whoever they might be.

Instead, we followed Coop's rather impulsive plan, and got here without my usual level of research.

"I'm not reassured by the phrase 'it should be,'" Mikk says from behind me. He's speaking to Coop.

"I didn't come out here," Coop says. "This is the planet that was initially chosen for Sector Base Y, but the base was just in the planning stages. If the team ran into difficulties, the base could have ended up somewhere else."

Mikk sighs.

"I don't want to take the *Two* into orbit and then search to see what's belowground," I say. "That might attract too much attention. I'd rather send a skip."

"The *Two* can orbit using your traditional cloak," Coop says.

He doesn't like our cloak, so I am surprised by his suggestion. We have adopted new language for the cloak. Everyone else—those who know nothing about the secret military research in the Empire or about the *anacapa* drive—call this technology "stealth mode." With all of our references to malfunctioning stealth tech and old stealth technology, we have finally moved to the very simple "cloak."

Although "cloak" doesn't really describe what this stealth mode does. All it does is mask our presence on another ship's instruments or on instruments functioning at ground level.

Coop has repeatedly voiced his hatred of the cloak precisely because it's standard throughout the Empire and the Nine Planets Alliance. He believes that someone has probably developed a way to pierce a standard cloak without others knowing about it—and he's probably right.

Plus the cloak is designed for our cultures, not for other cultures. The cloak might mask the ship from the cultures in the Nine Planets or in the Empire, but not mask the ship out here.

"I don't want to risk the *Two*," I say. "It can stay out here and remain cloaked."

Coop gives me an annoyed look. He knows I'm being practical; I'm doing exactly what he would do if he were in charge of this mission. But he's not.

"I don't suppose you'll let me go," he says in a deceptively calm tone.

"Hell," Yash says, "*I* won't let you go."

"I'm afraid you can't go either," I say to her.

She rolls her eyes at me, but the response isn't a mean one. I prefer to interpret it as somewhat fond. "I know, I know," she says. "I shouldn't really be on this mission in the first place."

I told her that time and time again. I really didn't want to risk her because it risked all of our *anacapa* research.

"I can only bend so far," I say.

"You're irreplaceable as well," Coop says.

I can't tell if he's speaking from his fondness for me or if he actually believes that.

"He's right, you know, Boss," Mikk says. "You're in charge."

"Actually," I say as I lever myself out of the pilot's chair, "we need someone on this trip who can make command decisions, who can pilot the skip, and who can act quickly. That's me or Coop."

"I can act quickly," Mikk says, and he sounds almost surly.

"But we're in unknown political territory here," I say, "and if anyone is going to do something that will get us in trouble, I would rather it be me."

The other three have no response to that. Yash and Coop have no right to respond, and Mikk just makes a face. Whether or not he agrees with me, he knows better than to argue.

"I want Rossetti with me. She'll know what to look for in a sector base if it's not entirely obvious. And I need a backup pilot." I raise my eyebrows at Mikk. "You want to come?"

"Without you," he says, "but I'll take what I can get."

EIGHTEEN

he skip, at least, is a completely familiar piece of equipment. Even though I've upgraded models since I started the Lost Souls, the improvements have been mostly cosmetic.

Skips are small ships designed for short distances. They fit a small crew. On overnights, four is a crowd. In a short run, like we're doing, three is relatively comfortable—at least for me

The skip has two main rooms: the main area, which includes the command center—a big phrase for controls set against the corner—and a back area that can be used for resting, recreation, or sleeping. All new skips have a thin galley between the two rooms, as well as a full bath, which is something new. Before, the skip only had a partial bath, and the galley—if there was one—was part of the main room.

I left the *Two* far enough away that it should be outside of Treffet's space—if Treffet follows the same rules that both the Empire and the Nine Planets follow. I still don't know.

What I have learned from my research team's quick scan of the information is that this sector of space has not unified. No big governing body coordinates anything among the planets, and some say that the area outside of planetary space is a gigantic free-for-all, favoring whomever has the most firepower.

There are several starbases nearby, but they're all privately run and not owned by any governments at all. If we can't find Sector Base Y, then those bases might be a good place to go for research and information. There might be some rumors or legends that hold the key to the Fleet's pass through this area thousands of years ago.

I've learned to rely on legends. They hold a kernel of truth. Of course, what part of the truth isn't always obvious. But they can at least point us in a direction.

Treffet is big and rocky with three visible oceans through a cloudy layer.

We settle into orbit, and I keep all channels open in case one of the governments below decides to contact us. We have cloaked, but I have no idea if the cloak works here.

If it doesn't and if someone controls the space around Treffet, then that someone will most likely contact us. If no one does, then we're free to do what we want.

If we get caught—if we're violating some law we don't know—then only the three of us are at risk. Mikk and I are used to these risks, and from what I understand, Rossetti took them all the time when the *Ivoire* was still with its Fleet.

Once the skip is in orbit, I relinquish the command chair—not because I'm relinquishing command, but because standing makes it seem less crowded near the control panel.

Rossetti sits down. She's going to use the scanning equipment we've added to the skip to see if she can find the sector base. On a planet as mountainous as this one, we're all assuming that the sector base, like the other two, is deep underneath some mountain range.

I stand beside her. I'm going to monitor her work, but I'm also going to scan the pad that Stone handed me before we left. The pad is filled with the research I requested. Even though the Six ran the research, Stone organized it as best she could in the time allowed.

I scan over it, looking for an ancient city, one with a history that goes back thousands of years. Vaycehn on Wyr had just that kind of history. There was no place on Ylierr, and of course, in my quick scan, I find no place here either.

So I look for stories of lost cities, and find hundreds. Apparently a goodly portion of Treffet is desert, and the planet's cultures have a history of settling in an inhospitable place, giving life there a try, and then abandoning the place for somewhere a bit more welcoming.

The mountains are even trickier. Not only are they incredibly high, but they have very deep valleys that also have deserts running through them. There isn't a lot of water in the mountain range, except rivers fed by spring snowmelt—rivers that apparently dry up in Treffet's brutal summers.

I'm not feeling very encouraged, but I don't say anything.

Mikk is pacing. He has no real patience for this kind of research, and I know that he would prefer we do it somewhere safe, like our own space station.

If we can't find anything quickly, I will recommend that. At some point, we'll be wasting time and taking unnecessary risks, particularly in a sector where we have no support whatsoever.

"I have something," Rossetti says.

"An energy signature?" Mikk sounds hopeful. Sometimes the only way to find a weak *anacapa* signal is through its energy signature.

"No," she says. "Some tunnels underneath one of the mountain ranges that look symmetrical."

"You're kidding, right?" he says. "Shouldn't you be looking for the base itself?"

She doesn't acknowledge him with a look. Her fingers remain on the control panel. In the past, the insubordination of my team used to irritate Rossetti. In fact, the insubordination irritated everyone from the *Ivoire*.

But over time, the members of the crew who remained with us have gotten used to our working method. They still don't like the questions, but most crew members have come to realize that the questions do not waste time. They clarify things so that my crew can work better.

Rossetti does wait a moment before responding. That's the only way I know that she did not like his question.

"I have been searching for the base, but I'm not finding anything," she says.

Something in her tone alerts me. I glance at her, studying her from the corner of my eye. She's one of Coop's most trusted officers, calm and collected even in the face of danger. I saw her in action years ago, and I realized she was the kind of person I would trust my life to. She doesn't let anything bother her. She works hard, and she thinks quickly.

But this bothers her. Her jaw is set and she's blinking hard.

What I thought was irritation at Mikk is actually a deep emotional upset.

"You should be able to find the base," I say so softly that I'm not sure Mikk can hear me.

"If it's here," she says tightly. The corridors have shaken her. Perfect, seemingly man-made tunnels, without a gigantic room that her people could have built.

"Is there any way that those tunnels could have been built by someone else?" I ask.

"Of course there is," she says, and straightens her back, as if the thought has given her strength.

"What about the sector base itself?" Mikk asks, but his tone is gentle. He must have seen her face too. It probably shook him as well. It's hard for us to remember sometimes our history is the crew of the *Ivoire*'s past. "Could the base be shielded somehow?"

"You mean is the *anacapa* functioning?" She looks up at him. Her expression is impassive now: the old Rossetti, not the emotionally fragile one. "No. We'd have some indication."

"What about some other kind of shield?" Mikk asks. "You know, something as primitive as ours."

To my surprise, she smiles at him. "No," she says. "We would never use something that primitive."

I can't tell if she's speaking the truth or just saying that to irritate him.

"Besides," she says, "that shield would have had to last for a very, very long time."

He nods once, seemingly unperturbed by her jab.

I'm clutching the pad. "Where are those tunnels?"

She shows me. She's run her scans repeatedly, and there doesn't seem to be a sector base. Nor does there seem to be any kind of ruin. Just those perfectly designed tunnels. The tiny map she's created looks like the map for the original corridors around Sector Base V.

No wonder she's feeling a bit unnerved.

"Let me see what I can find," I say.

I lean against the control panel as I tap on the pad, looking for an ancient lost city in the vicinity of those tunnels.

It takes only a moment to find one, primarily because the city factors into the mythos of several of Treffet's cultures. It is the ultimate lost city, the one that everyone discusses. It's referenced in myth and legend and histories alike.

No one knows exactly where it is, and apparently there is some debate as to whether or not it existed at all. But most scholars—at least according to the rather cursory information that Stone had time to find—believe it was located not too far from those tunnels.

I sigh. "I think I found something," I say, and hand the pad to Rossetti.

She looks at the information, then looks at me.

"What?" Mikk asks with impatience.

"There's a lost city in this area," I say to him. "It existed more than forty-five hundred years ago, and some legends say it was built by a race of superbeings."

"Lost how?" Mikk asks. "What happened to it?"

"They don't know," I say. "They don't know much about it at all. It might not have existed. It might have fallen through the ground."

Mikk straightens. He recognizes that. Sometimes malfunctioning stealth tech creates a plume of energy. If that tech is underground, then the energy flares outward, destroying anything in its path.

"According to this," Rossetti says, shaking the pad at us, "the city was destroyed in a cataclysm."

"Meaning what?" Mikk asks.

"Fire from the sky," Rossetti says.

We look at each other. We're all silent for a long moment.

Then I speak up. "You know what Stone would say. She would say we don't know enough about Treffet to understand if that's important. We don't know the various features of this planet, if 'fire from the sky' is some kind of natural phenomenon."

"You're right," Rossetti says. "We don't know. But I want to go down there and see what we can find."

NINETEEN

Normally, when we need to study something on a planet, we go to the appropriate government, request the appropriate permits, do the appropriate diplomatic dance, and follow the appropriate regulations. We don't always do this under our legal names. If the place we need to study is in the Empire, for example, we use aliases. So many of us are wanted there that it's just safer.

But Treffet isn't the Empire. Nor is it part of the Nine Planets. We know nothing about Treffet, and it hampers us.

Of course, following the rules anywhere would hamper us. Usually it takes months to run through official channels. I know without even asking that Coop doesn't want us to take months. He wants us down there now.

He has waited this long; he feels he can wait no longer.

The skip is back in the *Two*, and we're in the *Two*'s conference room. In my previous ships, I always used the recreation area as a conference room, but the *Two* is big enough to have one. I actually like the room, and I didn't think I'd ever like something that official.

The conference room is in the center of the ship, and has no portals at all, nothing that looks out at anything, including the ship's interiors. Instead, the walls are covered with screens and access ports and specially designed holoreplays that can turn the entire room into someplace else should someone want to. I can hit a button to bring various-sized tables and chairs out of the floor. The tables and chairs are collapsible and actually have weight limits, but I figure no one who travels with me should have any trouble meeting those limits. Divers, spacers, and explorers are generally too thin. Scientists who travel have learned spacer habits.

The only person we've had to worry about is one of the Six—Rollo Kersting. Despite all of his activity over the years, Kersting has never lost a pound. He stubbornly consumes more than he needs, and I have come to view that trait with more affection than irritation.

The Six are all civilians who got roped into working for me because of my father. My father, who once headed military stealth-tech research for the Empire, discovered that some people have a genetic marker that enables them to work in malfunctioning stealth tech. The marker was difficult for the Empire to find through genetic testing, so my father ruthlessly tested for this marker primarily by sending anyone he suspected of having the marker into a malfunctioning stealth-tech field. Many people—including my mother— died in those fields.

I did not. Neither did the Six.

All of whom came to work with me long before we met the crew of the *Ivoire*, who also have the marker. The marker guaranteed that anyone in the Fleet could survive if the *anacapa* drive malfunctions. Apparently those of us with the marker are descendants of Fleet members who chose to live on the surface of various planets rather than continue forward with the Fleet itself.

We're all in the conference room because we're about to take a risk, and I've learned the hard way that asking your people to take a risk without explaining that risk is a recipe for disaster.

The Six have stuck with me for years and have, over time, become completely different people than those who helped me dive Sector Base V. They have all gained a love of history, and some have found that they enjoy diving. Orlando Rea, in particular, has become one of my best divers, and so has, surprisingly, Elaine Seager, who was initially one of the most timid of the Six. Fahd Al-Nasir has become quite a linguist, specializing in the dialects of Old Earth Standard. Nyssa Quinte is now our dive medic, a role Squishy used to take back when I dove old wrecks. Julian DeVries is the only one of the Six who hasn't really changed much. He is still a bit of an outsider, reserved, a bit pompous and more reluctant to take risks than he initially seems.

For the most part, they're disappointed that they didn't get to see Sector Base W, and hope they get to go to Sector Base Y. The *Ivoire* crew members, for the most part, never let their wants and desires be obvious.

Most of the *Ivoire* crew members that Coop brought are not in this meeting. They're along in case we find an intact base or if we need them to shut something down.

The only *Ivoire* crew members here at the moment are Yash, Rossetti, and of course, Coop, who looks impatient. Mikk, Tamaz, and Roderick round out the potential divers. Lucretia Stone is here to advise about working on the ground.

At the moment, however, we're discussing how to get to the ground. I've already stated my desire to go in quick and dirty, to see if the site of this lost city—which Stone says is called Isstahn in most of the histories—is also the site of Sector Base Y. If we're going to go in essentially illegally, then I want to take two skips, have a pilot waiting in each, and have everyone on the team be prepared to run if something goes wrong.

"I'm not sure you're going in illegally," Stone says when I finish my presentation.

I look at her. I know better than to argue. Stone is much more rules-oriented than I could ever be.

We're all looking at her. She's been pacing as I've been talking. She clutches another pad as if it's a lifeline. She seems nervous, and I'm not sure why. I thought it was because she didn't approve of my unwillingness to go through channels, so her comment surprises me.

It also surprises Coop. He's standing near the door, his back against the wall. He has one foot against the wall as well, as if he's trying to look relaxed when he clearly is not.

I haven't sat down either, although my hands rest on the chair at the head over the long conference table.

"I'm not sure I understand, Lucretia," I say. "Does Treffet have different rules than other places?"

"That's the thing," she says, flashing a nervous smile. "Treffet is different. Not only is it not aligned with other settled planets in the area, but it has two hundred and forty different cultures that I've counted, and they appear to be unaligned as well."

"Okay," I say, "so there's no one central government to negotiate with. We ran into that in Vaycehn. We had to work with the locals."

"That's the most interesting part," Stone says. "There are no locals."

I frown at her. Coop turns his head toward her sharply.

Rollo Kersting, who is sitting near Stone, leans his head back so that he can see her better. "You just said there are two hundred and forty governments. Those people are locals."

"No, they're not." Julian DeVries adjusts his silk suit. He always prefers to dress as if we're about to go to some diplomatic function. This habit has gotten worse over time rather than better. He shifts slightly in his chair so that he faces Stone. "You mean that no one lives in this area."

"More than that," she says. "No one claims this territory."

"How is that possible?" Mikk asks. Like me, he was raised in the Empire. All land, in both the Empire and the Nine Planets, is owned. I'm aware that other places do not have the custom of ownership, but I've never run across it outside of historical research before.

"I'm doing this on the fly," Stone says, "so I could be in error. But everything I'm finding refers to this as a no-man's land, a dangerous place that no government has been able to conquer and hold. Partly, from what I can tell, because there's nothing here for a government—no water, no good places for settlements, nothing."

"But you said that the city had been there," Kersting says, "so there was a good place for a settlement once."

"And water," DeVries says.

"We use different methods of providing water to our sector bases," Yash says. "At some bases in the past, we have used underground springs to supply water to a base and the settlement around it."

"I think water is the least of their problems," Stone says. "There's mention throughout the record of how deadly the area is, and how it seems haunted."

Coop's gaze meets mine. The malfunctioning stealth tech made the area around Sector Base V deadly.

"Well, then," I say. "We have an argument now. We'll take your research, Lucretia, and claim that we thought there was no government to negotiate with—should someone try to stop us, which it doesn't sound like they will."

"I can be wrong," she says somewhat nervously.

"We all can, Dr. Stone," Coop says. "But you're quite cautious, which I appreciate. I would like—."

Then he stops himself and looks at me. He has trouble staying back and letting me run things.

"Go ahead," I say with just a bit of amusement.

He nods and smiles at Stone. "I would like you to figure out the best place to land, given the topography that we know. I'd like to be in the city if possible. If not, I'd like to be in the most likely site for that city."

"I already have that, Captain," she says. "I was about to make suggestions."

"Good," I say, because I can't quite tell Stone's mood, and I don't want another argument between the two of them. "Given the reports of danger in that area, our ground team can only include people with markers."

Mikk glares at me, but knows better than to say he'll be all right. People without the marker die horribly in malfunctioning stealth tech. Generally time passes faster for them. They try to get out, can't, and die, waiting for help that is—realistically—just outside the stealth-tech field.

Mikk, Roderick, and Tamaz have all seen that kind of death up close. They don't want to die that way.

"We'll monitor from up here. But you're going to need some good pilots," Mikk says. "And the pilots can't be the explorers."

With that last statement, he looks at both Coop and Rossetti. Then he gives me a solid glare just in case I haven't thought that through.

"I have some good pilots on my team," Coop says. "They don't need any risk assessment here due to Dr. Stone's assumptions. Besides, we might not be down there long enough to cause any problems. We aren't even sure we're in the right place for the sector base."

He says that last to everyone, but his gaze catches mine. We both know that there's enough detail here to indicate the presence of a sector base.

If it exists, we'll find it.

Maybe this very afternoon.

TWENTY

I am already nervous. Nervous and out of practice—not with flying a skip. I do it all the time. But with the crowd.

Eight people inside the skip, talking, moving, laughing. I try to concentrate on piloting. Coop sits beside me, hands resting on his knees so that he doesn't touch the controls.

We agreed that I'd fly the skip. When it comes to skips and single ships and the *Two*, I'm the best pilot we have. When it comes to gigantic vessels like the *Ivoire*, Coop makes me feel like a beginner.

But we haven't counted on the distraction of the crowd.

Theoretically, this skip, which is the latest model, is built for ten people to travel comfortably for short distances. For long distances, the skip can hold four, two in each cabin.

Four is about my limit, long or short. I can keep track of everyone and I can pilot.

But we need eight—including me—down on that surface, so we all pile in. No sense in having two skips, especially when the landing area is small.

I'm not out of practice piloting. I'm always taking a skip here or there. Sometimes I simply run a piloting program at its highest, most difficult level. I take skips to wrecks to see if they're Dignity Vessels; I visit abandoned space stations; I'm always on the move.

No. I'm out of practice handling distraction. I haven't had this many passengers in a skip since I was running tourist dives twelve years ago.

We've just gone through the atmosphere, and I'm going to need to concentrate. I've run the holographic model of our landing site and I've read the topological maps, but something feels off to me, as if I'm not seeing something.

"Tell everyone to go to the other room and strap in," I say to Coop.

He gives me a startled look. There really is no reason to strap in on a skip, especially a state-of-the-art one like this. The inertial dampeners are spectacular, and the gravity doesn't change. Even if the skip bobs and weaves, turns upside down, or suddenly loses altitude, we won't feel any effects inside the skip. Our floor will remain a floor, our ceiling a ceiling, and our balance will be perfect.

"Do I have to say please?" I snap.

He gets up, corrals them, and heads them to the other room.

I could explain to Coop that the conversation is ruining my concentration, but that's only partly true. I am feeling claustrophobic and uncertain, and that's just not like me.

I have never seen mountains like this. They loom large ahead of me. The information running across the cockpit tells me that they're sixteen kilometers high, and a couple of the peaks are even higher.

We've already mapped out a path through the peaks that sounded good when we were on the *Two*, although Stone kept making a face. Once she even said, "You're not taking into account the reality of mountains."

Coop shrugged. He said, "Boss has flown through much tighter spaces," and I have. But in space itself, not on land, where I have to deal with a different external environment.

Of course, the skip compensates for all the changes—if it didn't, we couldn't fly it down from space—but I'm a hands-on pilot. I usually do everything manually. It keeps the job fun, challenging, and it's saved our asses more than once.

But as those mountains approach and the readouts in front of me look very different from anything I'm used to, I realize that flying by feel is simply not possible here.

I set the automatic controls and remove my hands from the control panel just as a proximity alarm goes off.

My heart pounds. I should have expected the proximity alarm. The mountains themselves will cause half a dozen of them because we're essentially flying into a box. Our speed decreases, but even so, if we hit a mountainside, nothing can save us. We will die. The proximity alarm warns of that.

Coop comes back in and sits beside me. He glances at my hands, then at the controls.

"Do I have to strap in?" he asks, and I hear some humor in his tone. He has figured out why I wanted everyone strapped in, and that it has nothing to do with the actual flight.

"Only if you want to," I say as the ship banks around two peaks. We're flying in a space so narrow that there's barely six meters of clearance on either side.

"Oh, I trust you," he says. "Or should I say that I trust the skip."

I glare at him.

"I thought you were flying this because you're the best skip pilot . . . ?" Now he is grinning.

"The best skip pilot knows when she needs to rely on the equipment," I say primly.

He clutches his hands together. He doesn't like the autopilot either, but I note that he hasn't volunteered to take the controls—which is something he would have done if he felt the need.

Our speed has decreased to a crawl as we enter the canyon itself. It's small, and it's not really box-shaped. Its edges are more like triangles, although there is a large center area.

The skip has stopped completely and hovers. I search the ground for our landing spot. From space, we found an area that looked large enough for us that wouldn't send us into a pile of pine trees or on the river's narrow edge.

But what we can read from space and what we see on the ground are sometimes very different things. I see three bare patches, but only one is level enough for the skip.

I retake the controls and slowly lower us to the ground.

From the back room, I hear applause.

Coop's smile has become a grin. "You clearly scared them."

"I didn't mean to," I say. But I realize now why they were worried. The only reason to strap in—at least from their point of view—was because I was worried the skip would crash.

"Don't tell them the real reason," he says so softly I know they can't hear.

I grin back at him.

"Don't worry," I say. "I won't."

TWENTY-ONE

*I*t takes nearly an hour to unload all of our equipment. Lucretia Stone has given us specific instructions so that we can set up everything correctly. Instructions, it turns out, that we wouldn't have needed if we had been able to perform the proper scans.

There is no loose stealth tech down here, no readings at all that would show that someone without the genetic marker would be in any danger. We find no death holes either, and nothing on the surface that indicates trouble.

We find nothing on the surface that indicates a city either. The floor of the box canyon is covered with dirt and tangled vegetation, most of which I can't identify, and trees—hundreds and hundreds of trees.

Some trees are familiar. I've seen pine before on other planets, and they're mixed in with trees I've seen, trees with leaves, but then there are trees I haven't seen before, with silvery bark and reddish leaves. A few have ropy leaves—or are they vines?—hanging from branches.

I am stunned at the diversity near us because it wasn't evident as we came in for our landing.

This flat area where I've landed the skip extends for one square kilometer, which is good, because we need all of that space. From the ground, the box canyon looks huge. From the air, it had seemed small and terrifying.

The other part of the box canyon that astonishes me is how high the walls of the canyon are. I know of space stations that are bigger, longer, and wider, but no single room inside the station has walls like this, walls that extend as far as the eye can see. I know there's a sky above; I can see it, vaguely orange and pale pink, but I have to tilt my head all the way back, making my neck crack as I do so.

But our work isn't above us. It's below us.

We set the equipment in three different areas, forming a triangle exactly the way that Stone has told us to. Julian DeVries supervises the equipment setup. Archeology has become a hobby of his, or so he said on the skip, and he styles himself our resident expert.

He looks vaguely expert, in his brown pants and corduroy jacket, his hair combed back. He loves being in charge, even though he rarely gets a chance. He doesn't have the degrees that Stone does, nor does he have her authority, but he seems to know what he's doing.

We would all rather look around anyway.

It's cold here, and there is no wind. I'm surprised at the cold. I hadn't even bothered to look at the temperature before we arrived because I assumed it would be warm. The last mountainous area where I spent any time was Vaycehn, where we found Sector Base V, and that area was stiflingly hot.

For some reason, I believed that the Fleet would pick warm areas for its sector bases. I hadn't asked Coop about it, of course, nor had I done any research. I had simply done what I tell my divers not to do: make an assumption about an area we're going to explore without doing the proper research.

Not that we're really going to explore this. If we find anything, we'll return to the *Two* and figure out what to do next.

I did note the cold before we left the skip, and took a jacket from my emergency clothing stash. I'm glad that I have it; I fasten it closed and stuff my hands in its pockets.

I'm standing with Orlando Rea near one of the first pieces of equipment that DeVries set up. The equipment—which has some big fancy name that I really don't care about—is probing belowground. Not that Rea and I need to pay much attention to it. It will function on its own for a good fifteen minutes before we have the information we need.

Instead, Rea and I are looking across this valley, which slopes downward from here. The ground rises and falls like small swells, and in the distance, boulders stand like warning beacons, letting us know that the mountains around us are active and could crush us if they really wanted to.

Coop and Yash walk toward us. They helped set up another bit of equipment. Coop looks purposeful. He has already stopped and spoken to Rossetti, who is still tinkering with the third piece of equipment. Seager and Kersting hover near Rossetti, like people awaiting instruction. Since Stone trained us all in equipment setup, the fact that they're hovering like that tells me that Rossetti prefers to do this work herself.

She stops, listens to Coop for a moment, and then looks around, as if she can't quite believe what he's telling her. Rea hasn't noticed the interaction, and I don't say anything to him.

Instead, I watch Coop and Yash climb across a row of prickly little plants that seem to be growing out of rock. Coop gives me a grim look as he gets close, and I can't wait any longer.

I walk over to him.

"It was here," he says.

"The city?" I ask.

He nods. "Yash ran a test of her own."

She's clutching one of their handheld devices, some kind of scanner that's so much more sophisticated than anything the Empire has. She's given the specs to one of our engineering departments at Lost Souls, but we don't have the devices yet because we don't have access to all of the materials.

Some of these things that the *Ivoire*'s crew possess have become more precious over time.

"I ran the composition of the soil," she says, "with a special eye to things unique to the Fleet."

I have learned in the past five years that the Fleet develops some of its own materials.

"The nanobits that we use for building have a particular signature, especially after they degrade," she says. "There are faint traces in the soil."

This news seems to have depressed Coop, so I can't help asking, "You're sure?"

"Positive," Yash says. "We're in the right place."

I scan the area. I see no evidence of a city. No ruins, nothing. "Where was it, then?"

"About ten meters beneath us," Yash says. "We'll be able to map its footprint, just like Stone says."

"But there's no way to know what happened to it," I say.

Rea, who has been quiet until this point, looks around pointedly. "I think it's pretty clear," he says. "If cities change the way Vaycehn changed—you know, with no one remembering its exact history—then eventually, the city probably needed supplies from the outside. Getting out of this canyon has to be work."

"That's one theory," Coop says.

"But you don't agree," I say.

He shrugs one shoulder. "There's no *anacapa* signature anywhere that we can find. And we also learned from Sector Base V that the *anacapa* drive in a properly shut down base can last several thousand years."

"That's how they were designed," Yash adds.

"Yeah," I say, "but not everything works the way it's designed. Let's see what we can find."

The three different equipment points are doing three different things.

One is mapping the footprint of the city underground. The one that Rea and I helped set up is searching the nearby mountains for an opening that will lead to Sector Base Y. The third is mapping the tunnels beneath us, hoping that they will lead to the sector base.

The equipment will give us answers. That's what it's designed for.

And, I'm trusting, that's what it will do.

TWENTY-TWO

*I*t takes almost two hours, but suddenly we're standing in the middle of a beautiful fantasy. The default on the equipment Stone sent with us creates a hologram. It's a suggested image, something that's composed of all the information that the equipment has, plus a great deal of speculation.

Even so, it makes tears well in Yash's eyes.

The hologram envelops us. It spans the entire valley—or at least, the illusion created by the hologram *seems* like it spans the entire valley.

Around us, a ghostly city rises. It has the design structure of other Fleet cities, pulled from the records of the *Ivoire*. It follows the underground footprint that the equipment has mapped, and shows us what the city might have looked like in its heyday.

The hologram is accurate down to the ground level. We seem to be floating several stories in the air, the city sprawling below us, and climbing up the mountainside. The river that runs against the farthest mountain range has bridges and buildings beside it. Although, oddly, the bridges are underwater, because apparently when ground level rises, rivers rise as well.

The hologram includes properly dressed icons of people, and those make Coop avert his eyes.

The city must have been very lovely. If this suggested hologram is even half right, this place has a bit of magic. The buildings blend into the environment, the roads are made of bonded nanobits, and the people look like Coop's people, hurrying about their day.

No one else seems to have noticed what bothers me.

On a mountainside not too far from us, a moving staircase leads to a gigantic closed door. Every once in a while in this simulation, the door opens and a ship goes in or comes out.

The three crew members from the *Ivoire* haven't even looked at that mountainside yet. Neither, it seems, has anyone else.

Everyone stares gape-mouthed at different parts of the city, the artwork on the public buildings, the parks, the children. Kersting is staring at the children as if they're real. He looks shaken too. He's such a kind-hearted man.

"Now I understand why the people of Treffet consider this city legendary," DeVries says. He stands beside me, shoulders straight, hands clasped behind his back.

"Why?" I ask.

"It's lovely. It's the kind of city that would live in memory. Some cities just aren't worth remembering. This one would be." He speaks softly, as if he doesn't want the three members of the *Ivoire* crew to hear him.

But they can, of course. They aren't responding.

"I also see why it's lost," Seager says. She extends a hand toward the high mountain walls, which seem steeper and even more rugged somehow. "I don't see a way in, do you?"

"It doesn't look like there ever was a city here." Coop says. It takes me a minute to realize he's not looking at the suggested images of the lost city. He's looking at the way the ground has overtaken the ruins. "This is just another valley, as far as they're concerned."

"And if you looked at the topological map," DeVries says, "you'll realize that there are dozens of these closed-off valleys throughout this mountain range."

"All that worry about what might happen if we're discovered by some government on Treffet," Kersting says, "and they couldn't get to us if they wanted to."

"On the ground anyway," Rossetti murmurs.

"It does explain why no government has claimed this land," DeVries says. "Why claim something so remote?"

"In the Empire," I say, "remote places get claimed all the time. It's a way of owning the land before anyone else can."

Coop sighs. "This doesn't tell us what happened."

DeVries says, "Five thousand years—"

"Is a long damn time, I know," Coop snaps. "I know it better than anyone, and I wish you people would stop reminding me about that."

My cheeks heat even though I'm not the one who said anything. DeVries mutters "sorry" and turns away. Kersting looks down. Seager examines a see-through image of a building near her, as if she could go inside it. Yash wipes at her face, and I realize she's wiping away a tear.

I touch Coop's arm. Since he's already upset, I may as well make matters worse.

"Did you see that?" I ask, indicating the opening that the program created on the mountain wall.

He turns, freezes, then closes his eyes for just a moment.

Kersting says, "I didn't know that the entrance to a sector base would be so obvious."

Proving that he hasn't done all of his research. Even the opening into Sector Base V on Wyr once had all kinds of outbuildings and businesses near the entrance. The Fleet never saw a reason to hide the entrances to sector bases, since the Fleet expected only its own people, or people it approved, to be in the cities near the sector base.

Coop stares at that opening for just a moment before he goes to the equipment that is supposed to be searching for the sector base. He runs a hand along the screen, then glances sideways at Yash.

She goes to his side, as if she has been given an order. All traces of tears are gone from her cheeks. It's as if they never were.

I join them. She's using her pad to put the basic map of a standard sector base over that mountainside. It all falls into place, lining up to the remaining tunnels.

Coop says, "This stupid machine isn't finding any evidence of a sector base."

"That's because it's looking for the wrong thing," I say.

They all look at me. My cheeks grow even warmer. I hadn't realized there was a problem when Stone made her presentation about the equipment, but now I understand.

And I feel bad that I haven't thought it through.

"What do you mean?" Coop asks, a strange tone to his voice.

"If I understand what Lucretia was telling us," I say, "then this equipment is looking for evidence of a human presence. Something regularly shaped or a building's footprint or a garbage pile."

"So?" Yash asks.

I nod toward the image on the mountain's side, and as I do, I resist the urge to mention just how long five thousand years is. I need to trim that very phrase from my vocabulary.

"We haven't found any stealth-tech residue," I say. "There's no *anacapa* signature."

"So?" Yash says, and this time it's not a question. It's a command to get on with what I have to say.

"So," I say as calmly as I can, "the equipment your people put down there isn't working."

"But the tunnels still exist," Rossetti says.

I hold up my hand. I have no answer for that, at least not yet. "One thing at a time," I say. "The sector base itself is one gigantic room, with some rooms off to the side. Like a network of caves."

"That's where the initial idea came from, or so the histories tell us," Yash says, no longer trying to hide her sarcasm.

"Which means that there is no footprint. Lucretia's equipment will read those areas as if they're a natural phenomenon."

"Except that they're hooked up to the tunnels," Rossetti says.

"Only they're not," I say. "We would have found that."

I have their complete attention now.

"When we were in Vaycehn, we experienced one cave-in. The nanobits took care of the damage, but you said the nanobits weren't working in the remains of the city." I said this last to Yash.

She lifts her chin slightly. "That's right."

"So," I say, "if they're not working below—"

"They're not rebuilding after a rockfall," Coop says slowly, as if it's all becoming clear to him as well. "The natural footprint looks more and more like a cave."

"That's right," I say. "And we haven't programmed this equipment to look for Fleet technology."

"Our tech is good," Yash says, "but not good enough to survive thousands of years without the constant maintenance provided by an intact *anacapa* drive and a working nanosystem."

The three of them look at each other. Coop's shoulders drop, and he sighs.

"There's no way to know what happened here, is there?" he asks.

"Not without a lot of research," I say.

"We've found three sector bases so far," Rossetti says. "One was properly shut down and still worked. Another was destroyed probably by bombs. And this one could have just had some kind of malfunction."

"Stone loved the idea of a lost city," I say. "We can have her bring in a team, interview the locals, do some real excavation—"

"I don't want to wait that long," Coop says. "There've got to be histories we can access."

I bite my lower lip, then realize what I'm doing. I don't want to tell him he's chasing phantoms, but it's hard not to.

"It seems to me," I say slowly, picking my words carefully, "that a people who build a city in such a remote place, and put their most important on-land equipment underground, don't really want the locals to know that much about them."

"But if there was a giant battle, surely that remains in the lore," Coop says.

"How will we know if that battle we find in the lore is what destroyed this city?" I ask. "No one on Treffet even knows where Isstahn really is. They have theories. I'm sure they have theories about what happened to it as well. And theories aren't facts."

"Besides," Yash says, "we have no idea if this sector base was properly shut down and the equipment just gave out. Maybe Sector Base V was more of a fluke than we thought."

"Or the underground environment there was more conducive to the equipment," Rossetti says.

Coop stares at the holographic image of the opening on the mountain's walls. "We don't know if that image is right or if it's a guess."

"It's a guess that matches those tunnels," Yash reminds him.

He doesn't move for a long time. Neither do the rest of us.

The fake city continues around us, as if we're the ghosts and it's the reality.

Finally, Coop says, "I don't like not knowing."

Yash nods in agreement. I remain silent. As much as I think I understand what they're going through, I really do not.

"For some reason," Coop says, "I thought that history was an absolute. It happened, someone recorded it, and we should be able to get answers from it. I didn't expect all of this guesswork."

"We might never know what happened," I say gently. I've been wanting to tell him that for years.

He shakes his head. "I don't accept that."

But Yash does. She looks at me, and I can see the sadness in her eyes.

"Maybe we should let Lucretia work," she says to Coop.

"And wait years to find out what happened here?" he asks. "We have more sector bases ahead, a lot of history to cover."

"We can try to find the next one," Rossetti says.

"You want to tell me how?" he asks. "We didn't have a suggested location for Sector Base Z when our ship left the Fleet. If something happened—if Sector Base W was destroyed by an enemy's bombs—then the Fleet might have changed course ever so slightly. And ever so slightly magnified by centuries turns into a hell of a mathematical error."

His voice rises with frustration. My team looks at us. I met Seager's gaze, and she looks away. The others follow, as if they don't really want to know what we're discussing. Maybe they don't.

"I can put a research team on this," I say.

Coop glares at me as if I'm being stupid, but I continue anyway.

"We can investigate ancient cities in a radius you choose. Some might be Fleet cities. Vaycehn was."

He sighs. Then he glances at that opening again.

"I just thought this would be easy," he repeats. "I think, of all people, I should know how much time changes things."

And then he walks away.

TWENTY-THREE

We are almost to the *Two* when Coop says, "Starbases."

He has been extremely quiet up until now. In fact, the entire team that we brought to the planet has been quiet. I don't feel claustrophobic around them, even though they sit inside the cockpit and galley, instead of in the seats in the back room.

Once we loaded the equipment and took off, conversation stopped. I'm not sure what Kersting, Seager, and DeVries are thinking. I know that Rossetti, Yash, and Coop are thinking about the answers they didn't get.

Once I got us out of that box canyon, I was much calmer. When the skip hit Treffet's atmosphere, I felt even better. As we head toward the *Two* I feel even lighter. My hands are on the controls, I know what I'm doing, and I'm ready to go home.

I find myself thinking about something completely different from everyone else. I find myself wondering when Lost Souls became home, and how a woman who likes to wander has actually managed to settle down.

I am double-checking the distance between us and the *Two* when Coop makes his little outburst.

He speaks loudly enough to get everyone's attention.

"What?" I ask.

"Starbases," he says, but he's not talking to me. He's sitting in the copilot's seat, but he has his back to me. He leans closer to Yash, as if they're continuing a conversation that they've had before.

Maybe they are.

"We've been worrying about sector bases," he says. "We haven't given a second thought to starbases, and they're on a trajectory too."

"There's just fewer of them," Yash says.

"Which could work to our advantage," Coop says.

"You want to explain this for the rest of us?" I ask.

"I need to check the records," he says, still talking to Yash. "There should be a starbase somewhere in the vicinity of Sector Base Y. We might even have its specs in our database."

"Even if we don't," she says, "starbase trajectories are more precise."

"More precise than what?" I ask. I'm feeling quite confused by this, and since it's going to be my ships taking everyone where they need to go, I'd like to know what this discussion actually entails.

Coop swivels in his seat so quickly his knees nearly hit my right thigh.

"Starbases get set up first," he says. "So even if something bad happened to Sector Base W, the starbase would have already been established, and it would be farther out."

"Closer to Sector Base Y," Yash says.

"Or even Sector Base Z," Coop says. "Or the place where the Fleet initially planned to put Sector Base Z."

"Starbase Kappa is in its proper location," Yash says. "So we just map the next point from there, and see if we come up with anything."

Starbase Kappa is known in the Empire as the Room of Lost Souls, which is where my adventures with stealth tech began decades ago. The Room of Lost Souls is an empty base, filled with rogue stealth tech, and people have died there for centuries.

Including my mother.

I was just a child when I went in there with her. I came out. She did not.

And my father planned it. He suspected that my mother lacked the marker. He knew he had it. He was willing to sacrifice me to find out if I had it as well. If I hadn't, I would have died with her.

"A starbase could have vanished a long time ago," I say. It's really hard not to mention how much time has actually passed because it is relevant. I know of starbases that haven't lasted a hundred years, let alone five thousand.

Besides, the Room of Lost Souls isn't a starbase any longer. It's a curiosity, something spacers warn each other against.

"We were lucky to find Starbase Kappa," I say, using their name. "Even if the starbase that you're searching for still exists, it probably isn't a base. It might just be floating parts."

"We learned some things from Starbase Kappa," Coop says. He had taken the *Ivoire* there against my instructions because he said he wanted to shut down the stealth tech.

He had done that, but it took me a while to realize he was also trying to find some hint about his past.

That was early in our relationship, less than six months after we found the *Ivoire*, and he still had no comprehension about the dangers the Empire faced.

Fortunately, no one from the Empire saw the *Ivoire*. No one saw him; no one realized what had happened.

And as far as we can tell, no one knows that the *anacapa* drive that was malfunctioning on Starbase Kappa, causing the strange effects that made it the Room of Lost Souls, has vanished. The Room of Lost Souls is a safe place for ships to stop now, because Coop brought its *anacapa* back to us.

I sigh. "I'm not going to be able to talk you out of this, am I?"

He grins. "I don't even know why you tried."

I want you to be sensible, I nearly say, but I don't. There is nothing sensible about his quest. But I do realize that it gives him focus.

So many others on the *Ivoire* were more realistic. They lost their focus, and some of them couldn't face the new world that they were in.

I don't want to take Coop's main prop away from him, but I also hate wild-goose chases.

I'm about to say something like that, and then I remember: a find like that starbase would be something like the wrecks I used to dive. I could get in touch with my former self, which I have wanted to do.

"All right," I say. "We'll go back to the *Two* and do a proper search."

"Thanks," he says, and claps his hand on my shoulder. But he's not thinking about the rest of us. His mind is already on that starbase, and what he might find there.

I hope he finds something. I'm not sure how many more disappointments his crew can take.

TWENTY-FOUR

After I finished talking to Coop, I contacted the *Two* so that our team could start searching databases for anomalies near the suggested location of Starbase Lambda. We don't know what we're searching for, and we might not have all the information that we need.

I've just finished docking the skip when the fight starts.

The skip's external door is open and the team is leaving. I'm running the shutdown procedures, double-checking to make sure everything is off before I start the skip's cleaning routine. I already had it shed as much material as it could while we were in flight—I don't want to bring anything weird back from Treffet. But there's a secondary round of cleaning procedures that take place in the bay, and then a massive decontamination run.

The crew has to go through a new decontamination chamber, one our scientists designed with the help of the *Ivoire*'s engineers. We've learned so much from the *Ivoire*, and Squishy, for one, believes we should market all of it so that we make enough money to run Lost Souls.

I have already consented to marketing a few small items, but I prefer to keep some of this technology proprietary, particularly since I don't know how all of it works yet and what other properties it possesses.

So I'm deeply wrapped in thoughts of cleanup as well as the way that I'm going to handle the upcoming meeting, when Coop takes my arm.

"I'd like access to your personal database," he says.

Normally I don't mind it when he touches me, but this time I do. I shake my arm out of his grasp. My personal database is mine. It's leftover from my diving days, and no one has access to it.

"You heard me contact the team," I say calmly. I'm still running the shutdown procedures with my left hand while I keep my right between me and Coop. "We'll talk about what they've found when we get to the conference room."

"I don't want to have another meeting," he says. "They don't know what they're looking for."

I can't stop the work, although I want to. I want to look him in the eye as I talk to him. Instead, I have to let my voice show my displeasure.

"And you do?"

"Yes," he says.

I shake my head. "You would never have found the Room of Lost Souls."

"It was near its proper location," he says. "Its stabilizers worked well enough."

"If you were looking for a starbase, which it has never been listed as. It's always been an anomaly, a cautionary tale, not a place that people were supposed to stop. Most maps of that sector deliberately left it off, and set routes around it."

He's standing too close. I don't like being near anyone when I'm irritated with them. And I'm irritated with him. I can't believe he asked for access to my database.

"I'll find it," he says.

"*If* it still exists," I say. "*If* it's still in starbase form. *If* it has caused some kind of anomaly. *If* it's in any records at all."

I finally finish the shutdown, but I don't look up yet. Coop knows that I do most things manually, and he deliberately asked me while I was working. He was hoping for a distracted yes. Even if he had gotten it, he still wouldn't have been able to access the database. I've set up new protections on it, tied to my DNA. Once a person gets through those protections, then they have to go past my old protections, which are probably too low-tech for anyone from the *Ivoire* to even consider.

"I can figure it out, Boss," he says, emphasis on my name. At moments like this, the fact that he has to use the word "Boss" grates on him. "I'm not stupid."

"I never said you were." I hit the automated internal shutdown procedure. Then I tilt one palm toward the door. "Let's get out of here."

As he steps out of the skip, he says, "You're not going to let me near the database."

"No, I'm not," I say.

"I can search it faster than you can," he says. "There are things I can look for."

"*No.*" I push past him. Five other skips sit in the bay, all waiting for their own adventures. The *Two* is so much bigger than the *Business* that it startles me sometimes.

He grabs my arm again, and I shake him away. Then I hold up a hand so that he doesn't touch me again.

"Believe it or not," I say, "as primitive as I am, I know more about searching these sectors than you ever will. That's my job, that's my expertise, and that's who I am. You're an amateur compared to me."

He opens his mouth, then closes it as if he's rethought his comment.

"You cannot convince me by arguing with me or by grabbing my arm or by forcing me to do what you want. I know you're desperate to find out what happened. I get that." I'm so angry that I don't care about the promise I made about timelines and censored language. I want him to back off, and I'm going to use every verbal tool I can to get him to do so. "So, *Captain Cooper*, you need to remember that whatever happened here happened five thousand years ago."

He snaps, "I know that—"

"And," I say, not letting him go into his own rant about how familiar he is with passing time, "while it all seems urgent to you, it's not. The people you know died a long time ago. The Fleet is gone, and might only be a legend in the dust of history."

"I know that," he says, shaking now.

"My people are alive right now," I say over him, "and so is the crew of the *Ivoire*. Living *now*. And we just happen to be in a sector because of your lovely *anacapa* drive that I don't know a lot about. I have no idea if we're even in hostile territory or if someone would think we are."

"That doesn't matter—," he starts.

"It matters a great deal," I say. "First of all, we're in the *Two*, not the *Ivoire*, and we don't have much in the way of defense capability. Second, you're asking my people to risk their lives *on a historical quest*. You got that?"

He straightens as I speak, as if he's putting on his captain's mask. I made him do that; I'm provoking him back into his shields. I know that. But he needs to know what he's asking of us. I've tried to tell him before, and he hasn't heard.

He needs to hear me now.

"The information is important to you," I say. "I know that. We all know that or we wouldn't be here. Your team needs to know what happened to the Fleet as well. It's part of your survival. But you have to realize that what you discover will probably have no impact on your future."

"You don't believe I'll be able to find the Fleet," he says, his tone so flat I know he's deliberately leached the emotion from it.

"I believe you can find a version of the Fleet if you want to," I say, "particularly if we find the information you need."

"But?" he says.

"But it'll be nothing like your Fleet. The ships will be different; the people will be different. You won't fit in."

My face is warm, and it gets even hotter as I draw a breath. I shouldn't have said that. I shouldn't have said any of it.

Coop's cheeks are ever so slightly red. I have no idea how he controls his anger responses so well, but I wish he wouldn't. I wish he would yell back at me.

It probably has to do with his training. I suppose a captain who constantly yells at his staff is no good to them.

"Thank you for your help so far," he says. "I suppose it's time to return to Lost Souls. Then I'll take the *Ivoire*, and we won't trouble you further."

He walks away. I resist the urge to grab at him. That's what he has just done with me and it infuriated me.

Instead, I use my voice. "Jonathon."

He stops.

"You need me."

He shakes his head once. "We can find what we need."

"I'm sure you can," I say to his back. "But it'll take you months. It'll take me weeks, maybe less. You want to find out what happened? Then you need me to do the research, and you need my team to help yours."

He doesn't move. He doesn't turn around. He doesn't do anything.

"I know this is a matter of life and death for your crew," I say in a much softer tone. "I know how important it is that they find out what happened to their families, even if nothing can be done about it. I know how long you've put this off. So let me help, and let me do it the right way."

"What is the right way?" he asks.

"We've been to two different planets on this trip," I say, "and now we're headed deeper into the sector—a sector none of us knows much about—to find out if there's still a starbase nearby. We're skimming over the surface of what might be very valuable information."

"I don't have the time to wait for Stone's archeologists to figure out what happened at the sector bases."

"I know that," I say. "But we can at least learn the history of the region. It might tell us a lot."

He tilts his head ever so slightly backward. I can feel his frustration. "So let's go look up your database."

"My database is the most complete database I know of on Empire history," I say. "I know a lot about the Nine Planets as well. But I've never had cause to come out here. I haven't collected information on this part of the universe."

"So you have nothing," he says, and this time I hear the defeat in his voice.

"I have what all the other databases have," I say. "Nothing more."

His shoulders slump. I have always been aware that this quest has kept him going. I simply hadn't realized how much until right now.

"Each year that goes by," he says, "I feel less and less like a part of something, and more and more like a man out of time."

I wonder if he realizes that his words have more than one meaning. Knowing Coop, he probably does. And he probably means that he is both a man who no longer fits in one particular era and a man who is running out of options.

"If you let me help," I say gently, "we can get you some answers. But you have to let me run this mission, just like we initially said."

"You want to go back to Lost Souls," he says.

I do, but not because we need to work there. I'm just ready to leave this part of space.

"I think we should," I say.

He lowers his head.

"But first, I think we should stop at the closest starbase. I think we should get some information that's not in the public records."

He finally turns around to face me. He has gone pale, lines carved into his skin that weren't there a moment ago. "How do you propose we do that?"

I give him my gentlest smile. "See why you need me?"

He extends his hand.

"I need you for more than just that," he says.

I have to walk a few steps forward to reach him. I thread my fingers through his. "It's a strange situation we're in, isn't it?"

"Yeah," he says softly. "And it gets stranger each and every day."

TWENTY-FIVE

I don't know what to call the relationship I have with Coop. It's sexual and distant, passionate and cold. We never ever call each other partners. We rarely acknowledge that we're lovers. We don't live together, we don't always sleep together, and we sometimes don't see each other for weeks.

I think most of the crew knows that Coop and I are something more than colleagues, but I'm not sure how much they know. I'm not sure how much I know.

I do know that I'm his best friend outside of the *Ivoire*, and maybe his best friend period. Around me, he doesn't have to be "the captain" all the time. He can let go, at least a little.

I think, sometimes, that's one of the main things he lost when the Fleet vanished—he lost the ability to be anyone besides the man in charge. He lost a large portion of himself.

As for me, I'm in a relationship of equals. He doesn't want anything from me. He doesn't want me to give up my work or change who I am. He doesn't care about my past, and he doesn't even want me to promise him a future.

Neither of us is sure what the future is. And neither of us wants a commitment from the other. We take comfort in each other's presence—except when we're fighting with each other.

And we have had some spectacular fights. Today's, while blunt, isn't the worst fight we've ever had. It's not even close.

We walk through the corridor hand in hand. As we round the corner near the conference room, our hands slip apart. I'm not even sure who disengages first. I'm not sure it matters.

I push open the door to find the crew that we took to the surface, Stone and some of her team, as well as the remainder of the Six.

Stone looks frustrated, but I can't tell if that's because she didn't go to the surface or if it's because she's frustrated by the work.

"It's not simple," Yash says to Coop. She's standing near the head of the table. As I note her position, that's when I realize that no one is sitting down. They're either milling or standing back awkwardly, arms crossed.

There's tension in this room as well.

Coop moves away from me, and I'm glad of it. I always feel better when we approach our teams separately.

"What do you mean?" he asks Yash.

"There is no starbase where Lambda should be," she says. "There's no record of one either."

"There's no record of anything there that we can find," Stone says.

"I think that's unusual." Mikk is across the room from Stone. He looks angry, and his tone is belligerent.

I feel a few steps behind. "You think it's unusual that there's no starbase in that location?"

"No," he says. "I think it's unusual that there's nothing there."

"Yes," Stone snaps. "And now the city Isstahn on Treffet is a meadow. That's what happens over time. You can't have a meadow in space."

That's when I understand what's going on. They're having a similar argument to the one that Coop and I just had. They're arguing over the passage of time.

"She doesn't get it," Mikk says to me as if Stone isn't there. "She doesn't know anything about space."

"I know something about space," Yash says, "and I don't get it either."

I can't help myself. I shoot a glance at Coop, and part of my expression is a petty I-told-you-so. I also know he won't understand why I have that expression until later in this conversation.

"Nothing's routed through there?" I ask Mikk.

"That's right," he says.

"Recommendations in the travel charts to avoid the area?" I ask.

Coop moves his head ever so slightly. He's beginning to understand now.

"You got it," Mikk says.

"So what's there?" Coop asks.

"As far as the star charts go, a big fat nothing," Yash says. "Which is normal, if you think about the damn time passing."

"It's not normal," Coop says. "Boss has been informing me of that for a while."

He nods his head in my direction, a small movement that is both an acknowledgment and an apology.

"We can't find any reference to that part of space in the material we've scanned," Stone says to me. "Now, granted, we're scanning. I barely understand what this sector is about, let alone what we're discussing when we discuss that part of space."

"What is this sector about?" I ask.

Coop gives me an exasperated look. Yash actually rolls her eyes. But I don't care. The politics of a region are as important as what's in the region. If you don't know what you're up against, then you have no idea if you've done something wrong—or if there's a place to avoid.

"So far as I can tell," Stone says, "everything is nonaligned. Hell, even the cultures inside the various planets are nonaligned."

"So we can go anywhere," Yash says.

"It's not that simple," I say. "Who polices the sector? Anyone?"

"I don't know," Stone says. "I'm not even sure if the various planets trade with each other. A few cultures don't seem to have space flight, or if they do, they don't use it."

"That's the thing that worries me," Mikk says.

Stone gives him a look of complete exasperation. "It worries you for no reason," she snaps.

"That's okay, Lucretia," I say. "I've worked with Mikk a long time. He often has a good sense of things."

Stone sighs heavily and turns her back to him, as if she's going to disown what he has to say before he gets a chance to say it. Yash shakes her head as well, but Rossetti remains quietly observant, as if she's not quite sure who to believe.

Coop raises his eyebrows slightly and looks at me. Our teams haven't disagreed like this in a long time. Not since we had the Dignity Vessel arguments a few years ago.

This time, however, their discomfort isn't an echo of our discomfort. This time, the frustrations seem to come from this unsatisfying trip and from our groups' varying work method.

And, it seems, the people in this conference room haven't divided themselves by *Ivoire* crew and my crew. They've divided themselves by opinion, and the opinions seem based on varying experiences and expertise. That's new as well.

"So what is it, Mikk?" I ask. "What's bothering you?"

"There're hints in the public materials," he says, speaking directly to me, "that there's a group of ships that form a culture all their own."

"A Fleet?" Coop asks, and there's a bit too much hope in his voice.

"There's no evidence of that," Yash says. "Believe me, that's the first thing I looked for."

"It might be a group of cargo vessels that travel together for protection,"

Roderick says. I knew he was in the room from the moment I entered, but his presence didn't register until now. He's standing behind Mikk, half-hidden in the shadow caused by the overhead light.

"You don't believe that it's cargo ships, do you?" I say to him.

"It's hard to find information about them," Mikk says. "That worries me."

"Why?" Coop asks. "You say there's no information on our Fleet."

"That's something out of the past," Roderick says. "We're talking about right now."

Cargo vessels banding together are common in the Empire. But the cargo vessels travel together for protection—at least in the parts of space I'm familiar with.

"Are you finding some draconian laws?" I ask. "Or do you think there's a pirate problem?"

Coop lets out a grunt of understanding. Yash frowns at me, as if I shouldn't be giving these men any credence at all. Stone shakes her head slightly.

"We're not finding evidence of anything," Mikk says. "I don't like it."

Both the Empire and the Nine Planets have laws about who patrols which area of space. Those laws enable both sectors to deal with pirates rather ruthlessly. The pirate problem still exists, particularly in the Nine Planets, but it's not as severe as it was when I was a girl.

"Crap," I say. "We'll have to be cautious going in."

"Going in where?" Stone asks.

"To that dark area of space?" Mikk asks.

"We're not going home?" Rossetti says, and her use of the word "home" surprises me. I'm not sure if she's referring to the Lost Souls or if she's referring to the *Ivoire*.

"Not yet," I say. "We have one more stop."

Everyone looks at me.

"There's got to be a starbase somewhere near here," I say. "We're going to go there like a bunch of weary travelers and see what we can learn."

"We'd have to download their entire database," Stone says.

"There's no way to know if they're going to be friendly," Roderick says.

"Or if they will take our money," Mikk says.

I grin at everyone, pretending a calm I don't really feel. "Well," I say. "There's only one way to find out."

FLIGHT

TWENTY-SIX

Squishy had to program a whole new route into her control panel, one she had never taken before. Her hands were shaking. She had already activated her FTL, leaving Quint's pod far behind.

But she realized that when he was alone in the *Dane*, he probably accessed the computer logs. He couldn't get into all of them; most were coded to her DNA as well as to the poem she had learned in proper Ancient, thanks to the *Ivoire* crew.

However, the most recent flight records were easy to access because so many starbases and space stations wanted to download them before allowing a ship to dock. Squishy had always felt it better to make the information easy to access so she didn't have to go through a lot of regulations once she got into a policed part of space.

She made herself sit in the control chair and breathe deeply. The entire ship felt odd without him. He had a bigger presence than she remembered, and even though he had only been in two rooms—the cockpit and the main cabin—it felt like he had touched every part of the ship.

She had put all of the used medical equipment into her biohazard bin, but she hadn't yet jettisoned the waste. She didn't want to leave a trail, and she still wasn't sure what had embedded itself in his skin. Part of her—the stealth scientist more than the medic—wanted to know. She wouldn't be able to conduct any real experiments here—she lacked both the equipment and a safe lab on the *Dane*—but she wanted to do so the moment she returned to Lost Souls.

If she returned to Lost Souls.

And that "if" was a much bigger "if" than it had been before.

She leaned over the cockpit and stared at the star chart before her. She had several problems. The first was that the research station had been deep in Enterran territory, far from most settled planets. The Empire had learned that much from her mistakes. The research station had been an island unto itself.

In some ways that had played in her favor. No nearby population had seen the station explode. In other ways, it caused her problems.

Getting out of the Empire wasn't an easy task, especially now that Quint had alerted them to her presence.

If he had been efficient—and knowing him, he had—he had let the imperial authorities know that she would be returning to the Nine Planets. There were a thousand routes out of the Empire, a million ways to get to the Nine Planets, which should have made her task easy.

But it didn't.

Each culture within the Empire had its own police force, and most of those forces had some sort of space patrol. Add to that planetary and regional patrols, as well as subdivisions of the Enterran military, and suddenly each route she could travel had a dozen ways she could get caught.

She needed to dump the *Dane*. But if she did that, then they would know what ship she had replaced it with. If she wanted to get rid of the *Dane*, she had to go farther into Enterran territory rather than trying to get out of it.

The authorities would expect her to dump her ship on the way to the Nine Planets, but they wouldn't be looking for her to do it deeper inside the Enterran Empire.

But she wasn't sure she wanted to do that.

Part of her wished she had upgraded the ship with an *anacapa* drive. Then she wouldn't have to worry about getting caught at all. But she had deliberately not brought an *anacapa* drive into the Empire. She didn't want them to get their hands on that technology.

She stood up and rubbed a hand over her face. Then she paced the small cockpit, wandered back into the main cabin, saw the mussed-up bed without its usual coverings, and frowned. A red light glowed above the empty escape pod hatch, informing her that the pod was gone.

She grabbed the door and pulled it closed.

She was done with the main cabin for the duration of this trip. She would sleep—if she could sleep—in the other cabin.

That was probably part of her problem. She hadn't eaten since that morning, long before the evacuation of the station.

She would figure out her new route and then she would cook herself something.

The new route didn't have to be permanent. It only had to do two things: it had to steer away from the rendezvous point, and it had to get her as far from Quint's pod as possible.

She could change direction later. Right now, she had to get far away, whatever that meant.

And while she cooked, she could figure out if she wanted to replace the *Dane* or if she wanted to see if her luck would hold.

She made herself look at the star chart again, and then she charted a new course. It wasn't quite on the trajectory she had used a few moments ago, but it wasn't far off.

Her problem was that she didn't have a backup plan. She had gotten herself and her team into the Empire. She had figured out a way to destroy so much of the stealth-tech research that she would set the Empire back years in its research (and maybe put it on a new path). She had figured out a way to get her team out of the Empire, and she had thought she would join them.

But Quint had spoiled that, and she should have seen it.

Not Quint exactly, but her own failure to make a clean getaway.

After all, her task had been the risky one. She had taken it on for that very reason. She hadn't wanted anyone else exploding the station. Not because she didn't trust them (even though she didn't), but because she knew that job was the visible one, the tough one, the one that would take complete focus.

She should have planned on getting caught.

And she hadn't.

She hadn't planned on it at all.

TWENTY-SEVEN

Squishy found Boss next to her latest project, a reconstructed Dignity Vessel that Boss had deliberately kept nameless. Boss was preoccupied, her hair cut short, new lines near her eyes. But she didn't seem tired, even though she was working impossible hours. Lately, Boss seemed energized, as if the Dignity Vessel projects had revitalized a part of her.

The Dignity Vessel itself dwarfed everything else in the bay. The ship was huge. Squishy always forgot how big the Vessels were, even though she had now been inside several of them. The first Dignity Vessel, all those years ago, had been a derelict, floating in space, and even though it had taken a long time to dive it, the ship hadn't seemed as big as these. Space itself made everything seem small.

Since Squishy had come to work at Lost Souls, she had worked on five derelict ships. Then the *Ivoire* had arrived and some members of the crew had helped repair one of the five derelicts. This ship was another found ship, and it needed a lot of interior work, which Boss was supervising.

"We did it once before," Squishy said as she walked beside Boss, staring up at the Dignity Vessel. The ship jutted above them, shading them from the lights at the top of the bay.

Boss stopped walking. Squishy had made her entire presentation while they examined the exterior of the Dignity Vessel. Squishy felt a bit uncomfortable, arguing that they should take a team into imperial space, with the mission of destroying stealth tech. She was half hoping that Boss would take in a Dignity Vessel on a trial run, maybe even go in with the *anacapa* engaged, use the high-powered weaponry, and destroy the base that Squishy had discovered.

But Boss was frowning. "Why do you care? The Empire kills people in a variety of ways. We can't stop that. We're working to keep the balance of power in the sector, to keep the Empire from moving out here. That's more than enough."

Squishy swallowed. She had thought Boss would understand. But Squishy had forgotten how Boss could overlook disturbing things. Boss had done that on their first dives in a Dignity Vessel, ignoring Squishy's warning, and leading to the breach that had hurt their relationship for years.

"People are dying because of me," Squishy said.

"Nonsense," Boss said. "You haven't been part of stealth-tech research for decades, at least not in the Empire."

"But I'm the one who took them down this path. I'm the one who started all of these experiments. Everyone who died since then died because of me."

Boss shook her head.

"Don't be dismissive," Squishy snapped. "In the past, you've dismissed me and that was a mistake."

"One mistake," Boss said. "A big one, I grant you. But just one. And I've apologized repeatedly. This is different."

"How is this different?" Squishy asked.

"It's not personal, Squishy," Boss said. "I know you think it is, but it's not. A lot of people can hold the blame for all those deaths, including the people who continue the experiments in light of the disasters they're causing. It's not about you."

Squishy straightened. "You don't understand—"

"I do," Boss said. "I've lost people because of mistakes I've made. I understand. But the worst thing we can do is go into the Empire."

"You did it," Squishy said. "You went to Vaycehn, and found the *Ivoire*."

Boss nodded. "And it could have been a disaster. The Empire didn't catch us that time, but they might this time. We're fugitives."

"Not all of us," Squishy said. "I still get my military pension. It goes to my home in Vallevu."

Boss didn't say a word, but she was clearly struggling to remain silent.

"I can go back in with a team," Squishy said before Boss could say anything. "We can use the same explosives that I developed a few years ago. I did the research, Boss. The Empire has confined stealth tech to one gigantic base. We get rid of the base, we get rid of the tech."

"They're not stupid enough to keep all of the research on that one base," Boss said. "It's backed up somewhere."

"And once we find where the backups are kept, we launch the mission. I could go back, revamp my credentials, and work in the lab until we're ready to launch the attack. They wouldn't suspect anything."

Boss snorted. "You haven't worked in stealth tech in decades and then you return? How is that not suspicious?"

"I would blame the leaked studies." Squishy straightened. "I'm on the record—several legal records—protesting the way the experiments were conducted. That was decades ago. I would have complete credibility if I went back and stated that I wanted to return to correct the mistakes and make sure no one died."

"And they'd hire you?" Boss asked.

"They asked me to rejoin when I brought them that first Dignity Vessel." Squishy had claimed the vessel she had taken from Boss on that fateful trip for the imperial government to get it out of Boss's hands.

"And you said no," Boss said. "That was years ago. Things change."

Squishy shook her head. "I'm still considered the godmother of stealth-tech research. I'm mentioned in a ton of studies. I'd like to fix that."

"And what?" Boss asked. "Give the Empire the *anacapa* drive?"

"Make sure they can never catch us," Squishy said. "Make sure that their research goes a different direction."

"You can't control research," Boss said. "You know that."

"But you can alter it," Squishy said.

"And what if you get caught?" Boss asked. "They'll get you to tell them about the *anacapa* drive."

Squishy shook her head. "I'd die first."

"Don't be melodramatic," Boss said.

Squishy made a face. She wasn't being melodramatic. But apparently Boss wouldn't believe that.

Squishy needed a different argument, so she said, "I still don't have a great working knowledge of the *anacapa* drive. It's vast and complex, and I certainly couldn't build one from scratch. If the Empire catches me, the only thing they'd get from me is that the drive exists. They'd also learn how powerful it is. They'd learn that they're making a terrible mistake when they try to treat it as a cloak."

"And then they come after us," Boss said.

"They'll come after us eventually anyway," Squishy said.

"No," Boss said, and walked away.

Squishy scrambled to keep up. "People are dying, Boss."

"All over the Empire, for all kinds of reasons," Boss said. "Hell, people are dying in the Nine Planets for all kinds of reasons too. Some are too poor, some are too sick, some still live under repressive regimes. I'm not going in there to rescue those folks. Why should I rescue a bunch of scientists in the middle of the Empire? Scientists who specialize in weapons research, I might add."

Squishy was shaking. Her initial answers—*they're important, they're scientists for fuck's sake, there might be someone like me*—wouldn't be good enough for Boss.

"You wouldn't go in," Squishy said. "I would."

Boss stopped walking and turned around. "So I should send in the only one of us who isn't connected to the *Ivoire* who has any chance of understanding how an *anacapa* drive works."

"There are a lot of people here who understand it as well as I do," Squishy said. "And they're not all connected to the *Ivoire*."

"But they're not you," Boss said softly. "So my answer stands. No."

She started walking again. Squishy started to follow, then stopped. Boss had said no. She rarely revisited decisions, and only when faced with a great deal of evidence that her assumptions were wrong.

Her assumptions weren't wrong here. She was right: this wasn't a Lost Souls' mission.

This was a personal mission.

And it was one Squishy would complete. With or without the help of anyone else.

TWENTY-EIGHT

*T*wo course changes before she settled down enough to think clearly. Then Squishy put her head in her hands.

She thought she had been tricky, but she hadn't been tricky enough. Even though she had just acted like a covert operative on the research base, she really wasn't one. Her mind wasn't subtle enough.

But Quint's was. He had spent his entire life doing this crap. He manipulated people, he spied on them, and he bent them to his own will.

It was a measure of the respect with which he held her that he had actually told her what his job was. Most people in military intelligence, let alone someone in Imperial Intelligence, never told anyone.

He had told her and given her a warning, one she hadn't received until now.

She sighed into her hands, then let them run down her face. She glanced around the cockpit.

He had to have put tracers on it. Outside, inside, everywhere.

So the Empire was tracking her.

And she didn't have the equipment to find all the tracers.

Oh, she had the equipment at Lost Souls. Most of the ships owned by Lost Souls had it as well. Boss was paranoid about being tracked.

But the *Dane* was Squishy's ship, which she had bought after she took her leave of absence from Lost Souls, and she hadn't been paranoid enough. If she had been thinking way back then, and clearly she hadn't been, she would have put all of the up-to-date anti-tracer technology into the *Dane*. But she hadn't been thinking about that.

She had the anti-tracer tech the ship came with and nothing more.

That would have to do. She had learned a lot of tricks from Boss. Now was the time to use them.

Squishy took a deep breath and stood. She looked around at all the little nooks and crannies, then at the control panel itself. She had left the travel logs vulnerable on purpose, and it wouldn't take much to install something tiny in those. She would look there second.

First, she would take care of the ship's exterior.

She had gone onto the *Dane* repeatedly during her stay on the research station. Mostly she had brought back many of her possessions; they hadn't fit into the décor of her office. Besides, they distracted her, making her think of her real life.

But she checked everything from her locks to her readouts to her security systems.

Everything except the exterior of the ship.

She slid her hand to a part of the control panel she had never used. Somewhere in this thing was a series of commands that cleaned off the exterior of the ship. She probably had to drop out of FTL to do it, but it would be worthwhile.

Whatever she did might not remove every tracer that Quint put on the exterior, but it would remove most of them. His technology was probably much more sophisticated than the *Dane*'s.

But he hadn't had much time to put tracers on the *Dane* while the station was evacuating, and he hadn't suspected her of any wrongdoing before that.

She reviewed the ship's manual to make sure the ship could actually do what she hoped it could. Then she said a small prayer and dropped out of FTL.

She didn't recognize the part of space she was in, not that it mattered. She was still deep in the Empire. And she had to act fast.

She activated the external cleansing mechanism, hoping it knocked out or disabled whatever kind of tracer Quint had put on the *Dane*.

It would take five minutes, which was much longer than she wanted to be in this part of space, open and vulnerable. While the external cleaning program ran, she got up and grabbed one of her handheld medical scanners. She tuned it to read any kind of signal being sent, and then scanned the walls, the floor, and the furniture in the cockpit.

She found nothing. At least, not yet anyway. She would have to scan for different signals, different types of energy signatures, before she was satisfied that this room was clean.

The control panel beeped, letting her know the cleaning was done.

Then she resumed the same flight path, and launched the FTL again. It did her no good to change her flight plan before she scanned the computer system itself for tracers.

That was her next task.

She actually hoped she would find something. Because if she didn't, she would worry that she had missed it. And if she missed it, then Quint or his people would still be tracking her.

She sat down at the control panel again and took a deep breath. Maybe she was just channeling Boss's paranoia. But Squishy hadn't channeled that enough this trip.

A little bit of paranoia would do her some good.

Maybe it might even help her get home.

TWENTY-NINE

NINETEEN AND A HALF YEARS EARLIER

"**D**id they just fire on us?"

Rosealma floated to one of the portholes and looked out. She didn't see anything, but she was in some kind of side room. Turtle was in the corridor, clutching a door frame. The woman in charge of this silly dive, a woman who called herself Boss, was in the cockpit, such as it was, and she was the one who had spoken.

Rosealma's heart was pounding. She pushed herself off the wall and let the momentum take her, grabbing the doorway near Turtle as she went by.

Rosealma couldn't see Turtle's face through her helmet. In fact, the only way that Rosealma knew the person near the doorway was Turtle was the faint pink of her environmental suit, the suit's ridiculously broad shoulders, and Turtle's unnaturally small helmet.

The other tourists, five of them, were clustered in the corridor, clinging to the walls as if they might make the gravity return. This dive had been Turtle's idea, a prolonged date, something that enabled them to see a historic ruin while getting to know each other.

The training had been simple: taking a few tests outside Longbow Station, signing a few waivers, and forking over the money. Rosealma had to buy a special environmental suit; she hadn't had a good one since she left for college, and of course, she had abandoned that one when she left Vallevu. Not that she had worn it in years.

But a cargo monkey never forgot her origins, and throughout this entire dive, Rosealma felt like she had come home.

This ship, the *Hjalmar*, was two hundred years old. The corridors were narrow and uncomfortable, still scored by weapons' fire from the battle that happened inside the ship as well as outside. The *Hjalmar* had been a minor part of a major battle in the Colonnade Wars. A civil war had actually broken out among the crew.

It wasn't a mutiny: they didn't try to overthrow their captain. Instead, various rebel groups had infiltrated the Enterran military. On some command —Rosealma's history got fuzzy here—the rebels were supposed to capture all of the ships and bring them to a rebel stronghold nearby.

But the *Hjalmar* was the only ship where the fighting actually took place. In all of the others, the infiltrators had been captured long before they managed to get positions of power on any vessel.

The ship got disabled, a lot of people died, some pivotal battle occurred because of what happened here, and the remaining crew abandoned the ship. The ship itself got forgotten, like so many wrecks from the Colonnade Wars, only to be discovered by amateur historians, who claimed it as a tourist site.

And divers like this Boss took people on easy dives to see the bits of history.

Rosealma thought the dive silly. After all, you could just look at the holovids and imagine the battle yourself. Or you could go into one of those virtual reenactments, actually take on a historic persona, and live the battle, such as it were.

This exploring the old site, as if there were resonances here besides the dark and the cold and the emptiness of space, that was all just silly.

Although Turtle seemed to enjoy it. She claimed she liked historical sites. She had been looking forward to this for a week, as if it was all a grand adventure. Rosealma did not tell her that grand adventures generally did not happen two hours from a space station, in a wreck people had been diving for generations.

Still, Boss had sounded a bit panicked a moment ago. It was probably some kind of historical reenactment on a budget. This whole trip had been on a budget.

Boss knew what she was doing—her training was spectacular, and quick— but the ship she had brought them out on was minimal at best, and Boss wasn't the most personable of tour guides. She tried, but she wasn't amiable, and she clearly had no patience for more than one stupid question at a time.

She had tethered her ship, the *Skeessers*, to the *Hjalmar*. Rosealma had asked about the name of the *Skeessers*, and it turned out Boss had no idea what it meant. She had bought the ship on the cheap for short runs like this one, and she hadn't bothered to change the name when she changed the registration.

If this thing about being shot at was all a ruse, some kind of show for the tourists, Rosealma would have words with this Boss after the dive. At least, that was what Rosealma promised herself as she hurried to the cockpit. She felt a need to explain the sense of urgency she felt, without telling Boss or Turtle that too many people had died around Rosealma for her to ever feel comfortable with pretend death.

Rosealma propelled herself into the bridge, then grabbed a tether to stop herself from going any farther. Boss wasn't alone. Another tourist was in there with her, a slight figure, probably a woman. They were standing on the bridge, their magnetic boots on.

That surprised Rosealma. Boss had specifically told the entire tour group that they couldn't use their magnetic boots on this dive.

The other odd thing? Boss and the tourist were facing each other, not looking around like Rosealma would expect on a dive like this.

Rosealma did look around. She hadn't been to the bridge yet. It was large and mostly unfurnished, although someone—probably the tourist board that so many of these dive companies worked for—had installed tethers throughout the main route. The tethers kept beginners on the route, and prevented them from floating into too many hazardous areas. If tourists used tethers, they never had to worry about coming into a site too fast or missing a corner and hitting an edge.

Tethers marred all sorts of tourist dive sites. The tethers were just one of many safety requirements for an adventure dive site designation. The sites were inspected annually and deemed "safe" for beginners.

Or at least, that was what Boss told the entire group before taking their deposits for the trip, long before any of them got tested for their skill level.

The tethers hung from every flat surface in the bridge so if the ship rotated, something would float past an amateur, and the amateur would have something solid to hang onto.

Rosealma had just used the nearest one to stop her forward movement. Neither Boss nor that tourist even noticed she was there.

Rosealma saw nothing through the wide windows, jutting into space in the form of a two-level triangle. She had always thought the design on these old ships ridiculous: if someone wanted to defeat one, all they had to do was destroy the windows in the front of the bridge. Even though it was perched on top of the vessel, right smack in the middle, it was obvious which part of the ship was the bridge because no other part of the ship had that design feature.

One well-placed shot and the entire command crew would go down. That's what she would have done.

But she remembered from some of her military history that when this ship was in vogue, the Enterran Empire had no outside enemies, and rebel ships were too tiny to get close.

"I mean it. Someone's shooting at us."

Boss wasn't speaking. That voice belonged to the other person in the room, who, by process of elimination, had to be female. Rosealma looked around one last time. She could see the tail end of the *Skeessers*, hooked to the *Hjalmar*, but the space around both ships did not light up as it would if someone used a laser weapon.

Then she realized that Boss's hands were moving. Boss was talking to this tourist on a private comm link, but the tourist was too stupid to realize that she had been talking to the entire tour group.

Rosealma put a hand on her hip, then cursed silently. She didn't have a weapon. Boss had forbidden weapons on this trip, which had seemed silly at the time, and now seemed very wise.

Rosealma slipped farther in, then turned on her boots and slipped to the floor of the bridge, landing just outside the tourist's line of sight. Boss saw Rosealma, turned her head slightly, and Rosealma held up a finger to her helmet. Boss slowly moved her head back toward the tourist.

"They're shooting at us!" the tourist's voice was getting screechy. "Why aren't you doing anything?"

Rosealma knew she was still in Boss's line of sight. Rosealma pointed at the tourist, then made a circle with her forefinger around her own ear, hoping that Boss understood that as a sign for crazy.

Boss's head moved down ever so slightly, then back up. A nod.

Rosealma made a fist with her hand and shook it at the tourist. Boss nodded for real this time, and Rosealma couldn't tell if that was a response to the tourist or Rosealma's gestures.

But Rosealma was going to take it as a response to her questions.

"We're all going to die! Can't you see that?"

Rosealma didn't look behind her, but she wanted to. Had the other tourists come here? Or were they still cowering in the corridor?

She nodded toward Boss, hoping Boss could see that, then pointed at the crazy tourist again. Then she lifted a finger in a silent countdown.

One . . .

Two . . .

Three . . .

She and Boss both stormed the tourist, knocking her down and holding her in place. The woman started screaming and fighting hard. She kicked and slapped and moved her entire torso. It took all of Rosealma's effort to hold this woman in place—especially since her body was starting to float. They had knocked her magnetic boots off their anchor on the bridge.

"Do you have anything to restrain her?" Rosealma asked Boss.

"What do I look like, a cop?"

"No," Rosealma snapped. "I just thought you might be prepared for emergencies."

"I *am*," Boss said. "I have a medical kit."

"Oh, for God's sake," Rosealma said. "Hold her."

She got up, leaving the kicking, squirming crazy person to Boss. Rosealma shut off the boot magnets and floated to a tether, grabbing it and tugging. The damn thing didn't come loose. It was fixed quite well.

Rosealma tugged again, and couldn't get any traction. She needed a knife. But Boss hadn't allowed them.

So Rosealma held on to the tether, pointed her feet downward, and turned her boots back on. The boots' power sent her to the base of the bridge, and that dislodged the tether. Then she stomped her way to Boss, who was having as much trouble restraining the tourist as Rosealma had had.

Another set of hands joined them, another body got in the way, holding the woman down. The woman kept kicking and screaming, but Boss moved to her feet, grabbed them, and pointed them at the metal floor. The magnets held, making it hard for her to kick.

Rosealma looked up, saw that the third pair of hands belonged to Turtle. Rosealma grinned, even though she knew Turtle couldn't see her through the faceplate on her helmet.

"Nice of you to join us," Rosealma said.

"I wanted to see you one more time before you died," Turtle said.

"Who's shooting at us?" someone asked from the door.

"*No one*," all three women said together, and then Turtle giggled. Rosealma couldn't help it. She giggled too.

Boss didn't. She just grabbed the crazy tourist's hands, pulled them together, and said to Rosealma, "Were you planning to use that tether for anything?"

"Oh," Rosealma said, catching her breath. "I suppose."

She wrapped the tether around the crazy tourist's hands, and as she did, she realized she hadn't giggled in years. She was actually having fun.

"How are we going to get her out of here?" Turtle asked.

"I say we leave her," Boss said.

"No!" the crazy woman cried. "They're killing us! Why don't you believe me?"

"Why don't you issue sanity tests before allowing anyone to dive?" Rosealma asked Boss.

"You want to tell me how I can legally do that?" Boss asked.

"I have a few ideas," Rosealma said.

They looked at each other—or tried to, since the faceplates were vaguely reflective. Neither of them spoke for a long moment, not that it mattered. The crazy woman did most of the talking for them, about shootings, and dying, and how none of them would survive.

She was still thrashing. It would take some work to get her off this ship.

Boss looked down at the crazy tourist, then back at Rosealma.

"Okay," Boss said calmly. "She's convincing me. I'd love to hear your ideas."

"All right," Rosealma said. "We get her out of here, and you owe me a beer. I'll tell you then."

"I'll owe you a full refund," Boss said.

Rosealma shook her head.

"You promised an adventure," she said. "I didn't think you could pull it off. But you just did. So I'm getting my money's worth."

"You're nuts," Boss muttered.

"Nah, *she's* nuts." Rosealma nodded toward the tourist. "I'm just hard to please."

"I'm not nuts!" the tourist shouted. "We are all going to die."

"True enough," Rosealma said to her. "Just not this afternoon."

This afternoon, though, this afternoon, she had found something she thought she had lost, a sense of herself she had completely forgotten.

She had missed it.

And she was happy to have it back.

THIRTY

Squishy found two different tracers in her control panel, both in the travel logs. She had spent the last two hours digging through the logs, seeing if she could find anything.

She was hunched over the control panel, her back aching, not just from the position she was sitting in but from the tension. She was beginning to feel like eight kinds of fool. She always told the scientists working with her to envision the entire problem, not just the interesting parts.

But in planning this mission, she had envisioned it all the way to the destruction of the research station and not beyond.

She stood, stretched her back, and listened to her spine crack. Her stomach growled. Back before she thought of the tracers, she had planned to make herself a meal. She didn't have time for that now.

Instead, she went into the galley and got some dried fruit, bringing it back to the control panel. She made herself eat while she worked.

One of the tracers was easy to remove. It hadn't completely integrated itself with the travel log and, it seemed, that tracer was the most recent.

The other one, however, was much more intricate, and she wasn't even sure how long it had been there. Digging into the programming of a cruiser wasn't her area of expertise even though she could do it, but if she actually had some expert help, it would go faster.

Faster was what she needed. With each moment that she used to remove this tracer, she felt like the Empire was getting closer to her.

Besides, she probably hadn't even gotten to everything Quint had planted. He had to have done something simple as well.

As she had that thought, her mind flashed to his hands, resting on the side of the bed as he prepared to lean back so that she could operate on his cuts. His fingers had curled along the edge.

She got up, walked to that cabin, and pulled open the door. It still smelled faintly of blood and anesthetic. She took her medical scanner and ran it along the edges of the bed. She got four different hits.

Every time he touched the bed he left another tracer.

She frowned at that. Had he had some kind of substance on his fingertips? Or had he had a group of very small tracers in his uniform jacket?

She wagered it was the second. She would have to go to every place he touched, and somehow remove all of those tracers.

Or she could use them to her advantage.

She stopped and made herself breathe. The only way to use tracers to her advantage was to go somewhere unexpected.

She either had to go deeper into the Empire as she had initially thought or she had to abandon the *Dane*.

The problem with abandoning the *Dane* was that if she did it planetside, she would get caught. And if she did it here, in space, her escape pod wouldn't go far enough away from the ship itself.

She gathered the four tracers she found on the bed and took them to three of the remaining four pods. She planted two of the tracers in one pod, and the other two in different pods.

Her heart was pounding. She would release the pods at different points, but she had to wait to do so until she made certain all the tracers were out of her control panel.

It was no longer a question of if the Empire would find her; it was a question of when.

In fact, it was amazing that they hadn't caught her yet.

And then she froze.

Maybe they did know where she was. Maybe they were tracking her for another reason.

Maybe they wanted her to lead them back to the Nine Planets.

What had Quint said? *Don't worry. I couldn't track you inside the Alliance. They have good protections in place.*

Maybe he hadn't let her into the research station because he trusted her. Maybe he—or his bosses—knew about her association with Boss. Maybe they weren't after Squishy at all. Maybe they wanted Boss.

Her stomach churned.

If she wasn't careful, she would have led them right back to Boss.

And the others. Squishy's team.

Quint hadn't been lying when he said he was surprised about the bombing. She could almost imagine his presentation to his superiors: *She's no real threat to us. We'll catch her before she gives away any of our secrets. And she's squeamish. She doesn't understand that you have to lose some lives to save others.*

She closed her eyes and bowed her head.

You lose some lives to save others. He had said that to her outside the court. And she had known that, from a military standpoint, he was absolutely right.

And what if you get caught? Boss had asked her a year before. *They'll get you to tell them about the* anacapa *drive.*

I'd die first, Squishy had said.

And Boss's response had been automatic: *Don't be melodramatic.*

Squishy thought she hadn't been melodramatic.

But now she faced that very situation. She was going to get caught, because she certainly wasn't going to lead the Empire to Boss inside the Nine Planets.

What then?

Would she die before she gave away any secrets? Or would she try to bluff her way through?

She actually had no idea. And that very fact scared her more than anything else.

THIRTY-ONE

Squishy had never done anything this elaborate before—planning a mission of this magnitude without Boss. Squishy had never planned a mission of this magnitude, period.

She had taken the weekend off and organized a retreat for ten of her best people. They met in the island city of Topabano, on Ral, the planet closest to Lost Souls' newest science base.

Topabano had become a favorite resort destination for the science teams. The island was large, the city relatively new, the climate temperate.

Squishy had decided to hold her last mission meeting here at the recommendation of three of her scientists. She had planned to hold the meetings indoors—envisioning two days of discussions, without anyone leaving the (rather expensive) hotel.

Instead, she had relocated the meetings shortly after she arrived to a private beach, complete with tiled patio, an outdoor kitchen (staffed by the hotel), and some kind of roll-out roof in case one of the island's sudden rainstorms struck without notice.

Squishy arranged the tables and chairs herself, guaranteeing a privacy even when the hotel staff served the meals. Squishy had forbidden drinks on all but the last night. She wanted her team awake as they got their final instructions.

The hotel was set up for these kinds of meetings, which surprised her. What surprised her more was the fact that she could order surveillance equipment to go with the meeting. She did order a surveillance package, one that not only kept silent track of her team members, but also made sure no one kept track of her.

She didn't want anyone smuggling in recording devices or sending information back to Boss at Lost Souls. Nor did she want someone selling the information to the Empire.

She had handpicked her team carefully. She had followed all of their work for more than a year. But more than that, she had followed their attitudes.

Most everyone who worked for Lost Souls, at least in the beginning, had started out in the Empire. They had come to Lost Souls because of their dissatisfaction with the Empire, and Squishy made sure that the dissatisfaction was deep.

Boss also made sure that no one who worked for Lost Souls was some kind of imperial spy, and Squishy wasn't sure how Boss did that. All Squishy knew was that in Lost Souls' early years, a handful of people were summarily fired because they had too much contact with the Empire.

Squishy herself had had an interview with Boss's purity squad. In fact, Squishy had an interview every six months or so, when someone new came on board.

Squishy still got her military pension from the Empire. The pension went directly to her accounts in Vallevu, and the money went to her family there. Or the people she called her family. She kept care of them, even though she hadn't seen them in years.

She got notification through a variety of different sources, going through place to place, through addresses real and fictitious, to eventually get to her. None of it the Empire could trace—or at least, it couldn't trace any of it after the information left the Empire proper—but the purity squad worried.

Finally Squishy had given them permission to check the routes and to reroute some of her information if the addresses got compromised. She didn't want the Empire anywhere near her either, and she was glad that the purity squad was helping her keep track.

She used the purity squad to her advantage. And she made sure the purity squad helped her with her potential team members as well.

But she had to keep her own eye on the purity squad. Squishy had planned half a dozen retreats for various scientists this past year, and she had three more retreats in her future.

This was the only retreat with her mission team. All of the rest were ruses, so that this retreat seemed ordinary.

It didn't feel ordinary.

Some of that was the venue. The soft ocean breezes, the hot, almost sticky air, the white sand reflecting the sunlight, and the pale blue ocean made her feel like she had entered some kind of dream.

She hadn't thought she would be the kind of woman to find a place like this beautiful, but she did. She wished she had planned all of her retreats on

Topabano. But she had gotten it into her head that she should change venues all of the time, and she had.

So far, though, Topabano was the best.

The retreat had worked well so far. She had five teams of two. Each team would go to a different backup site within the Empire. It had taken a lot of research to discover where the Empire maintained its information on stealth tech.

The backup sites were often attached to other research stations. Her team members had to figure out a way in, and then figure out how to destroy the right material without destroying all of it.

She also wanted her teams to get out before anyone knew that something was wrong.

It had taken several planning sessions, most in captured moments with each individual team, to figure out how to get into those backup sites, how to get out, and how to target the right information. Each team had a different assignment, and none of the other teams knew what that assignment was.

That way, if someone got caught, the only person they could implicate for certain was Squishy herself.

She adjusted the linens on the table, made sure the settings were proper, and that a sheer drape enclosed the lunch area. She didn't want anyone on her team distracted by the ocean or by some kind of bird on the beach. She wanted their full attention.

Today was the day of the final speech, the one she had learned from Boss. The "this is a dangerous mission and we could all die" speech. The "you can quit now if you're afraid" speech.

She had learned how important it all was, and how necessary it was to give the team members the illusion of choice. Most of them were too deep into the process to quit, and even though she had told them that this mission could cost them everything, she wasn't sure most of them understood that.

She left the enclosed area to check on the meal. Grilled meats garnished with island fruits, fish for those who preferred something a bit lighter, a salad, and a few dishes native to Ral. Already everything smelled marvelous. The staff waited, keeping its distance.

Squishy nodded at them, not even hiding her nervousness. She had debated for a long time as to whether she would bring her teams together at all. She didn't want them knowing each other's missions, and she wasn't sure she wanted them to know who the other team members were.

Then she realized that they would all rendezvous to get out of the Empire, and if they didn't know who was going to show up, then they might panic when they saw a familiar face, even if that face was from Lost Souls.

She moved to the edge of the patio, where she could see the entrance to the private beach. Her team was starting down the steps: four men and six women, all in loose, white clothing purchased here, all laughing as if this truly was a vacation.

Later in the day it would become one. She gave them their last night free.

She waited for them, patting her pocket as she did. She had actually written down the rendezvous coordinates. She would give the coordinates to one team member and ask that member to commit the coordinates to memory. Then she would take the paper back and destroy it herself.

She had paired scientists with security personnel. The scientists all had eidetic memories. The security personnel were brilliant at systems. Most knew how to get in and out of anywhere. Most had served in one special forces team or another, either with the Empire or somewhere in the Nine Planets.

She didn't worry about loyalty. It was too late for that.

She worried that someone would die on this mission.

The laughter stopped as the teams came down the hill and saw her face. She was serious.

They had to be serious now too.

As they passed her, heading to the tables set out for the spectacular meal, she realized she didn't need to give the speech for them.

They had known the moment they decided to work for her on the side that they were taking risks. They understood the dangers.

Just like she had understood the dangers whenever she went diving with Boss all those years ago.

Still, Boss had given the speech, and Squishy had found it annoying. Particularly when everyone on the dive had gone with Boss on a previous trip.

For the first time, Squishy understood what Boss had been doing.

She had been talking to herself.

She had discussed the plan. Now saying it out loud, knowing that someone could die, might make her change her mind.

Squishy's heart pounded.

She wasn't going to change her mind.

Unless someone talked her out of it.

And she wasn't sure anyone could.

THIRTY-TWO

Squishy sat alone in the cockpit of the *Dane*. She had done this to herself. Boss had warned her.

Squishy herself had warned her team, and, in warning them, had warned herself.

This was not unexpected. And yet, oddly, it was.

She took a deep breath. Quint had thrown her off. Quint and his news about Cloris. Quint and his cuts.

She wiped a hand over her face, and as she did, she realized she didn't regret what she had done. She had meant to destroy the Empire's stealth-tech research, and she had done so.

Or at least, she had done her part. She hoped her team had done theirs. She would never know now.

But she had to assume that they had completed the task. She had to operate on that.

Those who had survived—and, if things had gone according to plan, that should have been all of them (considering they should have left their bases and research stations before anyone knew what they had done)—would have gone to the rendezvous point.

According to her timeline, they should have realized she wasn't going to arrive, and they should have left by now.

But had she been in charge of them, she would have waited—a few hours, an afternoon, maybe an entire day—before following that order.

So if they had stayed for a day, they were still there. They were just considering leaving.

She needed to prevent their capture. Because she knew where they were going—they were going to the Nine Planets—but she didn't know how they would get there.

And if it was standard procedure for bases in the Empire to put tracers in the travel logs of all foreign ships passing through Empire space, then those ships could be traced. But only if someone knew they needed to be traced.

So she needed to buy even more time. She couldn't tell anyone in the Empire about that rendezvous point until the ships had a good chance of getting out of the Empire. A few days, maybe a week.

She needed to plan for a week.

She sighed. Her hands were shaking. She glanced around the cockpit, her gaze resting on those places where Quint had left tracers. She wasn't going to pull the rest, if there were any more. She wasn't going to take any more tracers out of her control panel either.

She would chart a new course, heading toward the Nine Planets, and she would be dodgy about it, as if she were trying to lose someone following her.

Instead, she wanted them to follow her. That way, she could keep them from her team.

That was the first part of the plan.

The second—she had to decide what she would do. Boss had been right: Squishy wasn't the type to sacrifice herself for an idea. She wouldn't die first. But she might die down the road.

Still, she would give up information—and that might not be bad.

The Empire had to know it was on the wrong track. She could feed them information about stealth research without mentioning the *anacapa* for months, and that would direct the research in a direction that didn't cause hundreds of deaths, but also wouldn't compromise the Lost Souls research.

She had to die before giving up the *anacapa*. Or she had to escape. Or figure out a way to manipulate the Empire away from that information.

She would have to give that part some thought.

She stood, and as she headed to the galley for her long-delayed meal, she froze. She hadn't considered one other piece of this mess:

Boss.

When Boss found out that Squishy had destroyed the research base and hadn't come to the rendezvous, Boss would try to find her. Boss might not do anything more than figure out what happened to Squishy's ship.

But Boss was unpredictable, and she had been putting *anacapa* drives in smaller ships.

She might come for Squishy, and that would play right into the Empire's hand.

Boss would deliver a working *anacapa* drive right to them.

Squishy had to stop that. But she had to do it in a way that wouldn't lead them directly to Boss.

So Squishy couldn't just send a message to Lost Souls. She needed help. She needed someone she could trust. She needed Turtle.

THIRTY-THREE

We arrive at the nearest starbase nearly a day later. This trip is turning out to be much longer than I expected—than any of our team expected. Nerves are frayed, partly because of the length of the trip, and partly because of the things we've discovered. Or haven't discovered, as the case may be.

I research the base before we get there, and learn it doesn't call itself a base at all. It calls itself a resort, and it acts like one: we have to pay fees just to reserve a berth for the ship. Then we have to pay fees to disembark. We must choose our level of service, and because we're going to be asking a lot of questions, I choose the top tier, spendy as it is.

The resort itself, so far as I can tell, is unaffiliated with any nearby planet or any particular group. From the documentation and the history of the place available in the public records, the resort has been around for about seventy years.

A partnership with a corporate name bought the place for its location about eighty years ago. The partnership, called the Azzelia Corporation, used an existing starbase as its foundation and redesigned everything, taking its time, making everything "perfect" or so its literature says. The resort is now called, quite simply, Azzelia. I have no idea what that word means, if it means anything.

I've gone to resort bases before in the Empire, mostly to pick up repeat clients on the way to a tourist dive. On those trips, I deliberately never left the docking bay. I have always assumed these places are not for me, even though I've never had direct experience with them.

I do know, from dealing with high-end clients of my own in the past, that you get what you pay for in these places, and the more money you have, the fewer questions the staff asks of you.

I am supposed to submit financials, which I do under one of the aliases Lost Souls usually uses when we're in the Empire. I make a point, as I submit them, to mention that this is just one of my holdings. I also let the staff at the resort know that if there are any troubles, they must come to me.

The *Two* is included in those financials (as it is in many of my aliases), so that it looks like part of that particular business. I made sure I changed all the registration information in our systems long before we ever charted a path to the resort.

Since many of us are wanted throughout the Empire, I've learned to be cautious—even though we're as far from the Empire as most of us have ever been.

Docking is easy. These resorts make it possible for arrogant rich people to do the tricky maneuvers even if they have very little piloting experience. I learned on one of my earliest dive missions involving the superrich that it's better to follow the resort's automated docking glide path than it is to try to chart one on my own.

The resort's systems weave into mine, and generally leave tracers. I always turn that information back onto the resort (and starbases) themselves. I leave the tracers in, but disable their permanent implantation. Then when I leave, I make sure that my own tracers follow the same path back into the resort's (or starbase's) systems, so that I can find any information I need quickly.

Sometimes it pays to be paranoid. I have gleaned a lot of information that way, often without the starbase knowing I've even hacked into their systems.

Although, technically, I'm not sure it is hacking. They opened the channel—the computer dialogue if you will—between us, and I'm simply continuing the conversation.

I'm alone in the cockpit, doing the last of the work. Everyone else is waiting to disembark. I've already told them our plans. We're going to be here for two days. We need the rest and the break from each other. Since it's costing us a fortune just to visit this resort, I've decided to give the tense team a minivacation. We can't afford private rooms for all of them, so they can share. Some of us—me, Stone, Coop, and Yash—will have our own rooms, primarily because I need the privacy.

I've instructed everyone to do as much research on the sector as possible. Some individuals have specific tasks, things they should find. Others should do some general work. No one is supposed to call attention to themselves.

Except me, of course. I'll be asking some of the tougher questions. But I've done this many times before, and unless there are rules and regulations or things I don't know about, I should be just fine.

We're going to have a touch-base meeting twenty-four hours from now, and then we'll reassemble on the ship itself. I don't want to have long meetings, exchanging information, on the resort. High-end places can afford high-end security, and high-end security often means that surveillance exists in places we would normally expect privacy.

I don't want us to have any conversations about who we are or what we're doing while we're on this station. And I've let everyone know that.

I finish setting up the ship's privacy protocols and let myself out of the cockpit. As I walk toward the airlock, Coop joins me.

"Have you looked at this place?" he asks.

"Not beyond the specs." I grab my overnight kit from its place beside the door. "Why?"

"It's unreal," he says. "There are *swimming* pools here."

I shrug. I've heard of stranger things in high-end resorts. "Have you gotten off the ship then?"

"Not yet," he says. "I was waiting for you."

I don't look at him. I pretend that I haven't heard that last. I'll deal with that in a few minutes.

Instead, I say, "Is everyone else gone?"

"Like kids stepping into a dreamland," he says. "Each one was met by some kind of personal guard."

"It's a butler," I say. "It was in the specs. We all have our own personal guide if we want one."

"I don't want one," he says tightly.

"Then you can tell your personal guide when we get off the ship to leave you alone."

He catches my arm, then clearly remembers the fight we had the day before and lets his hand fall. He doesn't apologize, though. Coop rarely apologizes, which I rather like about him.

"This place is really expensive, isn't it?" he asks.

"It's not the priciest place I've seen," I say, going for nonchalance. *But,* I add mentally, *it's close.*

"Let me pay for this," he says.

If he were a regular client, I'd tell him that he would be paying for it. But he's not. "Don't worry about it."

"I do worry about it," he says. "You've covered the costs of so many things over the years. I have income now."

He does. They all do. The money that Lost Souls makes on the bits of technology and patents we sell based on Fleet technology gets split between the corporation and the crew of the *Ivoire.* If someone made a particular contribution, they get a higher percentage, just like they would if they were regular employees of Lost Souls.

So many of them are regular employees. I haven't put Coop on the payroll—his job is captain of the *Ivoire*—but he gets consulting fees. He has money so that, if he wants to, he can survive in this time without my help at all.

What he doesn't quite fathom is how little money he has in comparison to me. If I don't want to, I don't have to work again. But I want to. I can't imagine life without work. I'm just questioning the type of work.

"I know you do," I say. "But it was my decision to come here. I could have looked for somewhere else to stay. And it's my decision to let everyone off the *Two* for some R and R."

His hand comes up as if he wants to touch me again. "This trip isn't what you expected, is it?"

"It's not what you expected either," I say.

He nods. Then he straightens his shoulders, a clear sign he's going to say something he believes will be difficult for both of us.

"I have a request," he says. "I'd like to trail you while we're here. I don't want to work this place alone."

I feel my heart sink. I can't do the kind of work I do with a shadow. I'm shaking my head even before I realize it.

"I'm sorry," I say. "If you want some answers, then—"

"I have to find them on my own, I know," he says.

I'm not entirely used to this new, impatient Coop. I prefer the old, patient version. I realize, however, that I'm seeing the real man for perhaps the first time.

"That's not what I was going to say." I take his hand and hold it between mine. His skin is warm. "I was going to say that sometimes people give out more information to a person alone than they do to couples."

"Is that what we are?" he asks. "A couple?"

He's asking seriously, but I don't want to answer that. I can't answer it. I don't know what the answer is.

"That's how they would perceive us here," I say.

He sighs. Then nods. "No sharing rooms either, then, huh?"

I smile softly. "I'll make sure they're adjoining."

He smiles too, but the smile is somewhat defeated. I ignore that. I can't let his needs get in the way of what we're trying to discover.

"Now," I say, "you head out. I need to set up all the security protocols."

"Shouldn't you leave someone on the ship?" he asks.

That's standard procedure for the *Ivoire*. It's often standard procedure for my ships as well.

"If they want, they'll get in," I say. "We're far from home and we don't have a lot of defenses. We also don't have a lot to steal."

"Just information," he says.

"That will take them a long time to make use of," I say. "I make sure that we don't have a lot of proprietary information on any of the ships we take out of the Nine Planets."

"You're a strange one," he says to me. "Sometimes I think you're too cautious, and sometimes I find you too reckless by half."

"It's my lack of military training," I say, only half seriously.

"That's probably it," he says, then leans in and kisses me quickly on the lips. "Are you going to make sure our rooms adjoin or should that be my only request of my personal majordomo?"

"You can do it," I say. I kiss him again, then let go of his hand. "I'll see you at the twenty-four-hour meet, if I don't see you sooner."

He grins. "Oh, you'll see me sooner," he says, and heads into the airlock.

I watch him leave. I don't trust anyone with the *Two*'s secondary security procedures. Not even Mikk and Roderick, who are authorized to run this thing should anything happen to me, know all of the security I've added. And, should something happen to me, they won't know everything.

Some of the information on this ship will die with me, just like information on the *Business*, and information in the corporation itself. Not that I'm paranoid.

But I am cautious.

And there are things no one else ever needs to know.

I lock down the *Two*, and feel a slight pang as I leave her. I hope to find her in the exact same condition when I get back.

THIRTY-FOUR

By the time I leave the *Two*, I don't see Coop any longer. In fact, as I step out of the airlock, I don't see anything that I expect.

The resort has set up some kind of virtual projector, so that it looks like I'm stepping out of the *Two* onto a sandy beach, complete with ocean before me.

I know I'm in a standard docking bay, so the illusion, including the briny scent of the sea mixing with some kind of exotic flower, irritates me rather than pleases me.

So does my butler. The resort's promotional material carefully informed me that all of our butlers would be human, not android, as if that was supposed to reassure me. It did on some level. That reduces one layer of electronic security. An android or some kind of robotic servant could easily keep track of my every movement. So could a human companion, but it would be more obvious.

Or at least, it would be more obvious with technology that I'm familiar with. It's pretty clear that this resort takes technology to a level that's usually frowned upon in the Empire and, by extension, the Nine Planets as well.

My butler is male, which surprises me, given how many of the tasks the resort says the butler can help with are intimate and personal. He's also stunning—dark eyes, almond skin, and brownish-black hair. He's built like a man raised in gravity. His blousy shirt accents his broad shoulders, and his tight pants show off muscular legs.

His clothing is clearly formal; mine is not.

He makes me very uncomfortable. I now understand why Coop decided not to have a butler. I need the assistance, though, so I'm going to bluster my way through this.

I extend my hand and am about to introduce myself when I realize just how rudely I'll come across if I say my name.

"You must be my butler," I say. "Forgive me for asking, but is this really your usual appearance?"

His eyes widen slightly as he takes my hand. My question surprised him. "What do you mean?"

I've moved him off introductions, which was my intention. "Well, clearly, we're not on a beach. So I'm wondering if you're real as well."

"I'm real," he says.

"Well, then," I say, deciding that I'm going to play this rich and bossy. Back when I was running diving tourism, I experienced a lot of clients like that. What I'm beginning to realize is that it's not hard to come across that way, particularly when you've got an agenda. "Is it possible to get rid of this beach and just see the docking bay?"

"It's not that attractive," he says, taking my kit. "What else would you prefer?"

I almost tell him that I'm an old-time spacer and I prefer docking bays, but then I decide not to reveal that much about myself. "The bay itself is fine. I travel a lot, so I like to know exactly where I'm at. Which means I prefer reality to fantasy most of the time."

He gives me a sideways look that I'm not supposed to see. I've surprised him again, which is a good thing, I think. At least I'll keep him on his toes.

He touches a button on his wrist, and the entire illusion pinpoints down and then travels into that button, as if the button houses it. It's my turn to be surprised. I didn't expect him to be the source of the illusion.

The bay itself is huge. It's also gray and utilitarian. No wonder the resort doesn't want its customers to see the bay. There's nothing impressive about it, and there's no other way to enter the resort.

My butler takes me to the main doors, then up a side staircase. I don't have to check in. That happened before the *Two* even landed. I was told then that we would go directly to my room, which also felt odd.

I'm used to entering space stations from the docking bay, into a ring of restaurants and stores hawking various wares. It's always somewhat surreal, going from the quiet of the ship to the relative silence of the bay to the cacophony of merchants trying to capture the attention of everyone who arrives on the station before the money all goes away.

Here, instead, it's silence, except that my butler asks me if I would prefer stairs or a lift. I haven't exercised much since we left Treffet, so I opt for stairs.

They're opulent and shiny and look expensive. But that beach makes me question everything. I wonder if they're just gray and utilitarian like the bay, but overlaid with some kind of program from my butler's magic device.

I don't ask.

My room seems to be on its own floor. This I know is an illusion. No space station can afford to have a floor dedicated to just one room. But I wonder if the staircase can rotate so that it moves from room entry to room entry, or if there were stairs from the bay to each room separately.

For the first time, I regret telling Coop I wouldn't room with him. I would love to discuss how odd this makes me feel and see if he feels the same way.

My butler opens the gigantic doors, swinging them inward to reveal a living room as large as the main room in my skip. He takes my kit to a closet larger than my very first single ship was. I try hard not to act impressed.

After he hangs up my meager possessions, he bows to me, and says, "You may summon me any time you like."

That gives me the opening I want. "You forgot to tell me your name."

And then I brace myself. Because if he tells me his name is whatever I want it to be, I'm going to double-check to see what kind of service I'm paying for.

Instead, he smiles and says, "I am Rupert."

"Well, Rupert," I say, "I'm probably going to be one of your more unusual clients."

"That would be difficult, ma'am," he says, and I'm relieved he doesn't ask my name. Apparently discretion is part of his job.

"Nonetheless," I say. "You do know I came with several friends."

"Yes, ma'am," he says. "One of the gentlemen asked for a room adjoining yours, which we have given him. But the doors connecting the rooms will remain sealed unless you give us permission to open them."

He says all of this with just a bit of urgency, as if Coop has made some kind of mistake asking for the adjoining rooms. I wonder if Rupert's caution has to do with some kind of liability concern on the part of the resort.

"You can unseal them," I say.

He nods.

"But that's not why I mentioned my friends," I say. "They're here for relaxation, and they think I am as well."

That's a lie, of course, but it's one designed to put Rupert and the staff he's in contact with on my side.

"I'm actually here searching for my father." Another lie. "He's an old spacer, and I found some evidence he left the Nine Planets Alliance in rather shady company. I need a place where I can talk to people, preferably some of the spacers who stop here."

Rupert studies me, and I think he's actually seeing me for the first time. I wonder if he's recording this conversation for security. If he wasn't before, he probably is now.

He takes in my thinness, the fact that I haven't brought many clothes. It doesn't take much to realize that I have spacer blood in me, even if I tried to hide it, which I'm not.

But lifetime spacers don't have the kind of money I'm waving about, unless they're involved in something illegal. And someone involved in illegal activity wouldn't be as obvious as I'm being about her money.

"Spacers can't afford this place, ma'am," he says. That's the kind of sentence a butler usually speaks to reassure a rich client that there's no riffraff here. And he seems somewhat confused as he utters it.

I really am not what he expects, and that's a good thing.

"We both know that's not true, Rupert," I say. "Spacers come here all the time. They bring you food and merchandise. Sometimes they run security patrols, and often they handle currency exchanges. They also bring news of the sector—not the news that hits the public databases, but the kind of news that keeps a place like this alive. The gossip, the stories, the early warnings."

Rupert is standing very still. He's never had this kind of request before, and he's uncertain what to do.

"There are places behind the scenes," I say, "places where the normal clients never go. Places that we're probably not supposed to see. And in those places are the berths for spacers stopping here for a few days. There are bars and a few restaurants that do not cater to the upper-crust crowd. That's where I need to go. I need to find out what's going on with my father."

Rupert takes a deep breath, but masks it by keeping his body very still. He doesn't want me to know how uncomfortable he is.

"How about this, ma'am?" he says. "How about you tell me your father's name, and I'll research the information for you. If I find someone who has seen him, I'll bring that someone to you."

Implied in all of this, of course, is that I would have to pay for this special service. Probably a bribe to Rupert and a bribe to that someone he brings me. The information would be false, but I wouldn't know that until I've left the resort.

If, of course, I really were a rich daughter looking for her missing and somewhat delinquent father.

"Thanks," I say, "but that won't work. Because I have a few questions I can't entrust to just anyone. Do you understand me, Rupert?"

He looks trapped. He does understand me, or he thinks he does. He swallows hard. "Ma'am, I could get fired for taking you to that wing of the station."

I make my gaze flinty. I remember how the rich treated me all those years ago. I tilt my head slightly, so that our gazes are not on the same level. Mine is just slightly higher than his, so that I'm looking down on him.

"You could get fired for not doing what I want, too, can't you?" I ask.

"Ma'am, please," he says, and now I hear the panic.

I wave a hand at him, dismissing him. "Find me someone else. You're fired."

"Ma'am, *please*." He looks at me, and for the first time, I realize how young he is. It takes work for me to remain cold. I want to show him some compassion.

Instead I keep my expression neutral, as if I'm waiting for him to do my bidding.

"May I at least check with my superiors about this?" he asks after a moment.

"Your superiors will want you to accompany me," I say. "They'll want you to supervise everything I do, and they'll probably tell you to take me to the staff's dining lounge, and tell me it's the spacer bar. That's not what I want."

"No, ma'am," he says.

"If they give me permission to go to that wing at all," I say.

"Ma'am," he says, "I can arrange this, but I could lose my job."

"I'll make sure you're compensated." I almost say that I'll make sure he's compensated enough to tide him over if he does get fired, but I stop myself in time. God knows how much he's getting paid, and I don't want to put myself in that position.

Besides, I can't be the first client he's had who wants to go slumming. There are lower levels on every space station, and on resorts, there are the levels that cater to the darker impulses.

He probably won't send me to the spacers' wing that I've requested. He's going to send me to the bars that are shadier than the ones on the upper levels, the ones where I can find anything for the right price, something that will cater to all my deviate wishes, if I have any.

And that will be good enough.

In fact, that will be better than good, because I can find out what I need there.

"I'll bring you proper clothing, ma'am," he says, and lets himself out of my room before I can protest.

I smile softly to myself.

My quest for information is finally under way.

THIRTY-FIVE

*R*upert returns with a white blouse similar to his, a black vest, tight black leggings, and black boots. I excuse myself and retreat to the bedroom, which is even more of a surprise. The bed is large and covered in blankets. Entertainment screens cover the walls, and tiny black holounits rest on every surface. So I can change the appearance of the room if I want—maybe even making it some kind of cabana on the beach.

I slip into the clothing, not surprised that it fits. Rupert made sure of that when he put my clothes away. As I put on each piece, though, I make sure nothing is embedded in the fabric or in the seams. If I'm going to be surveyed, and I'm sure I will, I want it to be from the outside, not from something against my skin.

I stop in the gigantic bathroom and look in the mirror. I look like my younger self—the woman who nearly gave up after finding her first Dignity Vessel. All I need are bleary red eyes, a mug of ale in my left hand, and an I-don't-give-a-damn expression on my world-weary face.

I nod at myself, then head back into the living area.

Rupert raises his eyebrows when he sees me. Then he hands me some credit slips. "They're anonymous," he says. "Don't use your own money."

As if I would.

"I'm taking you through the staff corridors," he says. He seems comfortable. He has done this before. "Don't make eye contact, and don't act like you've never seen this before."

I nod. I don't care if he thinks me naïve. I let him take me back to that entry and then watch as he pushes open a wall panel. We step through.

He glances over his shoulder to make sure I'm following. In here, the corridors are narrow and darker than the area around my room. They twist, clearly avoiding any public area, and slope downward. No lifts, no stairs, just a ramp that is probably harder on the legs, not that anyone cares.

We walk for a good ten minutes before we veer sharply left. Then Rupert pushes open another wall panel, and the cacophony I expected when I left the docking bay hits me.

Voices everywhere, music of a dozen different types blending and clashing, the stench of too many bodies too close, mixed with perfume and incense and a few smoky scents I can't entirely identify.

As I follow Rupert into the wide bazaar, I note three obvious bars and a few places that cater to a less savory crowd. Several prostitutes of both genders and a few of indeterminate gender lean against the wall, watching me.

"The spacer bar is four down," Rupert says to me.

"Thanks," I say. "I can find my own way back."

"No, you can't," he says. "I'm staying with you."

I shake my head. "You won't get your money if you stay with me."

"Ma'am, someone has to keep an eye on you."

"Especially if you're around calling me ma'am," I say.

He sighs and looks nervous. I wonder how much of that is an act and how much of it is real.

"I'll be right over there," he says, nodding toward a pile of chairs near a stand selling jewelry.

His perch puts him in position to see the exits of most of the nearby bars. It also puts him near the obvious prostitutes. I don't complain. He probably does need to help me get back into the staff corridors, although I'm sure I could find a way to my room without him.

I wander past the stalls, looking at jewelry of questionable provenance, paintings, and of all things, rocks threaded with various colors. I wind my way around a few of the stalls so I'm not on the main path, and then I go into a bar two down from the spacer bar Rupert pointed out to me.

As I do, I feel a feathery brush of breath against my cheek. I reach backward with one hand and grab a wrist. Then I turn, yank the wrist upward, and use it as a weapon, to push the man who owns it against a nearby wall. He has spacer bones, fragile and easily broken.

"I don't like pickpockets," I say, taking one of the credit slips Rupert gave me from the man's clenched fist.

"I didn't do anything," the man says to me.

"Why don't you not do anything, and let your friends know that anyone who touches me will regret it."

He glances over his shoulder, and I see a woman clutching her hand to her throat. Apparently this couple doesn't get caught very often. I nod to her, then shove the man in her direction.

I glare at them and at a few of the others nearby just to make sure that no one messes with me. I've been in worse places than this, and I know most of the tricks.

I don't look up to see if Rupert is watching. If he is, he knows that the object lesson he was going to give me—*have you noticed your credit slips are gone?* he was probably planning to ask as we headed back to my room—is now moot. And he may understand that I'm as legitimate as I say I am.

Or maybe he is as buttoned-up as he seems and is sitting in his little chair, terrified that he's going to lose his crummy job.

I slip into the nearest bar, and blink as my eyes adjust. There's actual smoke here. I see the filters on the wall, sucking the smoke inward and probably processing it so that it doesn't contaminate the other filtration systems in the resort. I don't recognize the scent, but it makes my eyes burn.

I slip back out because I have no idea what kind of smoke that is, and if it'll give me some kind of high. I move one doorway over and find myself in a bar just as dark, but without the stinky, grayish ambience.

My entrance makes the conversation stop, and I silently congratulate myself that I have found the right place. There are no pretty people here, no one dressed up so that they can capture the attention of slumming tourists, no one who has a clean table and sharp, avaricious eyes.

The people in this bar come for privacy—privacy that I have just invaded. The only way to get accepted in a bar like this is to come with an invitation, which I do not have, or to let everyone know that I'm aware I'm out of place.

I take the only open table, tucked up against the wall, slide a chair over, and place my boots on it. I sit with my back against that wall, and survey the room with a half grin on my face.

In the past, a place like this would have made me nervous, but truth be told, I miss moments like this. I miss that feeling of danger, that sense of being on a knife's edge, where I just might fall off and hurt myself. I've allowed myself to be cocooned in what's right and proper, focusing on helping others and building something new, and I've been itching to be someplace like this, filled with adventure and a sense that I'm out of my depth.

I'm happiest out of my depth.

A real waitress approaches me, no serving units, no robots, no programmed tables that will then tell an automated bartender what I need.

She balances a tray on her hip. She's as old as I am, her face lined, her eyes tired. She isn't smiling, and I know what she's going to say. She's going to tell me I'm not welcome here.

"I want the house ale," I say before she can speak, "and answers to a few questions. Then I'll get out of here and let you people get back to your lives."

Surprise flickers across her face for one brief instant before she gets it all under control again. She doesn't say a word to me. Instead, she pivots and heads back to the bar.

There's a real bartender as well. He leans in as she approaches, probably to find out what the hell is actually going on.

An elderly man from a nearby table gets up, tugs his pants, wipes a hand over his mouth, and then stands behind the chair with my boots on it. He stares at me.

I grin and kick the chair to him, putting my feet on the floor.

He grabs the chair and straddles it. He rests his forearms on the back of the chair and stares at me with rheumy eyes.

"You're out of place, honey." His voice is gravelly. Apparently he's the designated speaker, which means he has a lot more power than is obvious at first glance.

I don't apologize for being here, nor do I acknowledge what he says. "I just want a few questions answered."

"I know," he says. "Missing father, sob story, big search."

His words make one thing clear: Rupert isn't buttoned-up. He's connected, and he probably told those pickpockets to go after me.

"Let me make it simple for you," the man says. "No strangers have been in this bar until you walked in. No one knows of any missing father. And you, sweetie, are awfully far away from the Enterran Empire. How did you get here?"

That last surprises me. Is it the way I'm dressed? Or did Rupert let them know that my ship's identification is Empire?

"The Empire?" I ask, keeping my voice nonchalant.

"You're certainly not from around here," he says. "You fly a fancy ship with a lot of people who are taking a short vacation here. You got money, and someone with money and Empire connections shouldn't be sitting in this bar."

I smile at him. His little threat calms me down. In fact, I've been expecting this. When he first mentioned the Empire, I worried that somehow—in this vast universe—I managed to walk into a bar far away from home where someone actually recognized me. It wasn't impossible, but it wasn't likely. Although I've had many unlikely things happen to me in my time. I don't rule anything out anymore.

But he hadn't recognized me. He probably uses this tone with every rich tourist who wanders into this place.

"I just need information," I say again, not confirming or denying anything.

"After you tell me what that energy signature is coming from your ship," he says.

The *anacapa* drive. I haven't even thought about the low readings it gives off, and how unusual they would seem at any station. This is the first time we've docked anywhere. I should've been prepared for this.

I shrug. "The energy signature is what it is."

"You tell me or you leave," he says.

"How about you answer my questions and then I'll leave," I say.

"Questions in exchange for some information on your ship," he says.

I shake my head. "When you sat down, you already gave me answers. Those don't sound like they're worth the air it took to speak them, let alone some proprietary information about my ship."

"Proprietary," he says. "Big word."

I don't say anything. I hook my foot around a nearby chair, slide it over, and then rest my boots on it. The chair is just slightly to his left, so I have to turn away from him just a little.

"Lots of missing people go through here," he says. "Mostly they don't want to get found."

He gave just a bit. He is interested in that energy signature. I'll have to be very cautious.

"Whoever told you that I'm interested in missing people was mistaken." I hold up my empty hand, curved as if it is around a mug of ale. "Are we going to have a conversation? Because if we are, I need something to drink."

He studies me for a moment, and then he grins. He twists slightly, raises a hand, and flags that waitress.

She already has my mug ready. She carries it over, and sets it on the table without even looking at me.

"Thanks," I say, reaching into my pocket for that credit slip Rupert gave me.

The old man shakes his head. "Your money's not good here. I'll take care of it."

Hoping to put me in his debt, ever so slightly.

"Thanks," I say.

"So if you're not searching for a missing relative, what are you doing here?" he asks.

"I want to hear some ghost stories," I say. "And I figure you people are just the right folks to tell them."

THIRTY-SIX

have the entire bar's attention now. No one is even pretending to ignore me. People I can barely see in the back of the room have stopped speaking and have turned toward me. The waitress leans one elbow against the bar, facing me, her foot on the rail running underneath it. The bartender clutches a single mug, as if he stopped working mid-drink.

"Ghost stories?" the old man asks, sounding incredulous.

I nod.

"You don't mean the kind that end with 'Boo!' right? You mean something else," he says.

"Something else entirely," I say. "I want to know about places where people die mysteriously, parts of space everyone ignores, those old wrecks that no one enters because they're supposed to be haunted."

He laughs, then shakes his head. "What do you really want?"

I am not laughing. "I just told you."

"Why?" he asks.

I know better than to answer him. I can't give a satisfactory answer to that question. "That part's none of your business."

"Then there's really no reason to talk to you," he says.

"There's no harm either," I say. "You're not ratting out a friend, you're not sending me after some existing ship, and you're not betraying any secrets."

"Ghost stories aren't worth the risk of coming to this bar," he says.

"To me they are."

He makes a disgruntled sound, gets up, and walks away. But the woman next to me, a slender thing who makes the waitress look young, says, "There's the Boneyard."

Everyone glares at her, and from the back, someone makes a shushing sound.

The woman rolls her eyes. "There's no harm in telling her. She can't get in there any more than we can."

172

I don't say anything. If I sound too eager, no one will talk to me.

"Besides," the woman says, "she might pass it."

"It's your funeral," a man farther back says.

The woman gets up and moves to my table. She has the look of a longtime spacer, too thin by half, brittle bones, eyes bigger than any other feature on her face.

"You're asking about ghost stories?" she says. "We got a big one. We have thousands of ghost stories floating for anyone to find."

Now's the time for the question, but only as a prompt. "What do you mean?"

"There's a ship graveyard not too far from here," she says. "You won't find it on any map. The maps steer you away from it. No route goes near it."

"Except one," another man says.

She waves a hand at him, shushing him without really looking at him. "That route's not even close," she says.

"But you can see the Boneyard," the man says.

"You can see the Boneyard if you head straight for it, too," the woman says. "Which I don't recommend."

"Why not?" I ask.

"Because of the field around it," she says. "The energy disrupts ships that get too close."

That really has my attention now, but I try not to show it. I don't move; I just study her, as if her information is only passingly interesting.

But my heart is pounding. I'm glad Coop's not here. Coop, who has become so impatient he can barely do an analysis from one place to the next.

I'm not going to ask about the energy, not right away.

"That gap shows up on every map, doesn't it?" I ask. I give her the coordinates of the empty region that Mikk found. "Is that it?"

She nods as that shushing sound echoes from the back again.

"It's been there forever," she says. "And you can only see it; you can't go in."

"Why not?" I ask.

"The force field," she says as if I'm dumb.

I tilt my head back slightly. Then I sigh. "Okay," I say. "I asked for ghost stories, I know. But I was kinda hoping they were true."

She frowns. I've clearly offended her. "This is true," she says.

"Nice try," I say. I almost add the dismissive *honey* that the old man used. "But either your ship graveyard only has a few ships or you're making it up. Because nothing has the power to maintain a 'force field' that would cover an entire ship graveyard, at least not in the way I'm imagining it."

She glances at the others. She has a stake now in convincing me because she went against everyone else in the bar to let me know this Boneyard exists.

"You can't imagine this," she says. "It covers an area bigger than Azzelia, bigger than most space stations. Bigger than some moons, I think."

I give her a skeptical half smile. "If you really want to know how gullible I am," I say, "let me give you a clue. I'd believe that there are ghosts flying through space and invading spaceships before I believe in this little fairy tale."

"You asked, honey," the old man says from the back of the room. "Now shut up and leave."

That makes my smile fade. If I truly believed what I just said—and I don't, I completely believe this woman—then his little outburst would have convinced me I were wrong.

I look back at her. Her cheeks are ever so slightly pink. She looks both mad and uncomfortable. For some reason, she decided to do me a favor, and I'm treating her badly.

"Your friends don't want me to know about this Boneyard," I say. "So maybe I am willing to give you the benefit of the doubt."

"Gee, thanks," she says sarcastically.

"It's the force-field part of your story that doesn't work for me," I say. "There's nothing in the known universe that could power a force field that big."

She shrugs one shoulder. "It exists."

"Everywhere on this graveyard?" I ask. "Because there have to be gaps."

"Go see for yourself," someone shouts.

She looks at me, and I can tell she disagrees with that person, but she doesn't want to say so. She no longer feels like she needs to talk to me. I've probably pushed her a bit too far.

"You've tried, haven't you," I say softly.

She nods.

"Did you find gaps?"

"I can't get close enough," she says. "No one can."

I take my boots off the nearby chair and put my feet flat on the floor. Then I sit up. "What do you mean, exactly?"

"The force field is really powerful," she says.

"I get that," I say.

"No, you don't," she says. "The reason the routes go around it isn't because we're trying to keep the Boneyard secret."

"Although it would be nice if we could!" the old man yells at her.

"It's because that field is dangerous."

"Yeah," I say again. "I get that."

"From a long distance away," she says. "Sometimes the field destroys a ship that gets too close. Sometimes it repels the ship and leaves the ship intact. There's no way to know what'll happen to you."

That sounds familiar. An *anacapa* field? A malfunctioning stealth-tech field?

"Has anyone ever gotten close?" I ask.

"People who get too close die," says a man on my other side. "There's no salvage to be had, if that's what you're looking for."

Good guess on his part. The fact that he's guessing means that they can't figure me out. Which is also a good thing.

"I'm not interested in salvage," I say.

"Yeah," says the old man. "You're interested in ghost stories."

"I am," I say. "I'm trying to track down some history."

They're quiet again.

"What kind of history?" the man near me asks.

I give him a sideways glance. "I take tourists on wreck dives. I look for good historical wrecks."

"There's plenty of wrecks in the Empire," the old man says.

"And I take out high-end tourists. The folks who can pay for a resort like this one. They want the latest, newest, most exciting thing. So they wanted to come out here, where no one from our sector has come, and they want to dive a few wrecks that none of their friends have even heard of."

"Sounds like a waste of time," the old man says.

I shrug. "It's a living."

"It won't be if you go near the Boneyard," the woman says. "Your ship could get ruined."

"Or," I say, "I could find exactly what I'm looking for."

"You're crazy, lady," someone says from the back.

I nod. "I've been called that before."

"It's silly to risk your life for a piece of history," the old man says.

I turn toward him. "But I only have your say-so that I'm risking my life."

"So check it out," the man next to me says. "But be warned: if something happens to you out there, you're on your own. No one will come rescue you."

"We're not like the Empire," the old man says. "We don't take responsibility for stupid people doing stupid things."

I grin at him. "I'll take that under consideration."

The woman is watching me intently. "I thought you were only interested in the stories," she says. "I didn't think you'd go there."

"You haven't told me any stories yet," I say. "What happened there to cause this Boneyard? Or is someone just storing ships there?"

"No one knows," she says.

I make that skeptical face again. "No one knows," I repeat as if I can't believe her. "*Someone* has to know."

She shakes her head. "The ships are just there."

"And more ships come in," I say, "and someone maintains the force field."

"That's just it," she says. "No one goes near the place."

"That you know of," I say.

"That any of us know of," she says. She looks at the others. "Right?"

There are a few reluctant nods around the room.

"So you're telling me this place just appeared one day?" I ask, my heart pounding harder. Coop would love to hear that. We might have the kind of field that is operating around the Room of Lost Souls, only in a kind of reverse. A field in which things are appearing instead of disappearing.

"No, I'm not saying that," the woman says. "I'm saying it's always been this way."

I turn my head toward her, no longer pretending at calm or disinterest. "What does 'always' mean?"

"Always," she says. "As long as anyone knows."

"Your lifetime?" I ask.

"Yes," she says.

"Your parents' lifetime?" I ask.

"Yes," she says. "And their parents', and their parents' parents, and on all the way back, back to the beginning of recorded history in this sector."

I have to clasp my hands together so that no one can see that I'm shaking. "And this Boneyard has had the force field the entire time."

"Yes," she says.

"Filled with ships," I say.

"*Yes,*" she says.

"And new ships come in when the old ones disintegrate into nothing," I say.

"No." Now she sounds exasperated again. "It's always been like this."

"Unless your recorded history is really short," I say, "those ships would eventually decay, even in space. They'd go away or dwindle down to parts."

"Why don't you believe me?" she asks.

"You're telling me a fairy tale," I say.

"I'm telling you the truth," she snaps.

"As she understands it," the man next to me says. "What we know is this: there's a force field, we can't get past it without losing ships or people or getting repelled from it. The Boneyard looks like it remains the same, but are those the same ships? Who knows. We also have no idea if those ships are coming and going within the force field. It's too large. We don't know anything about it. We have no idea if anyone is maintaining it or could maintain it."

"And no one is trying to find out?" I ask, no longer able to keep the eagerness from my voice.

"People have tried to find out throughout recorded history," he says. "And they've failed. You'll fail too."

"So why tell me about it?" I say to the woman.

"You asked," she says miserably.

"There's another reason," I say.

She glares at me, then she looks at the entire bar. Her attitude is defiant, as if she expects all of them to dislike her immensely.

Maybe they do. I don't know, and at the moment, I don't really care.

"I'll tell you why. It's what no one else will tell you." She nods toward the old man. "The strange energy signature your ship gives off? It has the same elements as that force field. If anyone can get inside that place, it's you."

THIRTY-SEVEN

Okay. Now I'm in trouble. I finally understand why Rupert was willing to bring me down here, why he provided clothes and advice and credit slips. Not to teach me a lesson about pickpockets and working above my station, but to help his friends figure out how to break into—maybe even steal—my ship.

I'm not even sure how to play this. I look around the bar. No one is talking. Everyone is staring at me, including the waitress and the bartender. They all want to know what I'll do.

What I really want to do is run, gather my group, and get the hell off this resort. But it's too late for that.

I'm stuck in the middle of this bar, with my back to the wall. I deliberately left my comm upstairs so I couldn't be traced. I'm not wearing any weapons—not that a weapon would do me much good—and no one on my team knows where I am.

So I decide I'm going to keep up my calm persona, the one that got me into this mess.

"You're kidding, right?" I ask. "You're making all of this up so that I'll tell you about my ship."

The woman shakes her head. "We're not making anything up."

I grin. "Nice try, folks. But my ship is pretty standard in the Nine Planets and—"

"No, it's not," the old man says. "If it were, we'd see more of it."

"Really?" I say. "How many spacers do you get at this swanky place? Not many, I'd wager. And I'll wager you don't get many who can afford a ship like that. It's high end, for people who are serious about their work. It's not a recreational vessel."

"We'd still see it," he says stubbornly.

I sigh. "Have you checked the manufacture? Because I didn't build that thing. I bought it."

This much is true. I did buy it, and I kept the name of the company that made the *Two* on its registration, no matter what identity I used. So far, no one has tried to trace the *Two* back to its manufacturer, not that it would matter. I went through several different companies to buy the *Two*, and the manufacturer would have no record of the retail outlet that sold me the ship.

The difference between the ship I bought and the ship docked here on Azzelia is simple: we added an *anacapa* drive and some defensive capability. We didn't remove anything or change anything. We just added a few things.

"You're lying," the old man says.

"Go ahead and check," I say. "I'm sure someone has some kind of database access here. I don't mind waiting."

The bartender nods once, but doesn't say a word. I'm not sure what that means, but the old man frowns.

"That energy signature is coming from your ship," he says.

I shrug.

"Tell me what's causing it," he says.

I shrug again.

"You can't tell me that you don't know what's going on with your own ship," he says.

"*If* I believe you that there's an unusual energy signature, which I'm not sure I do, and *if* I believe that energy signature is similar to this miraculous force field that you've been talking about, and I'm not sure about that, then I would have to say that I'd need to investigate. Because I purchased my ship about a year ago, and it's got every part that the manufacturer put into it. I haven't changed anything in the drive or the communications system or even in the cloak, as crappy as that is."

I'm looking at the old man, not at the woman or at the bartender.

"So," I say, "if there is some kind of strange energy signature, it's either part of the ship, which therefore doesn't make it strange to me, or it's something my passengers brought on the ship. They're quite an eclectic bunch, more interested in history than in the now, as you probably know already, since they stated their intention on this resort was to find out more about the sector. That doesn't sound like a vacation to me, but hey, I just get paid to ferry them around. I don't decide what they should do to have fun."

No one says anything. The old man looks like he swallowed something that tasted awful.

"However," I say, resting one hand on the table and the other near my hip as if I'm carrying a weapon, "I don't believe there is a force field or an energy signature, and I think you all are just another version of that pickpocket I nearly broke in half outside. You want my ship, you figure you can scare me into giving you the specs and security protocols, and you think I'll do it all in the name of some energy signature. I'm really not that dumb."

The silence is almost painful. No one moves, except the woman near me. Her gaze goes to my hip, then back to my face. I can tell: she's trying to figure out if I have some kind of weapon hidden there, a weapon she can't see.

"I also know that Azzelia is the kind of place that polices itself. If something happens to me, in this part of the resort, where tourists generally don't go, then no one will investigate or punish because the authorities here, such as they are, will figure I deserve whatever happened to me."

The old man smiles just a little.

"However," I say, as if I haven't noticed his look, "you folks should probably know that most of the folks I'm traveling with are former military, and they will have no qualms about defending my ship and figuring out what happened here. So take me on at your own peril."

"We're not like that, miss," the bartender says. He's not that convincing, but I suppose he has to say that for the authorities, in case something does happen. He needs to "prove" that he's not involved.

"Really?" I say. "Because the only way I'll know that's true is if I can get up and walk out of here, unharmed. No one follows me, and no one messes with my ship."

My heart is pounding, but my voice is calm. I look around the bar, moving my head so that I see everyone. They're all watching me, but no one has made a move.

I stand.

"Thanks for the ghost stories," I say, and walk toward the door.

I should have come in with someone else, because I can see 180 degrees— front and sides—but I can't see behind me. I can listen for movement, but if any of these folks are pickpockets or trained thieves, they can come up on me without making a sound.

I don't hurry, but I don't go slowly either. And when I reach the door, I push it open, then turn just enough so that they can see my face.

No one has moved, except to turn their heads to watch me leave.

I tip an imaginary hat to them, then slide into the bazaar. The noise here—music, laughter, conversation—takes away my aural protection. I'm in just as much trouble here as I was inside that bar. Maybe more trouble, if they contact someone.

I'm not going to go back with Rupert, but I do have to use the route he showed me. I don't know any other way back, and I'm not going to stumble around here searching for it.

I thread my way through the crowd, walk to that wall panel, and push on it.

It slides like any door.

I slip inside, bracing myself for another attack. But it doesn't come.

My heart is pounding so hard that I can't believe no one else hears it. I walk through the back area, doing everything I can not to run.

I didn't see Rupert in the crowd, but that doesn't mean he wasn't there. Nor does that mean he hasn't sent someone after me.

I wind my way through the passages, up the various stairs, and finally get to my room.

I can't stay here either. Rupert has access.

I open the door and stop. Someone is inside. I can tell just from the way the place feels.

I take a step toward the main room and see Coop, lounging on the expensive couch.

I let out a sigh of relief.

"Look at you," he says with a grin.

I hold up a finger, shake my head, and close the door. Then I say, "Everything's changed. Let's round up the group. We need to get out of here. Now."

FORFEIT

THIRTY-EIGHT

Six days had passed, and Squishy was nowhere near the edges of the Empire. She traveled through the less populated areas of Empire space, following a zigzag pattern, and occasionally changing it up, retracing her steps or finding a different way through the area.

She tried to remain as true to what she would have done had she not known she was being tracked. When she realized, somewhere about the second day, that she was being deliberately stupid, she stopped and went back to her original plan, such as it was.

If the Empire wanted to take her, they would. And they would probably do so closer to the somewhat porous border with the Nine Planets Alliance.

On the sixth day, she charted a course that took her directly to the Nine Planets. Not to Lost Souls. She didn't go anywhere near Lost Souls, nor did she try to go too far from Lost Souls.

Her brain hurt from all the second-guessing. She was usually a straightforward thinker, blunt and to the point. The idea of going around everything, of trying to outthink other people, was harder for her than simply pretending to do one task while doing another, like she had done on the research station.

Sometimes she wondered if she was making everything too tricky. And then she would have to remind herself that it didn't matter. She needed to buy time, and that was all she had been doing.

Besides cleaning the *Dane*. She had decided that if she knew she was actually being pursued (and without her backup plan), she would have continued to pull tracers out of the ship. She left the secondary ones she found in the control panel.

The tracers she focused on were the ones that Quint had left. First, she cleaned out her cockpit, going over it with several devices set at different levels. She found two more tracers.

Every time she found a tracer, she put the tracer in her garbage system, dropped out of FTL, and jettisoned the tracer. Then she resumed FTL, traveled a short distance, and plotted a new course, just like she would have done had she thought she had gotten away.

That was one reason for the zigzag course.

The other was the messages she sent.

She sent them in a single storm, as if she had panicked about her future. Most of the messages went to friends and family in Vallevu, along with a will, so that there would be a lump sum payment from Squishy's pension for the children. She also sent a revised will, bequeathing everything she had left on Vallevu in trust for the children.

She knew that would scare people, but there wasn't much she could do about it. They would end up scared no matter what Squishy did. Eventually the imperial military would show up in Vallevu looking for Squishy. Or maybe Quint would or his people would.

Everyone would wonder what Squishy did, and when Quint told them (if Quint told them) some of them would understand.

The rest would condemn her even more.

If that was possible.

Because no one condemned her more than she condemned herself.

THIRTY-NINE

She was actually starting to get fat.

Squishy climbed the road to the house. At first, she went up the steep hillside, and she thought she was out of shape—which she sort of was. After all, she had lived in manufactured gravity for years now, and did most of her exercise in zero-g. Diving with Turtle and Boss had become a lifestyle, one that she was no longer a part of.

But it had taken different muscles than living in Vallevu without any transportation. Now she used her real muscles, walking, lifting, just plain old existing, and breathing the fresh air.

She was starting to think she'd learn the name of the flowers that grew roadside. They bloomed for months, a riot of pink and purple and red against such a sharp green that it almost hurt her eyes. The sky beyond was a bluish purple covered with the occasional thin cloud.

Someone had told her the clouds were thin here because of the elevation. Squishy had no idea about any of that, and she should have known. After all, she had had a home here once before, a home that the city assessor told her Quint still owned.

The assessor said he had never received a notice of dissolution of marriage, so technically, Squishy still owned the home as well, and she was welcome to live in it.

Instead, she avoided it. She didn't even walk down that street.

She had enough money to buy a home here; prices were low for residents of Vallevu. The catch was that no one was considered a resident of Vallevu unless they had been born here or unless they had lived here during the Event.

She qualified, but she didn't want to own a home. Not a place where she would live by herself.

Instead, she had moved into the Refuge.

She had been appalled to learn that no adult lived there full-time. The children had a rotating group of babysitters, for lack of a better term. And their holographic nanny, who was worse than useless, in Squishy's opinion.

She had never lived with children before, and it had required a hell of an adjustment. Particularly with the teenagers, who had become used to running things over the years.

She had brought extra food in, tried to give the children some consistency, changed a few of the rules, but in reality, all she had done was become one of the babysitters. The only difference between her and the other residents of Vallevu was that she actually moved into the Refuge.

She rounded the corner, and stopped, partly to get her breath in the thin air, but partly because this view always made her stop.

The house was built on a cliff-face and had a 360-degree view of the entire area. It had been a VIP house for anyone from the Empire who showed up and needed to stay longer than a few days. The interior was still plush, despite all the years of children trampling it, but it was the exterior that always caught her eye.

Five stories, each smaller than the last, with the top little more than a single round room with a balcony that went all the way around. When Squishy came here the first time, she had been told that balcony around the fifth floor was a widow's walk.

Squishy had thought that in particularly poor taste, and only later did she learn that "widow's walk" was an actual architectural term, one kept from Old Earth. It was frighteningly appropriate, and it was stuck in Squishy's brain, something she thought about every single day as she crested this hill.

The yard was made for children, with its many paths, myriad hiding places, and well-kept plants, planted around all of the rocks. The plants covered everything, including the front of the actual porch. It looked, to Squishy, as if the porch had grown out of the ground.

The holographic nanny sat there, drinking her tea, which meant that some well-meaning resident was inside, keeping an eye on the children.

Thirty children lived here, scattered among all of the rooms. None of the children were younger than ten, and only one was older than fifteen. He would leave next year. He had already been accepted into Mehkeydo University, where his parents had gone to school. The only reason he remained was because Mehkeydo had rules about children under the age of eighteen: they needed to be accompanied by a parent or guardian, and technically, he didn't have either.

She sighed and walked the rest of the way, her legs aching from the climb. She wasn't used to hauling her weight up mountainsides, even though she had lived here most of a year now. The added weight didn't help, but the added weight was necessary.

Squishy had been much too thin when she arrived.

Squishy wouldn't have known that without her medical degree. The medical degree had given her life purpose here, and for that she was grateful, but she never thought of herself as a doctor, not even when she was treating people in her clinic.

She thought of herself as a lapsed stealth-tech scientist. And that gave her an almost palpable feeling of shame.

She was almost to the steps when a woman came out. Squishy recognized her. She was often in her favorite restaurant at the morning rush, sitting in a corner, drinking coffee and watching Squishy.

Squishy had known it would only be a matter of time before the woman came to see her, but Squishy hadn't expected it here. She had expected it at the clinic in town.

"Do you mind if I talk to you?" the woman asked.

Of course Squishy minded. She hated talking to the locals about anything except the weather, the children, and the future. But her very presence here reminded them of the past, and when they thought of the past, they needed to talk about their hopes.

Their hopeless hopes.

"Not at the house," Squishy said. "Come with me."

She gave the building one longing glance. Inside was a cool drink, a nice conversation with some of the older kids, a chance to put her feet up and catch her breath. Out here, she would have a conversation she'd had at least two dozen times in the past six months, one that would anger the woman and might make her Squishy's enemy forever.

Squishy didn't look to see if the woman followed her.

Instead, Squishy just trudged down a side path to the gazebo. It was on the very edge of the cliff-face. When she sat inside, she felt like she was floating on air.

She had loved that place initially, and now it was the place where she held the toughest conversations, a place that provided no refuge at all.

The gazebo was open on all sides, although she could pull panels closed in a storm if she wanted to. The chairs were made of some kind of bamboo and creaked when she sat. She favored one chair above the others—it had a high back and arms she could grip, so that she didn't tear fingernail holes in her palms.

She didn't have to have these meetings. She could refer people to the information center near the town hall. But Squishy knew they had all been to that information center, and they hadn't liked what they learned.

They were coming to her in the hopes that she had a different perspective.

She didn't. But this was, whether she liked it or not, part of her penance.

She sat in her chair, heard the familiar squeak, and looked out over the mountainside. Clouds and bluish purple sky, more mountains in the distance, nothing visible overhead.

She could remember when that sky was full of transports and other junk, when the sound of a dozen different vessels constantly echoed overhead.

"My name is Nianni Pavlovic," the woman said. "Maybe you remember me?"

Everyone thought Squishy should remember them. If she hadn't met them in Vallevu or on the research base, she met them during one of the trials. The meeting was significant to each and every one of them, but to her, after a time, the meetings had acquired a sameness.

She hadn't wanted them to, but they had.

"Yes, I remember you," Squishy lied. "But not all the details. You're related to Edan Pavlovic."

She didn't remember the survivors here in Vallevu, but she remembered the names of all the victims. She would never ever forget them.

"I'm his wife," the woman said as she eased herself into one of the chairs. "We still have two kids at home."

Lucky them, Squishy thought. *At least one parent survived, unlike the parents of the kids here in the Refuge.*

But she didn't say that. She was learning to be politic here, at least a little bit.

"I just was wondering," the woman said uncertainly, as if she didn't know how to broach the subject, "how your research is coming. It's been ten years, and I thought maybe you'd have an idea now as to when the cloak will let them go."

So many things wrong with that question, and Squishy didn't want to correct any of them. She didn't want to have this conversation at all.

"I'm not doing any research," Squishy said.

The woman gave her a conspiratorial smile. "Of course you are. That's why you came back. Everyone knows that."

Squishy sighed. She'd heard this now dozens of times. It didn't matter how often she corrected people, they persisted in believing that she was doing top secret research that would rescue their loved ones.

"I'm not," Squishy said. "I don't work for the Empire anymore."

"It's all right," the woman said. "I know they make you say that. But you can tell me. I promise I won't tell anyone."

Squishy shook her head. If she lied to make this woman feel better, the woman would tell her children, who would tell their friends, whose parents (if they had survived) would come to see Squishy, and then she would have to lie some more.

Or tell someone the truth.

She thought of this every time she was faced with one of these discussions, and she was always tempted. But she never lied.

She didn't dare.

"I'm not saying anything that the government wants me to say, Mrs. Pavlovic," Squishy said. "I'm not with the military anymore. I don't do stealth-tech research. I haven't since the court cases. I've spent the last few years working on a salvage team. I came home—"

She caught herself before she said too much. *I came home because of stealth tech, because we lost two more and I can't take it. This stuff haunts me, even more than it haunts you.*

"I came home," Squishy repeated. "I couldn't stay away any longer. But I didn't mean to bring expectations with me."

The woman's eyes were bright; it was clear Squishy wouldn't be able to convince her that her husband was dead.

"Someone is researching this, though, right?" the woman asked.

No one had asked that question before, and that one probably had some truth to it. But Squishy didn't know it for a fact, and besides, it would do no good. The research base was gone, destroyed, taken bit by bit for parts.

"I'm sorry," Squishy said. "I know the Empire refuses to make the declaration, but I can tell you one thing based on all my years in stealth-tech research."

The woman leaned forward. Squishy could feel her anticipation. Her mouth was open slightly, her cheeks flushed. She looked eager.

"Your husband is dead, Mrs. Pavlovic," Squishy said as gently as she could. "He's been dead since the day of the Event. We just weren't able to recover a body. That's all."

The woman leaned back and rolled her eyes. "Can't you get in trouble for saying that?"

If Squishy still worked in stealth-tech research, she probably would have. There were too many unanswered questions, and the Empire didn't want to deal with the repercussions.

"No," Squishy said. "I don't work for the Empire. I was, though, one of the primary researchers on that project. I know for a fact that your husband is dead."

The woman's jaw set. She was starting to get mad.

One of the reasons Squishy brought people here was that they often became unpredictable at this point. One man had actually slapped her across the face.

"He is not," the woman said. "If he was, the Empire would pay us our death benefits. But he's not. All I'm asking you is some kind of estimate. I won't even hold you to it. I just want to know how the research is coming so that I know what to tell my kids."

And the lies you can tell yourself as you're trying to fall asleep at night, Squishy thought.

"He's dead," Squishy said again. "If the Empire truly thought these people were still alive, no one would have dismantled the military base. Think it through: if the cloak goes away, then your husband and everyone else who was working that day would return to the same spot. Only there wouldn't be an environment to hold them. They'd be floating in space."

"You lie," the woman said with such venom that it took all of Squishy's strength to hold her position. "Everyone knows they brought the labs to another research station, completely intact, so that when the cloak fades, the survivors will be in a protected environment."

"Believe what you want," Squishy said. "But it would probably do you and your children a lot more good if you just accepted the truth."

The woman stood. "I don't know why I came here. I thought maybe you'd put the need of families before your oath to the Empire. I thought when you moved into the Refuge, you had some *compassion*. All I'm asking for is information."

"No," Squishy said. "You're asking me to participate in your own personal fantasy. I'm not going to do that. I'm not going to lie to you, no matter how badly you want me to."

"You're really just as evil as they say, aren't you?" the woman snapped. "You don't care about people at all."

Then she stomped out of the gazebo, making so much noise as she left that Squishy could track her progress through the crunching of leaves and the breaking of branches.

She couldn't reason with that woman, just like she hadn't been able to reason with the others before her. If Squishy didn't care about people, she wouldn't've even tried.

But she hoped that at least one survivor would listen to her, and get on with their life, rather than hope forever that their lost loved one would return.

No one had even given that any thought. What if Squishy was wrong? What if they did return, miraculously, on the ground here in Vallevu? Would they have lived all of those missing years? Or would they have been in a true stasis, the same person they had been when they left?

Their families wouldn't be the same. Nothing would be the same.

It wasn't some nice fantasy.

The best-case scenario was the true one: that everyone who had been in that wing of the military base that day had died. There were no ghosts; there was no cloak; there was nothing left.

Except this useless yearning for what had been—a world that would never ever return.

Squishy wished she could make people understand that. She knew they never would.

And she also knew that she would never stop trying.

FORTY

Squishy had to wait to send the messages to Vallevu until she tracked down Turtle, and that had taken more time than Squishy wanted. For days, she feared she wouldn't find Turtle in time.

Squishy had completely lost track of her. Turtle had quit Boss's employ when they returned from that first Dignity Vessel debacle. Boss had lost track of Turtle as well.

Maybe not lost track so much as didn't keep track. Even though the three of them had been friends, that last dive had been fraught. It had caused Turtle and Squishy's breakup, and it had led to a serious rift with Boss as well.

If Boss hadn't approached Squishy all those years later, that relationship would still be severed.

But Boss had needed Squishy. Apparently, Boss had never needed Turtle.

No one had needed Turtle. She had just slipped away as if she had never been. No diving companies had records of her, no resorts or space stations or starbases had any knowledge of a woman named Turtle in their midst.

It had taken Squishy two full days to remember Turtle's real name, because Squishy had only heard it once, and even that hadn't helped—not entirely. At first, Squishy believed that she had remembered it wrong, because it was so hard to track Turtle down.

But eventually, she did find Turtle. And it had been oddly easy. Because Turtle had returned home. She hadn't done anything after leaving Boss. Turtle had recovered her old name and moved back to the place she had been happy to flee.

It had taken Squishy a long time to figure that out because she hadn't believed that the woman she knew would go back home.

Maybe Turtle wasn't the woman she knew any longer. Maybe that fight on the *Business* had changed Turtle as much as it had changed Squishy.

Turning points were like that. They carved into everyone. A single decision, a single action, changing the future forever.

Or making that future inevitable.

Squishy wasn't sure which had happened here.

But she knew she had had a huge part in it. She could have stayed with Boss and Turtle and the rest of the team. Maybe if Squishy had stayed, she would have prevented yet another death.

Maybe. Or maybe she would have caused one.

There was no way to know, and no way to ever figure it out.

FORTY-ONE

She had been sick to her stomach for three days. She had a headache that wouldn't go away. Her shoulders were so tight that they felt like rocks.

Squishy should have left the moment she figured out that Boss had taken the crew to dive a Dignity Vessel. Or maybe she should have left the moment she realized that Boss didn't believe her when it came to crew safety.

Hell, Turtle didn't even believe her, and Turtle was supposed to be in love with her. The fight they'd had about that—well, it made Squishy's headache worse just thinking about it.

Yet she remained on Boss's ship, *Nobody's Business*, acting as medic now, while the rest of the team enthusiastically dove into that wreck. They believed they had found some kind of holy grail. Boss in particular seemed unrecognizable.

For the very first time since Squishy had met her, Boss seemed more interested in a thing than in her people. Or maybe, Boss just didn't understand the risks.

Squishy hadn't. Not even after losing Professor Dane all those years ago. Squishy had actually thought she could control those risks, just like Boss thought so right now.

Maybe that was why Squishy stayed. It wasn't because she wanted to say *I told you so*; she didn't. She wanted this to go well. It wasn't because anyone would need her services.

If stealth tech struck, it would most likely kill quickly and efficiently and no medic would be able to stop it.

She thought she owed it to Boss and the team, and more importantly, she owed it to herself. Maybe something minor would happen, and Boss would understand the error of her ways.

Then Boss would blow the ship like Squishy had asked her to. Damn the consequences.

Although Boss's discussion of the consequences—maybe it would cause some kind of rift in space, maybe it would make things worse—were exactly the things stealth-tech scientists had discussed for years. Things Squishy had discussed for years, before she ran away from the tech forever.

So she stayed on the *Business*, haunting it like a ghost. She wandered through the halls, twisting her hands against each other every single time Boss took a skip to the Dignity Vessel.

This time, both Squishy and Turtle remained, not that it mattered. She and Turtle had stopped talking to each other days ago. They had stopped sleeping together once Squishy figured out what the Dignity Vessel was. And they had stopped being civil to each other right at that point.

Turtle had taken Boss's side. Turtle somehow believed that Squishy had gone quietly nuts while she was working for the imperial military, at least on the topic of stealth tech.

And maybe she had. She certainly was much too intense. She had gone from protesting to screaming in the space of an hour once she had seen the Dignity Vessel.

And she had felt betrayed by the fact that Boss had even brought them all here, as if Boss could know about stealth tech.

Yet there was so much about stealth tech that Squishy couldn't tell anyone. She had agreed to confidentiality protocols all along in her career. Even worse, she had agreed to several as a condition for leaving the military with a full pension.

Legally, she couldn't tell anyone about the tech. She had already told Boss too much.

And it hadn't been enough to stop this damn mission.

She was in the *Business*'s cockpit, monitoring the communications array, even though she should have been in her cabin. Turtle was on backup duty, not Squishy. Turtle was the one who was supposed to fly out the second skip should the first skip get disabled.

But, even though Squishy was trying to avoid Turtle, she couldn't stay away, not when there was a mission. Not when people she knew were getting dangerously close to malfunctioning stealth tech.

She paced the *Business*'s cockpit as if it were the size of an exercise room. Twice, Turtle had told her to stop moving around so much, and twice Squishy had ignored her.

Then Boss's voice came through the comm. "Turtle," Boss said, sounding odd, "find Squishy for me."

"She's right here," Turtle said, and moved away from the comm.

Squishy's heart started to pound. Her mouth was dry. She walked to the communications control panel.

"What?" she asked, even though she knew.

She knew.

"Things have gone bad here," Boss said. "It sounds like Junior isn't moving. Jypé doesn't want to leave him, and I can't communicate with them."

Because the stealth field interfered with communications. Squishy had been to that Dignity Vessel; she knew. The person on the skip could hear what was going on in the Dignity Vessel, but couldn't contact the divers inside.

"I'm thinking of going in after Jypé," Boss said, and suddenly Squishy understood why Boss had contacted her. Boss had just admitted she planned to violate her own procedure.

If divers ran into trouble on a dive, trouble bad enough to kill another diver, then the worst thing the rest of the team could do was go inside and get caught in the same trap. The divers had to get themselves out.

That was Boss's rule. She knew it, but she was alone there, and she needed help enforcing it.

Squishy had to swallow to keep the nausea at bay. Boss was asking her for help. Boss, who had refused to listen to her. If Boss had listened, this wouldn't have happened.

Whatever this was.

"You need to get back here," Squishy said. "As fast as you can."

"Jypé's still in the Dignity Vessel," Boss said. "He's alive."

Squishy swore and looked at Turtle.

"I think he'll make it," Boss said. "But he's going to need assistance."

"He has to get to you," Squishy said. "He has to be able to get to you on his own. Right now, you don't have enough information. You need to have the survivor come to you."

She deliberately did not use Jypé's name. If she thought of him as a person, then she would be sick. Dammit. The inexperienced father-and-son team. The ones who brightened everything on this ship. Of course it would have to be them.

Because the universe was cruel that way.

"He'll need my help getting here," Boss said.

"No," Squishy said. "Think it through, Boss. There's no sense passing midway, is there?"

Meaning that Boss might not use the same route Jypé did, and they might miss each other. But that wasn't what Squishy was most worried about. When Boss got excited, she used too much oxygen. She got the gids.

She was already excited, maybe even panicked. She wouldn't bring enough oxygen, and then they'd have three dead instead of two.

Because Squishy knew Jypé wouldn't survive. How could he? His son was trapped in the field. Either Junior had vanished, or worse, he had mummified. Rapidly. And eventually his body would disappear as well.

If Jypé was a typical parent—and why wouldn't he be?—he would do everything he could to save his son. That Jypé was talking to Boss, saying he needed help getting out, meant he realized he couldn't save Junior.

And that meant Jypé had probably wasted all of his oxygen.

Boss couldn't go in there.

But Squishy was here, in the *Business*. She couldn't get to Boss in time to prevent her from going in. And she couldn't push too hard.

"Boss, look, we'll be right there," Squishy said, as if that were possible, as if she could actually get to Boss in time. "You wait for us. Okay? You *wait*."

"Get here fast," Boss said. She sounded furious. The last word was cut off because Boss shut down the comm.

But Squishy took heart in that anger. Boss had heard her. Boss hadn't liked what Squishy had to say, but Boss had heard her.

"Let's go," Squishy said to Turtle.

Turtle had already notified Karl so someone would monitor the *Business*. They were leaving now.

Turtle gave Squishy a cold glance, and Squishy had to look away. Why would Turtle blame Squishy for this? Squishy had tried to prevent it.

"If you had been there," Turtle said.

"Shut up," Squishy said. "Just shut up."

She didn't want to think about what they were heading into. She didn't want to have one or two or three more deaths on her shoulders. Deaths she could have prevented by insisting they leave, by forcing them to leave.

By turning them in to the Empire.

Her breath caught. She could notify the Empire of the Dignity Vessel, let them claim it. They were always willing to take unusual technologies, and they even paid a finder's fee.

Not that she wanted blood money.

But that meant that the Empire had a stake in these technologies and would get here quickly.

She wished she had thought of this earlier.

It would have ruptured her relationship with Boss, but this was already rupturing her relationship with Boss. They would never be friends again—not the kind of friends they had been, the friends who trusted each other through everything.

No one would ever trust Squishy again.

Once they rescued Boss and Jypé—if they could rescue Boss and Jypé—everyone would see Squishy's actions as a great betrayal.

And maybe it was.

But it was a betrayal she should have made earlier, a betrayal that would have saved Junior's life.

She was almost in tears by the time she got to the skip. But tears wouldn't do her any good. She had to be a medic. She had to be strong.

She had to end this farce once and for all.

FORTY-TWO

The message Squishy sent to Turtle went in a flurry of messages to Vallevu, Longbow Station, and several other places. Squishy even tried to send a message to the *Bounty*, even though she doubted anyone remembered her on the ship she had grown up on. She wanted whomever tracked her messages to think she planned to die and that she was sending good-bye messages.

Squishy spent hours at the control panel drawing up those messages. She was feeling surprisingly lethargic, ready for this part of the adventure to end. She walked the length of the cruiser, ate the best stuff on board, slept more than she probably should have—especially since she was sprawled in the second cabin, far from the cockpit and any messages or alerts she might receive.

Although she did have the cockpit set up to funnel messages to her. If any came. Which they did not.

She sent so many on her own, all different, that she lost track of what she said. Only the message to Turtle gave her fits. She needed to phrase it exactly right so that Turtle would understand. And Squishy had to hope that Turtle wouldn't just turn around and forward that message to Boss—if Turtle even knew how to find Boss.

Squishy had to trust that Turtle would send Boss a message from a secure place, somewhere different from the place she had heard from Squishy.

Squishy couldn't tell Turtle exactly what she needed. She had to rely on Turtle's memory of events that happened between twelve and sixteen years ago. She and Turtle had had codes back then, messages they wanted to send each other if something should go wrong, messages that coded the other person's reaction, just in case the first person was caught doing something illegal.

Well, Squishy had done something illegal. More illegal than either of them had imagined back in the day.

She had blown up a research station, maybe even killed a woman, not through her scientific experiments, but because of her bomb.

The other thing that had slowed her thoughts these last few days had been one other memory—that of the bomb she had made for Boss twelve years ago. Boss wouldn't tell Squishy if anyone had died when that bomb went off.

Boss said she didn't know, and Squishy had believed her—or at least, Squishy had wanted to believe her. She had never checked.

Just like she had never checked to find out if all of the signatures that had been on the station that morning when she arrived had managed to leave the station before the bomb went off.

Of course, that then led to Quint's questions: What would she have done if someone had remained? What could she have done?

She didn't like to think about that.

Any more than she liked to think about relying on Turtle. But she had to. She had to trust (how ironic!) that Turtle would remember their old codes, and then care enough to act upon them.

In the end, Squishy sent a fairly short message: She apologized for treating Turtle the way that she had. She then mentioned an incident that never happened—one of their codes—and said that she had thought that everyone involved shouldn't have taken any action at all, that they should have left each person to their fate.

It was as blatant as she could get without tipping off the Empire that she was worried Boss would come after her.

Then Squishy added one more thought: *I've always felt I did the wrong thing by giving that last ship to the Empire. Under no circumstances should any similar ship ever get into imperial hands. I'm sure you understand.*

She knew that Turtle wouldn't understand that part. But Boss would. And maybe, if Squishy was lucky and Turtle had forgiven her, Boss would get that message.

And Boss would do the right thing: leaving Squishy to her fate.

THE BONEYARD

FORTY-THREE

"**W**e're being followed," Mikk says. He sits near one of the control panels on the far side of the cockpit.

The cockpit of *Nobody's Business Two* is set up for twelve people to work the systems if need be, but I've never needed twelve to do so. I still don't have twelve people in this room. I have seven, counting me. That's everyone on board this ship who can be useful in space flight. I feel crowded, but I don't mind. I might need every single person before this trip is done.

Coop sits next to me in the copilot spot, but should things get dicey, I might let him command. I've never had a ship with full weapons before, and I've certainly never captained one, so I will bow to his experience if need be.

Yash is monitoring the *anacapa* drive. Right now, we have it on low. I'm not going to power it up until it's absolutely necessary.

Mikk and Roderick are at various seats throughout the cockpit, working the systems. Rossetti has charge of the weapons systems; she helped supervise their installation so that, besides Coop and Yash, she's the person who knows the most about them. DeVries is also here because he asked to observe. If he gets in the way, I'll make him leave.

My heart is pounding. I got us into this, but I'm not panicked. I'm a little more thrilled than I want to be. I have forgotten how addicting an adrenaline rush can be.

It took us nearly an hour to gather everyone and get to the ship. Coop and I went directly to the *Two*. We searched the interior for tracers. We figured there were tracers on the outside, and we planned to leave them for the time being. But we made sure we could jettison them quickly in flight.

Not that it mattered, in the end. Most tracers only worked short range, and we planned to get out of this area quickly—maybe even with the *anacapa* drive.

After we went to this Boneyard.

I told Coop about it, but not in detail. I didn't want to get his hopes up.

I just told him that it was an old graveyard of unworkable ships, and he was a bit disparaging to me. He figured, like I originally had, that the old graveyard was only old in modern terms, not in his terms.

He probably figured (and this is what I wanted him to assume as we left Azzelia) that the ships were old Empire ships or local ships from the sector. It hasn't been our experience in the short history of the Lost Souls to discover Dignity Vessels in a cluster.

In fact, we figured that the Dignity Vessels we've been discovering all over our sector of space have slowly eased out of foldspace, only to show up at various times throughout history. None of us—the scientists, engineers, and physicists—believed that the Dignity Vessels, no matter how well constructed, could survive all of that time in space.

But some clearly had, and with certain systems intact.

I have often wondered if the *anacapa* drive made that possible, that it provided some kind of protection, like a shield. Yash pooh-poohs that, but she hasn't dismissed it entirely.

We're dealing in things we don't understand, and that makes our work difficult.

In fact, we're dealing in things that the *Ivoire*'s crew doesn't understand either. More than once, Yash has wished she could consult with the experts on the *Pasteur*, the Fleet's main science vessel. Experts got scattered throughout the ships of the Fleet, but the science vessel still had the bulk of the reputable scientists.

And Yash seems to believe, with an almost religious fervor, that those scientists could have figured out all the things she can't.

I'm not so sure. But I'm not an expert in anything except the ever-fluid unknowns of history itself. I have spent my life constantly surprised by the way that actual events aren't actual at all, and the things that we believe to be true often aren't.

"Should we do something about them?" Mikk asks. "I count three ships."

I glance up at the screens. The ships are as large as this one. One is a modified tourist cruiser that shouldn't be able to keep up with us (but is, hence my knowledge of the modification), another is a cargo ship with a bunch of parts added, and the last is a ship of a configuration I don't recognize.

I have no idea which is the greatest threat, so I'm going to assume they all are. I don't want to engage them, and at the moment, they clearly don't want to engage me.

I say, "They want us to know that they're there."

We aren't very far from Azzelia. We're on a course to the Boneyard. I had expected ships to ambush us there. I hadn't expected any to follow us.

"We can still lose them," Mikk says.

He doesn't like being followed any more than I do.

"There's no point in losing them," I say. "They know where we're going."

Half the people in the cockpit look at me in surprise. They probably think I should be more panicked than I am.

"Is this place worth going to?" Coop asks.

"If what the folks in that bar told me is accurate, then yes," I say. I haven't had time to brief the crew about my experience. I only said that based on a discussion I had in a bar, we could be in trouble, and we needed to leave immediately.

"Were the people in that bar just following your lead?" Roderick asks. "I mean, this could be some kind of trap."

Roderick understands how these things work. My divers have all spent time in space stations and starbases. There are a lot of shady characters in those places, some of whom like to get a ship to an unpoliced part of space, and then board it and strip it of all valuables, sometimes killing the crew.

"You think the people in that bar set me up?" I ask, trying to keep the smile off my face. Roderick should know better. We've both watched that game a million times. We understand it. And the fact he thinks I've forgotten is amusing. "I'm sure they did set me up."

Roderick clearly isn't finding any of this amusing. He turns slightly in his chair so that he can make eye contact with me. This is Roderick Sincerity Mode.

"Then, Boss," he says, "I respectfully submit that we shouldn't go. They probably know what you were asking about and just fed it to you."

I shake my head. He's finally managed to insult me. "I'm not that naïve. They didn't know exactly what I was asking for. I kept changing my information. They told me a few things that they would have no idea mean anything to me."

Now Coop is looking at me. "What, exactly?"

"We're almost there," I say. "We can see for ourselves."

Coop glances at Yash, who is frowning.

"I don't like the idea of flying into a trap," Roderick says stubbornly. "We're not a fighting vessel. We're a bunch of scientists and divers."

"I know," I say gently.

Coop puts a hand on my arm. The touch is light, a warning to stop the argument.

I'm about to remind him that my people aren't military and can question command decisions when he says, "If it's a trap, we have the *anacapa*. We can get away from them quickly."

I'm surprised. He's actually engaging in a discussion about a decision.

"No offense," Roderick says, "but I want to avoid that *anacapa* thing as much as possible."

Coop grimaces, but of course Roderick doesn't see that. "No offense taken."

I suspect Roderick is simply voicing how all of us feel about the *anacapa*. Some of us have always been wary, and Coop's people have a healthy respect for the drive that they hadn't had before.

"I wouldn't be surprised if there are other ships waiting for us when we get to this Boneyard," I say. "Coop, you and Joanna need to be ready. They might fire on us. They think we have something valuable here."

"Valuable where?" Mikk asks.

"In the ship," I say.

"Oh, this is just getting better and better," Roderick mutters.

I ignore that, even though Coop stiffens beside me. That comment has gone past his disobedience threshold.

"What would they find valuable about the *Two*?" Yash asks in a tone that shows how much contempt she has for my ship.

I haven't had time to brief the crew.

"They've seen the energy signatures from the *anacapa* drive. They want to know what it is," I say.

"What did you tell them?" Yash asks suspiciously.

"That it's a miraculous drive from the past that the Empire has been trying to re-create for generations," I say, then I roll my eyes. "Seriously, you guys, I'm not that stupid."

Yash grunts and turns away. Apparently she doesn't approve of my little adventure. Maybe Coop's way is the better way.

"Why would they be interested in the energy signature?" Coop asks. "You said no one knows what it is."

I give him a sideways look. "They've seen it before."

Stunned silence greets that statement. Coop is clearly thinking about it. "They've seen it at this Boneyard."

I nod. I'm not going to explain any further. Let him think there's one Dignity Vessel among the dead ships, not an active shield around those ships that has a similar signature to the *anacapa* drive.

"The upshot is this," I say. "They want this ship. They have no idea what's causing that energy signature, but they want it."

"So why didn't they keep you in the bar?" DeVries asks. Of course, DeVries is the one to ask that. He hasn't had this kind of experience before.

I smile. "They think we're more vulnerable out there. If they attacked us in the resort, they might have lost their clearance. Out here, we're an easy target."

"Or we would be without the weapons systems and the *anacapa*," Coop says.

I realize that I had unintentionally lied to the patrons in that bar. I had told them that we hadn't modified the *Two* from her factory specs. But we had in an obvious way. We had the weapons.

Maybe this group of space pirates—if, indeed, that's what they are—understood adding weaponry.

I find it funny that I worry about telling the bar patrons one untruth while I was telling them another. It isn't that the bar patrons matter; it's that they needed to think me as sincere as possible—I wanted them to believe I had no idea what that signature was, and that it had come from something the scientists had put on board my ship.

I wanted the advantage; I didn't want to give it to them.

But I say nothing to my team now. We're in this situation, and frankly, I want to see this Boneyard. Even if it's half of what the bar patrons said it was, it's worth all the time and expense we've taken.

Of course, there is some risk.

"There's a fourth ship now," Mikk says.

Coop nods. He doesn't ask me if I want him to take over the ship, but I can sense that he wants to.

"Oh, my God," Yash says.

We all look at her, except Mikk.

"Yeah, their weapons systems are pretty amazing," he says.

"No," she says. "Look at this, Coop."

He leans over, and I swear, his face turns pale. I've never seen anyone's face do that before.

"What is it?" I ask.

"I don't know," he says, "but I haven't seen readings like this since we left the Fleet."

Before his *anacapa* malfunctioned. Before he came here.

"Is it another Dignity Vessel?" Roderick asks.

Coop shakes his head, but answers, "I don't know."

"Is it another damn ship?" Mikk asks, because he thinks we're outgunned now.

"I have no idea," Coop says.

I look at him. There's something in his face I can't read. Hope? Fear? I'm not sure. He's trying to keep the emotions off his face.

"If this is your Boneyard," he says, "we could be in a hell of a lot of trouble."

FORTY-FOUR

"**Y**ou want to tell me what you mean by trouble?" I ask.

Coop isn't answering. Instead, he leans against Yash, and they confer. Rossetti joins them. I can hear a few words—*big, significant, impossible*—but I'm not sure of the context.

"You want to share with the rest of us?" Roderick snaps.

I wave a hand at him for silence. "We have enough to do."

A fifth ship has joined the others.

I know that the bar patrons could have lied to me. I know that there might be nothing here, and I had actually been afraid of that. Until just now, when Coop had his reaction. Something is here. But what, I have no idea.

Then it shows up on my screen, but it shows up oddly. It's as if there are no readings at all. I see everything that's in this little part of space, except for one large swath. It reads as nothing.

Literally nothing. Like there's nothing there. Not even space itself. It is as if someone has ripped a hole out of the universe and left a blank spot.

"What the hell?" I ask.

Coop looks over. I tap the screen. "Is this what you're seeing?"

"No," he says. "I'd tell you to come look, but you have to pilot."

Screw piloting. I want to see what's going on.

"Six ships," Mikk says tightly.

One is arriving underneath us.

"Are any of these ships some kind of law enforcement or military vessels?" I ask him.

"Not that I can tell," he says.

"Do they have their weapons systems engaged?" I ask.

"How the hell should I know?" he asks. And I realize then where his panic is coming from. None of my team are trained for this. They're trained to run when things get bad. And instead, we're flying right into it.

"Let me," Rossetti says.

She moves over to the space beside Mikk and taps a few things. Then she moves back to her post.

"They're all armed," she says, "and none of them have any kind of military or law enforcement insignia that this ship recognizes."

Which we all know means nothing. We're not used to this sector of space.

"Make that no insignia of any kind," she says.

"Pirates," Mikk mutters.

"Probably," she says. "Given our circumstances."

She doesn't sound concerned, and her lack of concern seems to calm Mikk. A little anyway.

"We need some kind of plan," Mikk says to me.

"Don't worry," Coop answers. "We have one."

I want to raise my eyebrows and say in an incredulous tone, *We do?* but I know better. He probably does have a plan, and his assurance just calmed my crew.

"I'm piloting," Coop says to me, then bumps me as if he wants me out of the chair.

My face flushes and I'm about to argue, when I realize that if what the bar patrons say is true and if those ships really want our *anacapa* drive, arguing with Coop right now is incredibly stupid.

"You want me to copilot?" I ask in as humble a tone as I can manage. "Or is Rossetti better at the moment?"

"Joanna's good where she is," he says, tapping my screen as if he invented it. "Take a look at what Yash has."

Everyone on my team is watching us gape-mouthed. Apparently they've never seen me acquiesce to orders before.

I look up at them before I turn to Yash's screen. "I'm not the interesting thing here. Those ships are."

They return to their jobs, chastened.

I lean over and look at Yash's screen. It shows a series of numbers and codes, something that fizzles and reappears like Yash can't hold the signal. I've never seen anything like it.

"What the heck is that?" I ask.

"The thing you want us to fly to," she says.

"Good Lord," I say. "It shows up blank on my screen."

"Yes, I know," she says. "This one is modified to monitor the *anacapa*."

I knew that but hadn't given it any thought. Still, something is odd here. "The *anacapa* doesn't read like that."

"This is a small ship and we installed a low-level drive," she says. "Whatever this thing is, it's overwhelming our equipment."

"Is it an *anacapa* signature?"

"No," she says. "It's too big for that."

"Meaning what?" Roderick asks.

"Is it something you'd find on one of your vessels?" I ask.

"No," she says. "It's too big for that too. You want to tell us where the hell we're going?"

"It's a ship graveyard," I say. "I've been truthful about that."

"But?" Yash snaps.

"But the bar patrons say it's protected by some kind of shield," I say. "They recognized the shield's signature and say it's on our ship as well."

Coop curses in his own language. Then he says several more things, and Yash answers him, too fast for me to follow, not that I've ever become good with Old Earth Standard.

"You want to share with the rest of us?" Roderick asks again.

"Nine ships," Mikk says, as if he expects us to die at any minute.

"Look," Rossetti says, and taps something in front of her.

The wall screens inside the *Two* fill with an image I'm the only one even slightly prepared for, and I can't believe what I'm seeing.

Dignity Vessels, as far as the eye can see. They're clearly unmanned, clearly dead, with holes in their sides, or blown centers, missing wings or missing entire back halves. They're scattered haphazardly, as if they were left just the way they had fallen in battle.

Although if that were the case, they'd be spread out farther.

"How big is this thing?" I ask.

"I think it goes the entire length of that area those maps avoid," Rossetti says.

"That's not possible," I say.

"It's possible," Coop says tightly, "if someone attacked the Fleet."

FORTY-FIVE

Yash's hands are shaking. Rossetti's back is perfectly straight. Coop's face seems to be made of stone.

"It's been five thousand years," DeVries starts.

"God," Coop says in a withering tone.

But DeVries doesn't stop. "Couldn't someone be storing the ships here?"

"I don't like how all of these ships are gathering," Roderick says to me.

I nod. I don't like it either.

"I think we should get out of here," he says.

"We will when we're done gathering data," Coop says.

"Maybe someone collected these ships like we're doing at Lost Souls," DeVries says, as if the other conversation isn't happening.

"Then you want to explain how the field around these ships is one of ours?" Yash asks.

"It is?" DeVries says.

"It is," Yash says. "We've used fields like that in space for countless things."

"Damaged ship storage?" DeVries asks.

"Sometimes," Yash says, "but not that big. This isn't the entire Fleet, not even close, but it's the largest damn ship graveyard I've seen. To make this work, there would have to be some kind of station in the middle of it."

"Does that make it modern?" DeVries asks. "Because it would seem to me that a field like that—"

"Enough," I say. "We *don't* know anything. We don't even know how long an *anacapa* drive keeps functioning."

"Yes, we do," Coop says. "We discovered that on Vaycehn. At least five fucking thousand years."

It's his tone that shuts us all up. I look at the images in front of me, then down at my control panel. We're getting closer to this area, and it does seem to go on forever.

This Boneyard is huge.

"Can we get in there?" Coop asks Yash.

"With this little ship?" she asks. "I'm not sure—"

The images flicker for just a moment.

"Shit!" Mikk says. "There's a tenth ship, and it's shooting at us!"

"Stations," Coop says, although it doesn't mean a lot here because most everyone is in their stations. But I think he's used to giving that command.

His fingers are moving quickly, and I'm monitoring everything, and we're still heading toward the Boneyard. We have shields up and they're working for now, but if all ten ships fire at us, we're in deep shit.

"This is important," Coop says, and with a shock I realize he's talking to me. "Did you get any indication that those bar friends of yours got into this Boneyard?"

Suddenly I realize what he's asking. He's asking if their weapons are even stronger than they seem. These people might have stolen something from the Boneyard.

"No, they didn't," I say. "Unless they were lying to me. But honestly—"

The images flicker again. I snap them off and bring up the images of the ships. I count eleven now, none of them the same, all of them surrounding us.

"—if they had gotten into that Boneyard, I don't think they'd be coming after us."

"That's an assumption," DeVries says.

"But it sounds like a good one to me," Coop says. "They don't want us. They want the *anacapa* drive to see if they can use it to break that field around the Boneyard."

"Can we?" Mikk asks.

"How the hell should I know?" Yash says.

Another shot hits the shields.

"Target the ship that's firing on us," Coop says. "Get rid of it."

"Yes, sir," Rossetti says, and suddenly weapons' fire leaves the *Two*. It hits the ship in a spot just to the left side, a spot I never would have fired on, and blasts a hole through the middle. The ship lists, then tries to right itself. Some kind of reaction is going on in the center of it, and the damn thing is probably going to explode unless they contain it.

Another ship moves forward. Its weapons appear along the side—something older, that have to jut out of the ship itself.

"They're not going to quit!" Mikk says.

As if to prove his point, another shot, this one stronger, hits our port side.

"Yeah," Coop says, "but they're not trying to destroy us. They have enough firepower to do it, given enough time. Boss is right. They want our *anacapa* drive."

Another shot hits us, ringing the shields and doing something to them that I've never seen before.

"Crap," Roderick says. "They're trying to alter our shields."

"They do that, we're in serious trouble," Yash says.

"As I see it," Mikk says, "we only have two choices. We try to get into that Boneyard—"

"This is not a debate," Coop says. "Yash, activate the *anacapa*."

"If they fire on us, it'll be like Ukhanda all over again," she says.

And suddenly I realize that Yash is as terrified of the effects of the *anacapa* as the rest of us.

"Then do it between shots," Coop says.

"Where are we going?" Yash asks.

"We're going home," Coop says.

FORTY-SIX

The order makes no sense. Home? Does Coop think he can replicate that shot that will take him and his crew back five thousand years? And why would he want to do so?

"The math alone, Coop, is impossible," Yash says, clearly misunderstanding in just the same way that I have. "Especially in the amount of time we have."

"*To Lost Souls,*" he says so harshly that the words feel like weapons.

"Done," she says, and slaps her hand on the console.

Then the ship does its little foldspace dance. Everything skitters, including my vision—including my heart—and I find I'm holding my breath.

Suddenly the weird foldspace star map appears before me.

"Well," Coop says with more relief in his voice than I like. "That's how the damn thing is supposed to work."

Someone laughs nervously—I think it's DeVries—and then I make myself take a deep breath.

"You know," I say, "we don't have to go back to Lost Souls. We can just show up on the other side of that Boneyard. Then you can investigate further."

"No, we can't," Coop says. He's not looking at me. He's looking at the same foldspace star map that I am.

I'm holding my breath again. Did something go wrong that I didn't see?

"Why?" Mikk asks, and in his voice is the same worry that I'm feeling.

"Because we need the *Ivoire,*" Coop says. "If anything will get us into that Boneyard, she will."

CAPTURE

FORTY-SEVEN

*T*hree days later, the ships came.

By then, Squishy was half-mad with anticipation. She spent hours questioning herself, questioning her plan, questioning her ideas. She paced the *Dane*, going from the small cockpit to the galley to the second cabin, and back to the cockpit.

Only once did she try the door to the main cabin, and then she stopped.

She was beginning to worry that Quint had died in his escape pod, that she hadn't done enough to save him, and she knew, she *knew*, that his death would haunt her most of all.

Sometimes she thought the Empire really had no idea who or where she was, and then she would have to remind herself about the tracers. Then she worried that they weren't working or that no one had monitored them or— worst case—that the Empire would simply monitor her until she gave up and went back to Lost Souls.

She would never, ever go back to Lost Souls. She didn't dare.

She hated being by herself. She used to think she loved being by herself— not as much as Boss, maybe, but more than most. And now Squishy knew that this kind of enforced solitude wasn't for her. It could never be for her.

She was starting to question everything.

Or maybe, just maybe, she had never ever had so much time alone with her own thoughts.

Either way, it didn't matter. She wasn't being paranoid, no matter how much her mind wanted to convince her she was.

She was thinking of giving up, saying that her conscience couldn't handle the guilt from the explosion, something, anything to keep the attention away from Lost Souls, when a voice blared across her cockpit:

Prepare to be boarded.

It was some kind of official announcement, filtered through her systems. It told her exactly what to do to comply with the boarding.

Failure to follow these instructions could result in damage to the ship, injury to its passengers, or death.

"Death," she muttered. "To me or the ship?"

Not that it mattered. It might be better for all concerned if she died. But of course, as Boss had known, Squishy didn't have the courage to go through with that.

At least, she hadn't summoned the courage yet.

She sank into the command chair in front of her small control panel, then called up images of the ship's exterior. Five imperial war vessels.

Five.

She supposed she should be flattered. She was one tough, dangerous woman in the eyes of the Empire, and it needed five gigantic ships to take down her little cruiser.

Although, if she thought clearly, maybe the Empire wasn't so far off. Maybe she was that dangerous. After all, she had blown up one of their science vessels years ago even if she had done it through a proxy.

And then she had destroyed one of their major research stations.

She wondered if the Empire knew she had also had a hand in destroying all of the backup materials relating to stealth tech. By now, maybe they did have an idea. Maybe that, in addition to the explosion, was why there were five ships.

Or maybe there were just five in the vicinity.

Second warning: You are about to be boarded. . . .

The instructions repeated just like they had before. She was going to comply, and then she thought, *Why make it easy for them?* She lifted her hands off the control panel. If they destroyed the ship or damaged it or injured her, then so be it.

And if this silly boarding procedure caused death, then she was willing to accept that too.

Although she knew, deep down, that they wouldn't kill her. They believed she had too much information.

The little ship shook as a grappler attached to the outside. Something scraped, and she winced. A warning light went on along her control panel, telling her that the exterior hull near the main exit had been damaged and if whatever it was that had caused the damage was removed, the ship would need to seal up the exterior door to prevent a loss of environment.

"So," she muttered, "the damage is purposeful."

She debated: Sit? Stand? Stay in the cockpit? Go to the door and greet them? Hide in the back room?

In the end, she decided to stand near the control panel.

She watched as the exterior door got breached, then as someone used something to open the *Dane*'s interior door by force. The environmental controls remained on, and nothing on her control panel told her that the ship's integrity had been compromised.

The control panel informed her that seven people had entered the *Dane*, and more followed. She wondered how many human beings they thought they needed to capture just one. Did they think she was going to stand here with some kind of laser rifle and pick them off one by one?

They probably did.

She smiled to herself: paranoid bastards. Somehow their caution made her feel stronger. She no longer felt like the half-mad woman who had been stalking around this ship for days.

She had been right. Her assumptions, her actions, everything she had done had been right.

They stomped through the narrow corridor and poured through the cockpit door, wearing battle armor so heavy they didn't look human at all. One, two, three—she stopped counting at five, and watched a group of them line up near the doorway, military fashion, weapons pointed at her as if she was going to blow them apart.

She actually felt a second of regret: she hadn't thought of attacking them.

Then she remembered: everyone who had died in stealth-tech research here in the Empire had all been working for the imperial military, including Professor Dane, even though he wasn't strictly military. She had been part of the military. Maybe that was why she hadn't thought of attacking them.

These soldiers left the doorway clear, and after a second, a man slipped through it. He didn't have a weapon at all, but then, he didn't need one.

He looked thin and tired, his face red with little cuts. He hadn't gone to a surgeon after all.

"Quint," she said softly.

"Surprised to see me?" he asked with such anger that her heart started racing.

But she kept her voice calm as she said, "Not this time, no. I doubt you can ever surprise me again."

FORTY-EIGHT

Rosealma came out of the meeting room and crumpled onto a bench beside the door. She hated this building. It was part of the military complex, but it was supposedly the Justice Building. It had been designed in the old style: a lot of expensive wood, imported from all over the Empire, and some marbled stone covering the floors.

The problem was that all the stone made the corridors an echo chamber. The wood dampened some of it, but not all of it. And then, lined up against the walls, were the regulation uncomfortable benches.

Just like the uncomfortable chairs inside that meeting room.

She put a hand to her face.

She was tired. She had been tired for more than a year, living and reliving the failed experiment, the problems, the attempted rescue, and finally the shutdown. She had testified and argued and fought. She had wondered if any of it was fair, particularly when the court decided to jail Hansen.

For a while, she kept going back to Vallevu between cases because that was where her off-site home with Quint was. But eventually, she couldn't face it any longer.

She stopped going home. She got an apartment near the courts and she stayed. At first she drank, because she needed her mind on something else. Then she realized if she kept doing that, she would go crazy, so she went back to school.

Medicine provided a good penance. It wasn't stealth tech. It wasn't related to weapons work at all, and yet it appealed to her scientific mind. It kept her thinking about something else.

She got to think about something else now. She was done. And it felt . . . odd.

"Rosealma?"

The voice belonged to Quint. She didn't want to face him now. But she could hear footsteps coming closer. That damn echo.

She'd been living with that for months as well.

She steeled her shoulders, rubbed a hand over her face, and stood.

Quint had come down the hallway, but he was alone. "Did they take your recommendations?"

"No," she said. "But they offered me a job. They want me to be director of Stealth-Tech Research."

He came over to her and put his arm around her. Somehow it didn't feel comforting. "Good. You can make changes when you get back to the project. Sometimes the best changes are made from within anyway."

"I'm not making changes," she said.

He looked at her. She slipped out of his embrace. He stood with his arm upright for just a moment, as if her movement surprised him. Then he let his arm drop.

"What?" he asked.

"I turned them down."

"Why?" he asked.

She looked at his face, broad and familiar, and wondered how she had ever found it attractive.

"I told you," she said. "It isn't the methodology. There's something wrong with the way that we conduct the research itself. Our assumptions are flawed. We're playing with something so dangerous that it could destroy all of us if we're not careful."

"You're being melodramatic," he said, and her breath caught.

He was supposed to be the one who believed her. He was supposed to be the one who understood. He had been with her from the beginning. He knew she had changed the direction of the research, and when she had done that, the deaths had started.

Or, as the committee had said, the disappearances. *No one knows if they're dead, Quintana,* one of the generals said to her. *You have simply made that assumption.*

They're dead to us, sir, Rosealma said. *We'll never get them back.*

"No," she said. "I'm not being 'melodramatic.' If we continue this research, many more good people will die. And that's something we could stop."

"So change the direction of the research, Rose," he said.

"I did that once already," she said. "I made things worse."

He was frowning. He didn't seem to understand what she was saying. "The research is important. This technology will help all of the ships in the Empire."

He was giving her the company line, and that made her even more tired.

"No, it won't," she said. "It won't help any ship except military vessels. If we ever get the stealth tech to work, it'll just make the Empire stronger. It won't do any good at all."

He shook his head slightly. Either he didn't agree with what she was saying or he really didn't understand it. She liked to think he didn't understand it. But she was beginning to fear that he wasn't agreeing with her.

"Quint, this technology, it's not worth all the lives. People shouldn't have to die because we're trying to re-create an old weapons system."

He studied her for a long moment. Her breath caught. She had spent a long time with him. She had trusted him, trusted her future to him. She had pledged her life to his.

Surely that had to be worth something, even if it was just a chance to give her the benefit of the doubt.

Then he said, "People die, Rose. They die for thousands of reasons, some good, some bad, some utterly stupid. They die in accidents and they die too young and they die because they went the wrong way or chose the wrong path. People die."

She was shaking. "Not because of something I developed."

"You didn't develop stealth tech," he said.

"I thought I understood it. I don't. And people are dying because of that. And those assholes in that room won't stop the research. They won't let us rethink our entire strategy. They say we've had too many breakthroughs."

"We've had more breakthroughs because of you than we ever had before," Quint said.

She was staring at him and wondering when he had become a stranger. What was he arguing? That she continue?

"The breakthroughs come at too high a cost," she said.

"You lose some lives to save others," he said.

"Stealth tech won't save lives!" Her raised voice shocked her. She had never yelled at Quint before. She cleared her throat. "Stealth tech, if it works, will cost lives. The Empire will use it to move into the Nine Planets Alliance."

"You don't know that," Quint said, but as he spoke, he looked away. *He* knew it. He knew she was right, and he wasn't willing to say that to her.

"It doesn't matter," she said, walking around him. "They didn't listen to me."

"So you do what I said." He kept pace with her. "Take the job. You change the experiment from within."

"Even if I had the stomach for it—which I don't," she said, "I can't do it now."

"Why?" he asked.

"I resigned my commission, Quint. I'm done with all of this."

He grabbed her arm so hard that it hurt. "Don't do that, Rose. Go back in there. Tell them you made a mistake."

"I didn't make a mistake, Quint," she said. "I did what I had to do."

He grabbed her other arm and pulled her toward him. He brought his face close to hers. "You can't do this, Rose. You're our best mind. You're the secret to stealth tech. You can't leave."

"I already have, Quint." She tried to keep her voice calm, even though he was hurting her.

"Those people, they don't matter," he said. "They're expendable. You're not."

"What people?" she asked. "The ones who died? Or their loved ones who want to believe their dead relatives will come back?"

"All of them," he said. "You can't care about them. Your work is too important."

"Do you care about them?" she asked.

"Hell, no," he said. "Why should I?"

She wrenched out of his grasp. Her upper arms ached where his hands had dug in. She lowered her head and walked away.

"Rose, wait."

She didn't. She kept walking. He grabbed her one more time, and she tried to yank away, but he held her too tight.

"Why should I care about them?" he asked.

"Because science is supposed to be for the public good, Quint," she said. "Not to help the Empire gain more power."

"There's nothing wrong with the Empire, Rose." He sounded convinced.

She looked down at his hand. "Let me go, Quint. You're hurting me."

He released her. She shook her arm, trying to get the circulation back.

"And, for the record, Quint," she said, "any time a government believes that it can sacrifice people for the greater good, then there's something wrong with that government."

He frowned as if he was trying to understand. The look on his face hurt her more than anything. He hadn't understood. He hadn't understood from the beginning. And she should have realized it.

She turned her back on him, and walked away.

And she hoped she would never ever see him again.

FORTY-NINE

Squishy should have found all of those military uniforms, all of those laser rifles, intimidating, but she didn't. She actually felt relieved.

But she didn't let the emotion show, not even when she realized that in addition to the uniformed imperial military inside her small cockpit, even more stood in the corridor.

Quint remained in front of the door. He was wearing a uniform too, but no battle armor. He wasn't holding a gun either.

"I have to arrest you now," he said.

"I know," she said.

"This isn't some simple charge," he said. "You committed treason against the Empire."

She waited.

The people around Quint didn't move. She could hear some of the armor creak, though, as if just staying still was too much for it.

"The punishment for treason is execution," he said.

"I know," she said.

Then she braced herself. Did he mean he would kill her here and now? Could he be that cold?

Her gaze met his. They stared at each other for a long moment, and then he looked away.

"If you cooperate," he said, "you might live longer."

"Cooperate how?" she asked, not because she planned to cooperate but because she was curious.

"Tell us the names of the people you work with," he said. "Tell us what you've discovered in the Nine Planets."

She smiled. "That's easy," she said. "There's a lot of salvage in the Nine Planets."

He sighed. "And don't lie, Rose. It won't help."

"I'm not lying about that," she said. "There *is* a lot of salvage in the Nine Planets."

He took out his cuffs. They had a design she hadn't seen before. "If you tell us everything you can about the rebel operations in the Nine Planets, you will not only live, you'll probably go to some cushy place that's more of a resort than a prison."

"Probably?" she asked.

He walked over to her. The weapons tracked him. Or to be more accurate, they moved in a wordless instruction to her: *Try anything and you will die.*

She thought about it for just a moment—dying as he tried to take her into custody—and then she heard Boss's voice: *Don't be so melodramatic.*

Or was that Quint's voice? They had both said the same thing to her in a different context.

She had never thought of herself as melodramatic, but maybe she was.

Or maybe that was just how she presented herself to the world. Maybe that was why Boss hadn't listened to her on the *Business* all those years ago.

Quint took her hands. His fingers were callused. He held her hands for just a moment, and then he raised his head and looked at her.

Her breath caught. They had stood like this years and years ago and promised to love each other forever. They had been in front of friends and family, and she had meant every single word.

At the time, she thought he had too.

He gently put the cuffs around her wrists. They adjusted to her skin, molding her wrists into one wrist. They didn't hurt, but they did seem warm, a constant reminder—besides the position of her arms—that something held her wrists in place.

"You know the other reason to talk with us, don't you?" he asked.

She didn't answer. He would tell her if she waited long enough.

"We have your ship. We'll know everyone you contacted."

"You know that already," she said.

He looked surprised. Then he cleared his throat and added, "And anything you've tried to get rid of, we'll just reconstruct."

"The only thing I tried to get rid of was those tracers you put all over this ship."

He was still holding her hands. "You found them."

"I'm sure I didn't find all of them," she said. "If I had, you wouldn't be here."

She wanted him to think she believed the lie.

"You know, Rosealma," he said after a long moment, "I really have no idea who you are."

"I know," she said quietly. "You never did."

HOME

FIFTY

*T*he trip home takes only a few minutes. When the ship skitters out of foldspace, I hold my breath.

Then, before me, the Lost Souls complex spreads like a beacon in the darkness. It startles me that I have developed a gigantic corporation, and that this corporation lives in a complex. Two research stations, several floating labs, and a base that has most of the Dignity Vessels we've found, unless they're under repair.

The *Ivoire* is docked against what I call our home base, mostly because it's a small station that my people built with comfort in mind. It has apartments that extend around the inner rings and cafeterias, entertainment plazas, and shopping areas that extend around the outer rings. The people who run the businesses on the outer rings are generally family members of the folks who work for Lost Souls—and a lot of those businesses are actually owned by the corporation.

Like the cafeterias. Designed to cater to a variety of tastes, the cafeterias were Mikk's brainchild. He doesn't like cooking, and he hates spending money for food, so he opts to have part of his paycheck taken as a food allowance. Everyone has that option, and a surprising 75 percent take advantage of it.

Of course, it's all too big for me to run, but back when I did control each aspect of it, I found myself saying yes a lot more than I should have just to get people off my back. Financially we were all right because of patents and the scientific developments that sold, and sold big, throughout the Nine Planets, but finally some accountant types convinced me that even with what seemed to me to be unlimited funds, Lost Souls would eventually spend all of its profits.

That was when I decided to get a chief financial officer. Even though I still monitor the books, I don't make all of the day-to-day decisions. I don't even make half of them, which is how I can stay away for so long.

Still, being back makes me relax in a way I don't like. I tell myself I'm just relieved we didn't get stuck in foldspace.

We dock near the *Ivoire*. I expect Coop to run out of the *Two*, gather his crew, and head back to that Boneyard. In fact, I'm braced to argue with him when he catches my arm.

"We need to plan this trip right," he says.

I look at him, startled that he even suggests this. "Yeah, we do."

"I think we take a few days and make an actual plan. I have some ideas, but I want to sketch them out before we implement them."

I'm openmouthed. I was just getting used to the impatient Coop; that the patient Coop has returned surprises me.

I can't keep silent about this. "I would have thought you'd want to leave immediately."

He shakes his head. "There's too much data to sift through."

His mood has lightened, and I don't think it's because he has returned "home," to use the word he used. I think it's because he believes he finally will get some answers.

Or maybe it's because he sees a possible path into the future now.

"I want to call a meeting in two days," he says to me. "I'll have information by then."

"Maybe you and I should talk first," I say.

"Oh, we will," he says. He stands, stretches, and his back cracks from the stress of sitting in the same position.

The rest of the cockpit crew is watching him, some with the same surprised expression that I must have had a moment ago.

"The adventure isn't over," he says to them when he realizes they're all staring at him. "But this part of it is."

Then he leaves the cockpit ahead of the rest of us.

"What's that?" I ask Yash.

She shakes her head, still staring after him. "A changed man," she says. "That's all I can tell you. He's a changed man."

FIFTY-ONE

As usual, I'm the last to leave the ship. I want to make sure everything from this trip has been removed, and the ship's ready to be cleaned for the next trip. In addition, I need to double-check our information files, and make certain I have all the materials I need to make a proper record of what happened on this particular journey.

I close up and step into the docking bay, which is much more elaborate than anything I had ever envisioned for a company I'm connected with. This section of the bay is built for smaller ships like the *Two*. We have other sections built large enough for Dignity Vessels, which are the largest ships I've come across outside of the imperial military fleet.

When I arrived here a few hours ago, I was relieved to be home, but when I step off the *Two*, I feel completely overwhelmed.

And it doesn't help to see Ilona Blake standing at the edge of the walkway, her signature electronic pad clutched to her chest.

Ilona runs this place, and does a much better job than I ever would. She also keeps me in the loop, which I rarely appreciate but do understand is necessary. She's slight and pretty enough that the men notice her as she walks past, before she stops and orders them about for the first time. She wears her long black hair the way she has worn it since I met her, tied behind her head and cascading down her back.

"I'm glad you're here," she says, and I sigh inwardly.

When she uses that tone, it means there's a problem she can't deal with. Problems she can't deal with are usually vast.

"I don't suppose I can get dinner, take a shower, and maybe have a nap," I say.

She doesn't even smile. That's what's changed about Ilona since she's taken over most of the duties connected with running Lost Souls. She hardly ever smiles anymore.

"Well," she says, as if she's actually considering my request. "It's better if you answer at least one question first. Do you know someone named 'Turtle'?"

She says the name as if it's somehow dirty. But she has my attention. I haven't heard that name in nearly ten years.

"Yes," I say, sounding as startled as I feel.

"Then there's no time to shower," she says. "Come with me."

We take the back route to her office—not because it's shorter (it isn't) but because we want to avoid seeing other folks who work here, most of whom will want to know how the "adventure" went. I can only imagine what Coop and the rest of the team have gone through as they integrate themselves back into the life here at Lost Souls.

The back route is a series of corridors that I designed for my office in the beginning, so that I didn't ever have to talk to anyone. Ilona's office, which was once mine, is in an older part of this station, and the office itself is hard to get to, again because of me.

Initially, when I gave it to Ilona, she talked about moving the main offices elsewhere. Now she understands the value of privacy.

"This woman," she says as we walk, "this Turtle, she says she has a message for you."

"You sound skeptical of her," I say. I'm intrigued by that. No one who met Turtle ever thought of her as anything but honest. I can understand people worrying about me or worrying about Squishy, but no one ever questioned Turtle.

"I looked her up as much as I could," Ilona says. "She's invisible."

"Meaning?"

"Meaning I can track her journey here from one space station away. Otherwise, she doesn't exist."

I frown a little. "She didn't give you her real name."

"She says I don't need it. She says you'll know her. The only reason I even let her into my part of the station is because she says she has news about Squishy."

Now I'm confused. "Squishy? She's on vacation, I thought. Did she go see Turtle?"

"Why would she do that?" Ilona asks.

"Because she and Squishy were in a committed relationship for about seven years," I say.

"I don't remember that," Ilona says.

"Back when Squishy and I were dive partners," I say with a smile.

Ilona grunts. And I realize that she keeps forgetting that Squishy and I have a long history that predates her.

"I would have stashed her somewhere until you got back," Ilona says, "maybe even sent her to some hotel somewhere, except for one thing."

Something in her tone catches me. "What?"

She stops walking. We're only a few meters from her office now, so she clearly doesn't want anyone to overhear this.

"Squishy apparently put a team together," Ilona says quietly.

"A team for what?" I ask.

"To destroy the Empire's stealth-tech research."

The breath leaves my body as if Ilona has punched me in the stomach. I put my hand against the wall behind me, but its smoothness doesn't hold me up. I lean on it and close my eyes.

Dammit, Squishy. Damn.

I open my eyes. Ilona is watching me, a slight frown creasing her forehead.

I take a deep, painful breath, and say, "I told her not to do that. A year ago, I told her it was silly."

I also told her I wouldn't help. So not just damn Squishy. But damn me. I should have known that she wouldn't take no for an answer. She's always been that way.

"She's not capable of leading something like this," I say.

"Ah, yeah," Ilona says. "Half of her team made it back. The other half didn't."

Now I'm cold. I suspect I know who her team was. A group of people had asked for more than six months off. Most of them were folks who had joined us early on, and I understood their need for a sabbatical. We do a lot of tough work here, and we expect a lot of our people. Sometimes a person just needs a break from all of that.

"What did the people who made it back say?" I ask.

"That they had a rendezvous site, and instructions on how to behave once they got there. They were supposed to leave within a few hours of arrival if no one else showed, but they waited a full day. Half the team didn't show—and Squishy didn't show."

I take a deep breath.

"And now we have a message from Squishy, sent via Turtle," I say. I'm confused by this. Why Turtle? I didn't even know they had been in contact all of these years.

"Yes," Ilona says.

"And what's the message?" I ask.

"That's the point," Ilona says. "She won't tell me. She says she'll only talk to you."

FIFTY-TWO

We step into the side door of Ilona's office. At first, I don't see anyone sitting in the comfortable chair arrangement to the far side of the room. That's where I've always had the visitors sit, and where I assume Ilona does as well.

The office is large. Ilona's workspace is private: behind another door, and much smaller. She keeps all of the confidential information there. But this space has a desk and three separate seating arrangements, as well as a clear wall leading to a room that houses a large conference table.

Ilona seems to thrive here. The very size of the office defeated me.

Partly because I can't see anyone. Then Turtle stands up from the second seating arrangement on the far side of the main door.

At least, I think it's Turtle. I wouldn't recognize her if I passed her on the street. At first, I think it's because she looks old, but she doesn't. Not when I really look at her.

She has some features of the very old. She's thin to the point of gauntness. She's always been too thin, but now she seems skeletal. The bones of her face stand out in sharp relief, and her hair is so short that it's impossible to tell at first glance if she's male or female.

Her hair has turned completely white, and she's let it do so. She wears baggy clothing, which also makes her seem older, as if she had once worn this clothing on a much bigger self. But I remember Turtle from ten years ago. She never would have fit into that clothing.

She either borrowed it or she wears it as a costume.

Only her eyes are the same. They soften when they see me.

"Boss," she says.

"Turtle." I hurry across the room. She leans toward me as if she's going to hug me, then leans back, seeking permission.

She remembers me well.

I do hug her, carefully, startled that she feels as fragile as she looks.

As the hug breaks up (quickly), she says, "This is some place you've built."

"Yeah," I say. "It's not what I would have expected from myself back in the day."

"You always put together things to get a job done," she says. "I assume this is the same thing."

I look at her, somewhat startled. I'd never thought of Lost Souls that way. But it's true. I did put this place together to get a job done, to figure out Dignity Vessels and stealth tech long before the Empire did.

And I achieved that. A bit accidentally because of the *Ivoire*, but I did achieve that.

No wonder I'd been feeling restless. This job is done.

"So," I say, indicating that we should sit down on a nearby sofa, "you saw Squishy."

"No," Turtle says. Then she looks over my shoulder. She doesn't sit down. "I think we need to have this conversation somewhere private."

"This is fine," I say.

"I've got some things to look into," Ilona says, and goes out the door we entered.

"I still think we should leave," Turtle says. "This room looks too official."

"It used to be my office," I say. "We're fine."

Her mouth thins. "I just don't want this recorded."

I'm startled again. "These are my people, Turtle."

"And I don't know any of them," she says.

"Except Squishy," I say. "I thought you had a message from her. So if you didn't see her, how did she contact you?"

"Through a hundred back channels," Turtle says. "And believe me, I'm hard to find these days."

"I know," I say. "Ilona wanted to check you out before she let me know you were here. She couldn't find anything."

Turtle glances at the door. "See? I think we should go somewhere else."

"Relax," I say. "Sit down. We're talking here. Why are you so paranoid? Is it Squishy's message?"

Turtle sits slowly, as if the couch is going to bite her when it touches her baggy pants. "I was supposed to figure out a way to send it to you, but I had no idea if your people would even give it to you. And it's important."

She hands me a handheld, a small one with a design I don't recognize. On the screen is a written message from Squishy. In it, she apologizes for the way she treated Turtle. And then she mentions something that rings a bell, something that—

I look up at Turtle as heat flushes my face. "It's one of our codes," I say.

She nods. "It took me a while to remember all of it."

I stare at it. I remember it all now. We designed these things for risky dives in bad places, dives that could cause political problems, difficulties with governments, dives that could have put us at risk of attack from rogue gangs that roamed certain areas.

The messages generally weren't calls for help. They were advice, warnings, get-the-hell-out-of-here codes, designed to make certain no one else got hurt.

This was the strongest: *I'm in trouble. I'll probably die here. Do not (repeat) Do not come after me.*

Since the code mentions both me and Turtle, and Turtle had no idea where Squishy was before this message arrived, the code is directed to me.

And it was written as if Squishy expected someone else—not the two of us—to read it.

"How did you find me?" I ask.

"It took some work," Turtle says. "If you hadn't used an old alias on Vaycehn, I might never have found you."

I had forgotten that the name I used there had been one devised in the last days of my diving business. Careless of me. Fortunately, I abandoned that name five years before.

"Still," I say. "You—"

"Your ships came back from that mission to the Nine Planets Alliance," Turtle says. "I tracked them using the Empire's own system. You do know they now track every ship that goes through their space."

"I suspected as much," I say.

"Once I got here, it took a while to find you, but I managed." She wasn't going to tell me how.

"How come Ilona couldn't track you?" I ask.

"When I don't want to be found, I can't be found," Turtle says mysteriously.

"Then how did Squishy find you?" I ask.

"Just like I found you," Turtle says. "Sometimes old friends have access to information no one else does. She found me through some business I did in my own name years ago."

I nod. That makes sense. "Do you know where she is?"

"The Empire has her," Turtle says. "And she probably thinks they're going to kill her."

"You don't?" I ask, interested in this new Turtle, the one who makes me seem like I'm not paranoid at all.

"I don't think they'll kill her," Turtle says. "She's too valuable. Have you looked at this place? They want to know what you're doing. They'll pull information out of her brain for years."

I bow my head. I warned Squishy about this. I said they'd try it, and she'd flippantly told me she'd die first.

But Squishy isn't that person. She won't kill herself for an idea. She's too pragmatic for that.

"You going to follow her orders?" Turtle asks, and I wonder if she uses the word "orders" on purpose. The old me would have bristled at that.

The new me knows that there are more risks here than I can contemplate. I can't afford to get angry over words.

"I have no idea what I'm going to do," I say. "I need more information."

"Like where they're holding her?" Turtle asks.

"Do you know?" I ask.

"No," she says. "But I have a pretty good idea."

FIFTY-THREE

"**H**ere's what I know," Turtle says, leaning into me, her elbows resting on her knees, her hands clasped and dangling in the air between us. She's speaking softly as if she still expects Ilona to overhear. "Squishy went into the Empire to destroy stealth tech."

I stiffen. "Did she tell you this?"

Turtle glances around Ilona's office. We haven't been disturbed, and I doubt we will be. But I can't reassure her of that. I wonder what has made her so paranoid and am not sure how to ask in such a way that will get information from her.

"One of the major science labs exploded," Turtle says. "It was completely destroyed. No one talks about the kind of research that was done there. Then in a handful of other stations, information got targeted and destroyed by some kind of virus or download or something—I'm not privy to what—before anyone figured out what was going on. In fact, the only way they knew that the backups had been destroyed was because of the explosion at the science lab on this research station."

She's speaking so softly I have to strain to hear the words.

"There's one other lab," she says. "It's on a base so top secret that it's on a need-to-know basis. If Squishy wanted to destroy their stealth-tech research, she failed. She had no idea that the bulk of the cutting-edge research is in this place."

I'm still stuck on need-to-know. "Are you with the Empire now, Turtle? How did you get need-to-know information?"

She gives me a thin smile, then runs a hand through her hair. "I forget you're not in the Empire any longer. I'm not with the Empire. I'm not in the military. I'm working with an organization that feels the key to loosening the Empire's control is loosening its control on information."

I frown. "What do you mean?"

"There's a lot of things no one living in the Empire has a clue about, things being done in their names. I leak that information."

I can't quite reconcile that with the Turtle I knew. The Turtle I knew loved diving and adventure and—

Suddenly I understand. This is a different kind of risk.

"That's how you found me, then," I say, "through some kind of information network."

"It's not some kind of network," Turtle says. "It's my network. I started looking into things after Squishy left. I didn't understand what she was talking about, and she got so mad at me that I just decided to investigate it. It didn't bring her back, but I understood more. And that's when I realized just how important information is, and how so few people have it, even when they need it."

My heart hurts just a little. It's been twelve years since the breakup and Turtle is still in love with Squishy. So much so that she's come to me when she simply could have sent me some kind of message.

"You think they want me," I say.

"The Empire believes you know more about this technology than they do," Turtle says, "and they're willing to do anything short of invading the Nine Planets to get it."

I nod. That's important information, but not as important as the other thing that Turtle has told me.

"You say there's a secret lab? One Squishy missed?"

"Yes," she says.

"And you're certain of this?"

"Yes," she says.

"And forgive me," I say, "I have to ask this even though we're old friends. But you know the codes just as well as Squishy did, and if you're collecting information, then you probably learned that she was behind that bombing. So how do I know that you haven't come here from the Empire just to get me into imperial space?"

Her cheeks flush, but she doesn't protest the question. I think she understands it. "The message tells you not to come," she says.

"But anyone who knows me would think I would disobey that order," I say.

"Unless they were there the day we set these messages up. They are hard and fast, you said. And we don't violate them. If the person inside thinks it's too dangerous for us to go, we don't go."

I did say that. I said a lot of things that I didn't always follow. But I remember that day now, and I remember how forceful I was. I actually believed what I said.

I believe it now, in theory.

But I have more information than Turtle does. I think I understand what Squishy is thinking. Squishy is worried that I'll bring a Dignity Vessel into the Empire to rescue her, and then the Empire will know that the Vessel functions, that we've solved the stealth-tech problem, and we're ahead of them in various research.

I'm sure they know about our peripheral research, but I've carefully monitored information that has left Lost Souls, and we've never let on about the *anacapa* drive or our stealth-tech research.

Except, oddly enough, in this last trip outside of the Nine Planets. At the Boneyard.

But Squishy knows all about the Dignity Vessels and the *anacapa* drive and the stealth tech. And while she may not be able to build an *anacapa* from scratch or even draw up the specs for one, she can let the Empire know that the drive exists and all the various functions the drive has.

Then the Empire would search for the ships and once it found one, remove the *anacapa* drive and try to reverse-engineer it. They might succeed.

Either way, they're going to know about the drive.

They might learn about a lot of other things if they spend too much time with Squishy.

She'll try to resist them. She'll lie, and she won't cooperate. She might even try to kill herself after a while. But they'll prevent that. And they have interrogation techniques that will pull information out of the most stubborn subject eventually.

Eventually, everyone talks.

"You're just going to leave her there, aren't you?" Turtle says into my silence. "That's what she wants. She's trying to protect you."

"Yes," I say, "she is."

"Are you two involved now?" Turtle asks, her voice plaintive, finally the Turtle I remember. "Is that why she's trying to protect you?"

I shake my head. "We've never had that kind of relationship, Turtle. You know that."

"Then why is she so worried?" Turtle asks. "Is it something to do with this place?"

"You're the information expert," I say. "I would have thought that you already knew."

She looks at me. "I haven't focused on you. I focus on the Empire. And they're going to hurt her, Boss. Badly. No one deserves that."

"I know," I say.

"I have the specs to that station," Turtle says. "I'm going to go back and put a team together. I'm going to try to get her out. You're welcome to come as an old friend, but I have a hunch you'll just piss her off."

I smile. "I always piss her off."

But I'm really not thinking about Turtle's rescue effort. I'm thinking about what she just said. She has the specs to the station.

She has information.

And maybe, just maybe, I have a plan.

FIFTY-FOUR

"**A**bsolutely not," Coop says.

He's in the captain's suite of the *Ivoire*. He has been in the ship ever since we got back from the Boneyard. He's preparing the *Ivoire* for a flight back, and maybe for a prolonged stay.

He could have waited for a week or so, taken his time to put things together, but he's clearly not going to. On the *Two*, I thought he was being surprisingly patient.

Now I realize he's not patient at all. He just has a better strategy than I thought he had.

The captain's suite is bigger than any land-based apartment I had when I was diving. It's certainly bigger than any captain's cabin I've seen on any of the ships I've owned.

This suite has five rooms, a private galley, and a full kitchen off the dining area that can be closed off if the captain so desires. That's so he can hold formal meals here if he needs to.

Most of the crew quarters on the *Ivoire* are spectacular because this ship isn't just transportation; it's home. So even the lower-level crew quarters have at least two rooms and are called apartments.

However, none of the quarters are as elaborate as this one.

It always takes my breath away whenever I enter it.

Coop is standing in the middle of the main room. He has full screens on all the walls, playing some of the footage we recorded near the Boneyard. He's studying it—or he was until I asked if I could come on board.

Now he's turned to face me. He has converted the table into a workspace—the surface now has a control panel, and maps blaze up at me. One chair is pulled back, the other pushed forward. The couch faces the wall screens, and so do two of the chairs.

He's thinking of making some kind of presentation, although not to me.

So I've jumped right in. I've told him that Squishy has been captured, that Turtle believes she's in that science lab, and that I've done what I can to verify the news.

In fact, I've spent the last two hours retracing Turtle's research without her purported connections, and certainly not following her steps. She's nowhere near me.

Squishy's surviving team members have come back, and they're a mess. They're apologetic and frightened and worried that they've abandoned friends to a fate that they shouldn't have done.

But they've also confirmed that Squishy was trying to destroy the stealth tech in the Empire. One two-man partnership also confirmed that they'd seen evidence of that second science research station. It's not a lab. It's a base, and it's huge.

They were going to tell Squishy, but of course, she never showed.

I tell Coop about all of this. I tell him that I've verified it. And then I tell him my plan—or at least, my *ideal* plan.

I want to use the *anacapa* drive and all of the *Ivoire*'s resources. We'll arrive at the base in an instant, send in a team to pull out Squishy, then destroy the base, and leave. I tell him I think this will add two days to the timing of his return to the Boneyard, maybe less.

But Coop doesn't think that's a good idea.

"You told her that she couldn't go on this mission, right?" he asks. He looks like a full-fledged captain now, in this space with the images of the destroyed Dignity Vessels behind him. "You told her you didn't sanction this. You told her that she risked being caught."

"I did," I say calmly. I knew he would make this argument.

"And she went ahead and did it on her time," he says. "Disobeying you."

"I don't own her," I say.

"But she's smart enough to know you were right," he says.

I sigh. "She does now."

"It's not humorous, Boss."

"I know that," I say. "But we need to get her out of there. She will eventually tell them whatever they want to know."

"What does that matter to us?" he asks.

I glance at the ships behind him. He's already gone back to the man he was.

"I don't think it means anything to you," I say. "But if the Empire gets its hands on an *anacapa* drive, it'll change the balance of power in this area. It will defeat the Nine Planets."

"Unless we give the Nine Planets the *anacapa* drive and our weapons systems," Coop says. "There is no downside."

"Except full-scale war," I say quietly.

He glares at me. Then he shakes his head and glances over his shoulder at the images.

"You want me to jeopardize my entire crew for a woman who doesn't follow orders," he says.

"No," I say softly. "I want you to use your expertise to save my friend."

"Dammit, Boss, don't manipulate me. I know how much trouble you have with that woman."

"I also have known her for more than twenty years," I say. "I owe her."

"If your friend Turtle is to be believed, you don't. Squishy doesn't want you to come."

"Yeah," I say. "She hasn't thought it through."

"Isn't that a surprise," he says. Then he comes closer, and puts his hands on my shoulders. I've seen him do this with his crew before delivering bad news.

I slip out of his grasp. Not just because I'm not a member of his crew, but I hate being touched like that. It's patronizing, whether he knows it or not.

He lets his hands drop.

"Boss, look, this war you fear between the Nine Planets and the Empire is going to come no matter what you do. In my study of your history, it's become pretty clear to me that this war isn't a new war, but a continuation of the Colonnade Wars. Sometimes groups fight until one wins—no matter how long it takes."

"I'm not going to be responsible for this," I say.

"You're not. You did what you could. *Squishy* will be responsible for it."

Now—suddenly—I'm mad. I didn't expect to get mad, but that hand-on-the-shoulder thing started it, along with lecturing me about my own history.

"When I first met you," I say, "you got really upset when you realized that we believed stealth tech was just a cloak."

"So?" he says.

"So the Empire thinks maybe it's just a cloak, or maybe it's a weapon. They're not going to change their thinking because Squishy also tells them it's a drive. She can't build the drive. She can't show them the safeguards. Those death holes we saw in Vaycehn, the deaths that happened in the Room of Lost Souls, there will be things like that all over the sector because the Empire will try to advance its technology. And you say that has nothing to do with us? Yet you were willing to risk everything to shut down the *anacapa* in Sector Base V when you realized what was going on. You even shot at Empire people to save my people."

He's waiting patiently. I *hate* that. It's as if I'm having a tantrum and he's a grown-up.

It's part of his command self, and I hate that too.

"It's different, Boss. The Empire would make mistakes anyway. I can't control them. They have nothing to do with me or my people."

"Because you're heading to the Boneyard," I say.

"Yes," he says quietly.

I expected it, but I'm disappointed. No, that's not fair. I'm furious. We gave him a home for five years. We helped his people learn how to survive in this culture. We helped them mourn the loss of their friends, the ones who couldn't cope with the change. We gave them jobs and income and a place to come back to.

He had called this place home not twelve hours ago.

But I don't say any of that. Because I expected him to turn me down.

I had hoped he wouldn't.

But I had expected that he would.

"Okay," I say quietly, hoping my disappointment and anger doesn't show in my voice. "Then I need you to take those two days to help me learn the systems in my ship."

"You know the *Two*," he says.

I shake my head. "I have working Dignity Vessels." I deliberately use the phrase he hates. "I'm going to take one to rescue Squishy. I need help understanding the full weapons system, and I need someone to show me the ins and outs of the *anacapa* drive."

"You can't do that," he says.

"Why not?" I say. "It's my ship. I can do whatever I want."

He stares at me. Finally he says, "You don't have enough qualified people to run it."

"I'm sure a few of your people will help me," I say. "We don't need a full crew. Just enough to man the bridge, work communications, handle weapons, and monitor the engine room."

"Good Lord," he says, almost to himself. "You're serious."

"I'm going to get her," I say. "I'm taking a ship in that the Empire is not prepared to deal with. I figure surprise will get us a lot farther than anything."

"Surprise will get you into that base," he says, "and then you're done. You're proposing a commando raid on a military base to rescue your stupid friend."

Now he's angry. He wouldn't normally have called Squishy stupid no matter how much he thought she was.

"You don't know how to run the ship and you don't know how to use the weapons and you sure as hell don't have anyone qualified to take on trained soldiers in their home territory."

I shrug. "Then maybe I'll go in and blow the base myself."

"With Squishy on it?" he asks.

I ponder it for a moment. "Probably not. I probably won't blow the base. One of my team will when I haven't come back from my 'commando raid.'"

"You'll die too," he says.

I nod.

He stares at me. I can see a series of warring emotions on his face. Anger, disbelief, fear. Then he gets his expression under control.

"You'd die for Squishy?" he asks.

"I've always been prepared to die for my team," I say, and he knows I mean it. I might have died the day we met, if things had gone a little differently. "But in this case, I wouldn't be dying for Squishy. I'd be dying to make sure she achieved her mission, which, no matter what I said to her, is a good one. I don't care what you say about the Colonnade Wars or the inevitability of the fight between the Empire and the Nine Planets. Right now, we're in a stalemate, and I want it to stay that way."

"You realize if we bring the *Ivoire* in and destroy their research base, this will no longer be a stalemate," he says. "It'll be an act of war."

I shrug. "We'll have superior firepower."

"We have three ships with weapons systems," Coop says, "two of which you refuse to name let alone staff."

"We also have your weapons systems and a variety of fighter jets. Believe me, the Empire won't be able to keep up. They'll claim it's an act of war, but they've never seen anything like the *Ivoire* before, and the Nine Planets will easily be able to claim ignorance. They have no idea about the *Ivoire* either."

He stares at me. He's assessing me. "You realize you'll be doing this at the risk of your own life. You'll probably die on this mission."

"I know," I say.

"Is your life that worthless?" he says with more force than either of us anticipated.

"I didn't know dying for a cause was worthless," I snap. "Isn't that the antithesis of what they taught you in Fleet school?"

He looks away from me, then turns toward those destroyed ships. Ships on which—I can guarantee it—people died. For some cause or another. One we have no idea about.

"Damn you, Boss," he says quietly.

I don't smile, even though I want to. "So you'll teach me?"

He shakes his head. "I'll lead your little suicide mission and we'll get your friend back. And then I'm heading to the Boneyard."

I nod. He didn't have to add that last bit. I know it, but I don't want to think about it.

"Thanks, Coop," I say.

"Don't thank me until we're done," he says, and shuts off the screens behind him.

CUSTODY

FIFTY-FIVE

They brought her on board one of the larger military vessels and marched to a side wing. Now they had her in some kind of brig. Squishy had never been in a brig before. She had never even seen one. This was bigger than she expected and more elaborate.

The walls were smooth and could easily turn into screens if need be. She suspected people were watching her, but she wasn't certain. There was a long bed on the far wall. The bed extended from the wall, and its supports were hidden inside that wall.

She couldn't take the bed apart if she wanted to.

She didn't want to.

There was also a place to sit—just another platform extended from the wall—but she appreciated it. Someone had even placed a light above it for reading. She got a reading pad when they put her in the brig, which surprised her. Most people didn't read, and she didn't expect the kindness.

But they didn't want her to go onto any network or view any vids. And when she finally picked up the reading device, it warned her that any attempt to take it apart would set off an alarm and cause her to go to a different cell entirely, one—apparently—less comfortable.

This one wasn't that comfortable. There was a toilet on the far side of the room and a little pump that released cleansing fluid nearby. She had no privacy, although she could pretend she did. No guard stood outside the door.

But people watched, *cameras* watched just the same.

This was her future. No matter what she did, no matter how much she talked, she would spend the rest of her life in cells of some kind, either alone or with unsavory types, people who had somehow angered the Empire.

As if she hadn't done unsavory things. At least two hundred deaths could be laid on her. Not counting Cloris. Plus the destruction of the research station had probably destroyed a bunch of lives. Not because the people died, but because she had completely ruined their life's work.

She wanted to say she didn't mind being in here, but she did. She hated being confined. And she hated having nothing to do.

That's why they had given her the reading device. They figured that no one could sleep all the time, and they certainly couldn't ruminate forever. So they gave her "entertainment," even though it wasn't.

Before she could open anything on the device, she had to read the list of crimes she was charged with, along with the statutory punishments. She wasn't surprised by any of it. In fact, some of the punishments seemed too lenient to her.

But she dutifully read them, and then she looked at the reading options. Mostly nonfiction, mostly propaganda on how wonderful the Empire was.

If she got desperate enough, she would read that too.

She had half expected Quint to come here and try to convince her to cooperate with the imperial authorities. He had tried a little in the *Dane*. She had expected him to try even harder here.

But maybe he was giving her time to reflect.

Not that she needed it.

All she needed was time to figure out what had happened to her courage and her bravado. She should have destroyed the *Dane*, while she was in it. She should have done a lot of things.

And she always seemed to let the opportunities go right by her.

FIFTY-SIX

"**Y**ou did *what?*" Rosealma asked, standing behind the clear double panes. She was queasy, hands on the control panel, feeling like she was going to be sick.

Not again, she thought. *Not again.*

She had helped design this military base. She was the one who had suggested putting it in orbit above a sparsely populated planet. She was the one who had suggested that the families live in Vallevu, a very pretty city on the ground below, so that they were nowhere near the experiments.

She had set up the sections of the base, keeping various experiments away from other experiments. The dangerous stuff was so far away from the operational and housing parts of the base that people joked about it, saying they needed a shuttle just to get to work in the morning.

She wanted it that way. She had even worked on the committees that set up the procedures and regulations—no one worked alone, no one worked on stealth tech in isolation, no one experimented on human subjects without a mountain of approval, no one made decisions without some kind of failsafe.

And now she stood in the deepest, darkest, most distant stealth-tech lab, and saw—nothing. No lab techs, no furniture, no walls. Even part of the interior of the damn base was missing.

Her stomach hurt and her hands trembled. The scientist beside her was just a baby, round-faced, wide-eyed, barely old enough to have a graduate degree, let alone the kind of credentials that allowed him to work in her lab.

Not that she was much older, in years anyway. But in life—she had aged fifty years in the past five.

"What did you do?" she asked again.

She knew it was him because he was the only one in the staging area, and he was the one who had called her, which pissed her off, because he should have contacted an entire team when something went wrong.

"I—" His voice broke, and she wasn't sure he would be able to get the words out. She needed him to get the words out, because if he didn't, she would have to review the logs, and that would take time—time she suspected they didn't have.

"I can't fix this unless you tell me what you did," she snapped.

He opened his mouth, then closed it. She cursed, and turned to the control panel. She'd even had a control panel installed in each of the labs as if they were separate laboratory ships operating in deep space. If anything went wrong, the labs should have isolated themselves even farther, but this one hadn't. She had no idea how many people had been working in the next lab over, the lab that was no longer there, and she wasn't sure she wanted to know. But she was going to have to find out.

"You said we actually got the cloak to work," he said.

She whirled on him. What was his name? Robbie, Reggie, Ralphie? She glanced at the name badge along the front of his uniform jacket. Hansen. Radley Hansen.

"We got the cloak to work in a limited fashion," she said. "Meaning it masked a single item, very small. A coin. That was it. Nothing more elaborate than that."

"Yes, ma'am, I know, ma'am, I'm sorry, ma'am."

She went cold. "You came in here, by yourself, and ran the experiment again, didn't you?"

"I'm sorry, ma'am, truly. I was just thinking—"

"Of yourself, of promotion, of the fact that if you succeeded, you would own stealth tech, you would be the one who everyone came to because you knew how it worked, isn't that right?"

"Sort of, ma'am. I thought I saw an anomaly in the data from the first experiment, and I came in to double-check it—"

"Alone," she said. "You came in alone."

"Yes, ma'am."

"Against direct orders. No one was to work alone."

His face was red. "Everyone does it, ma'am."

Anger surged through her. She wanted to hit something—hell, she wanted to hit him. Everyone did it? And she wasn't aware of it? If this were a minor infraction, she would check right now. But it wasn't minor, it was major, and she needed to deal with the crisis first, not with the group of idiots who broke the rules and might just have cost dozens of lives.

"So you ran the experiment again," she said.

"First I read the data, and really, ma'am, there was something wrong. When you shut down the cloak, the coin reappeared but it wasn't the same coin."

"Of course it was the same coin." She had checked it herself.

He shook his head. "It was an older coin. I can show you the scans—"

"I don't want to see the damn scans," she said. "I want to know what you did."

He closed his eyes, knowing he was admitting to something that might be the death of his career at best, might get him court-martialed at worst.

"I brought in one of my own coins," he said, his entire face trembling. His eyes popped open. They were red and round and filled with fear. "I knew every marking, I recorded everything I knew about that coin, I even wrapped it in a strand of my hair, so that I would know it was mine."

She stayed very still because if she didn't stay still, she would lay this asshole flat, and then pummel him, maybe to death.

"I put it in there," he said, his voice breaking again, "and I set it in the same position as the other coin had been in during the first experiment, and I came out, and I ran the experiment again, only this time, the cloak didn't work, it sent out this pulse of energy and it was big and it demolished the back half of the room, and I tried to shut it down, and it won't shut down, it's still growing I think, and I tried to reverse it, and when that didn't work, I called you."

"So you fucking tampered with the tech before contacting me?"

"I was trying to fix it," he said.

"You are eighteen different kinds of idiot," she said. "You need to call in the rest of the team, right now."

"But ma'am, I think the field is growing and what if it pulses again, we'd lose anyone who showed up here."

She whirled on him. "So you figured *I* was the expendable one?"

"No, ma'am, no. I figured we had to solve this with the fewest people and you were the only chance of doing that. You're the one who knows this stuff backwards and forwards—"

"And I'm the one who put in the safeguards that you didn't follow to pre-vent precisely this kind of thing from happening," she said, turning back to the controls, shaking now because she was only just beginning to understand how catastrophic this all was, all because some kid wanted to further his career and figured he'd be forgiven when he discovered the secret to everything.

"Yes, ma'am, I'm sorry, ma'am, I didn't intend it, ma'am."

"You didn't intend it," she repeated with deep sarcasm. "Of course you didn't intend it, you idiot. You intended to be complimented and told how damn brilliant you are. Well, that'll never happen now. It just depends on how many people have died as to what kind of stupid they'll consider you."

He took a step backward, as if her words had the force of blows.

"Have you contacted anyone else like I just asked?" she said, knowing he hadn't. "Have you?"

"N-N-No, ma'am."

"Then get on it." She was shaking with fury, and the anger wouldn't do her any good. But dammit, she had done everything she could to prevent something like this, and it had happened anyway, and if what she saw was any indication, it was worse—it was worse than the first time.

She had believed in this stuff once, and it had brought her here. To a room with no back where an entire wing of the science lab had just vanished. Or maybe (best case) maybe it had simply been cloaked.

But she doubted it, and she knew she didn't have the ability to figure all of this out on her own.

Hansen did have a point: the more people who came here now, the more people were at risk. But she needed help—*they* needed help.

She hit the command button that she had insisted be installed in every lab. Her staff joked about it, saying Rosealma wanted instant access to the head of the facility because she didn't feel important enough.

She did want instant access, because she needed instant access in moments like this. Nonessential personnel had to leave the base, and she couldn't make that call. She needed permission to have some staff help her with the crisis.

And she needed everything done Right Now.

FIFTY-SEVEN

*Q*uint didn't come to see her for two days. At least, she thought it was two days. There was really no way to tell. She counted meals: she had just finished her eighth. She figured that eighth meal was lunch, and the type of food confirmed it: a sandwich with bread she hadn't had since she left the Empire, some kind of fruit she didn't recognize, and a glop of something whitish that smelled like cheese, but she was too uncertain to even eat it.

But she really wasn't certain. The food had been coming at irregular intervals—or so it seemed. She wasn't sure if she believed the intervals were irregular because her time-sense was off, or if they truly were irregular to keep her off-balance.

Maybe both.

Either way, she had just put the food back on the little table that jutted out near her chair, and slapped the wall like the reading device instructed, when Quint entered.

She wasn't quite sure how he did that either. She was surrounded by walls on all four sides. Suddenly he appeared in front of the door—the wall—where she had entered.

He looked less battered. The cuts on his face were no longer red and appeared to be fading. Apparently the surgeon on board this military vessel had enough equipment to work on his injuries. She was a bit surprised the surgeon hadn't removed them altogether.

Maybe Quint had waited too long. Maybe it would take some kind of specialist now.

He was wearing his uniform, but he had left the jacket outside the cell. His brown shirt was open slightly, and his black pants fit perfectly. He looked good, better than she had seen him look in the last six months.

Or maybe she was just that lonely.

"Had time to think?" he asked.

She gave him a tired smile. "You know I have."

"Change your mind?"

Change her mind about what, exactly? She didn't ask. She just sat on that strange chair and watched him.

He stood awkwardly in front of the door. "You're still considered military, you know."

"I resigned," she said.

"And retained your pension. You're retired military."

She sighed softly. She'd read the complaints. She wasn't going to face a civilian court, which might actually have sympathy or consider her a bit impaired because of all the things that had gone wrong since she started working in stealth tech. She would face a military tribunal and be charged with murder, mass murder, and a bunch of minor counts, including destruction of government property.

But the mass murder charge came from the problems at Vallevu, the ones in which she had initially been found not-involved. Because this time, she had opted to blow up a military research station where weapons work was being done (or so Quint had said), the military was revisiting the early charge, changing it.

According to the complaint, she was showing a pattern now, starting with—of all things—Professor Dane's death. Even though she hadn't been in charge of that experiment, just a lowly post-doc. Even though she hadn't been present when things went awry in Vallevu.

The only thing she had done—and granted, that was big enough—was blow up the research station.

And kill Cloris.

"You'll be punished to the full extent of the law," Quint said. "And just your military position will show that you knew what the law was."

She sighed. "I read the complaints."

"Then you know what they're charging you for."

She nodded. "I assume I'll get access to an attorney when we get where we're going."

"That's what I'm here to talk with you about." He looked around the room, as if he was trying to find a place to sit down. His gaze rested on the bed for just a moment, and flicked away. "You get to decide where we're going."

"I do?" she said with a bit of surprise. "I have that much power, do I?"

"If you cooperate," Quint said, "then I can get the mass murder charges dropped."

"So can a good attorney," Squishy said with a bravado she didn't feel.

"Rosealma, please," Quint said in a tone of annoyance. "Take this seriously."

"I am taking it seriously," she said. "I just don't know what you want me to do."

She wasn't asking, not really. She wasn't going to change her mind. She was going to fight some of the charges, but not the ones from this visit to the Empire. She was going to go to prison, and maybe she was going to let them kill her.

But she was curious.

"I know you continued stealth-tech research in the Nine Planets," Quint said. "There's been a lot of rumors about breakthroughs. I believe rumors don't exist without truth behind them. Which means that there have been breakthroughs, and I believe you're behind those breakthroughs, Rose."

She studied him for a moment. He seemed serious. "You have a lot of faith in me."

"You're brilliant, Rose. I've said that all along."

She sighed. "Do you actually think I would have come here if I had a good career under way in the Nine Planets? Why would I throw that all away?"

"Why don't you tell me?" he said. The sentence, sympathetic and warm, would have worked a lot better if he had been able to sit down and make eye contact, instead of shift from foot to foot in front of that nearly invisible door.

"You're making a lot of false assumptions, Quint," she said. "You're assuming I know anything about the Nine Planets. You're assuming that I resumed my research career, abandoning my medical career. You're assuming everything."

"You wouldn't have killed anyone if you were still in medicine, Rose," he said.

"I'm not sure anyone died," Squishy said. "I only have your word for that."

He raised his eyebrows, as if she had startled him.

"Look," he said after a moment. "Here's the choice. We have one final research lab, one your people never found. I'd like to take you there and have you update our experts on stealth tech."

Her stomach knotted. Her face held the same expression it had before—she hoped—but she was so nauseous, she wasn't sure she had held it.

Another lab? She thought she had destroyed everything.

What he said just meant this entire trip was for nothing.

"Or," he was saying, "we take you to a maximum security military prison, and you'll disappear inside with some pretty hard cases until your trial, which will be at least a year away."

She was such a fool. How could she think one woman could demolish all of their research? She should have figured out that they had leaked that information about the deaths to attract her.

Of course, she wasn't that self-involved. That was the biggest issue. She would never have recognized it if someone was targeting her, because she didn't think she was worth targeting.

"Rose," Quint said, his exasperation getting more and more evident. "Just agree to go to the base. Because they're going to get the information out of you anyway, and believe me, it's better for you if you volunteer it."

She frowned. "You're threatening me?"

He shook his head. "I've seen what happens to people who go through the interrogation process. You won't be able to work in medicine or in science afterwards, Rose. You'll be lucky if you remember your name."

The nausea was growing worse. She made herself breathe. Sometimes oxygen shut down the gag reflex.

She had opted for this. She had been warned. And then she had failed to follow through.

"Make the right choice, Rose," he said. "Please."

"That's the thing," she said, more to herself than to him. "I already missed the chance to do that."

FIFTY-EIGHT

TWENTY-ONE YEARS EARLIER

Sixteen of them, sixteen scientists—the best in the Empire—working their asses off. Rosealma coordinated all of them, dividing her own mind into a thousand pieces so that she could think of the implications of stealth-tech science and manage her team all at the same time.

She couldn't look at the missing labs, at the emptiness where people should have been. She made herself focus on the control panels and the screens and the research in front of her, on what was *there*, not on what was missing.

All sixteen scientists were working fast, because they were all afraid that whatever Hansen had unleashed would grow and grow and eventually envelop the station. There was an energy signature that Rosealma didn't recognize buried in the middle of the reaction, something she knew her people hadn't created, and she was afraid that the experiment had morphed into something she didn't recognize.

Sixteen scientists, struggling to contain the reaction. Once they contained it, they would shut it down. But it kept growing, and she was afraid it was going to pulse again.

She had looked at the records. Hansen's description was spot-on. The experiment had pulsed.

But she suspected he was wrong about the reason. He said he had tried the experiment again—and he had. But it looked like her successful cloak, the one she had celebrated the night before he contacted her, had never really ceased. She thought she had shut down the experiment, thought that it was confirmed by the reappearance of that coin. Hansen was right: the coin *was* different. But he was also wrong: the coin was the same. It was older, and it shouldn't have been. If she had to guess—and hell, that was all she was doing these days, she was *guessing*—then she would guess that the coin hadn't been cloaked at all, but it had moved forward, then backward in time. When she had shut down the experiment, or moved to shut down the experiment, or initiated the shut-down that she thought would turn off the damn cloak, she had brought the coin back to its starting point.

The coin had experienced time differently than she had, and that alarmed her.

It also gave her hope. Because if she could move a coin forward, then backward in time, maybe she could move people forward, then backward in time. She might be able to recover the folks who had gotten lost.

"Might" being an operative word.

And she tried not to think about all the pitfalls, including the most important one: coins were immobile by nature; people were not. So if all of those people got moved to a different time period or they experienced time differently (more rapidly?), then they had probably moved away from the experiment area. They wouldn't all be in that area when the experiment got shut down.

She proposed that solution to her team and no one argued with her. The key was to shut down the experiment—all the way down—because her fear (their fear) was that it would grow and create some kind of rift or keep growing, even after it had consumed the station itself.

Somewhere in the middle of all this chaos, while she was thinking of a thousand different things, and trying to concentrate on each one of them, Quint came into the lab and scared her to death.

"What the hell are you doing here?" she asked, blocking him with her body.

He lifted bags that he had been holding in both hands. The bags smelled of garlic and fresh bread. "Bringing food."

"Get out," she said. "You can't stay."

"I can do whatever I want, Rosealma," he said gently. "I outrank you."

"It's dangerous here," she said. "I want you gone."

He gave her a small smile, then set the bags on a chair. He knew better than to set them on any tabletop, near any experiment at all. The scents grew stronger, mixing with the smell of cooked beef and thyme. Rosealma's stomach growled, and she realized she was lightheaded.

"How long has it been?" she asked him softly.

"Twenty hours," he said, and pulled her toward him. He held her tightly, and she tried not to squirm away.

He had always worried about her, always told her not to let the dangers of her job ruin their lives. He meant let the dangers of her job ruin his life—he was afraid she would be the one who died, just like her professor had. Quint had probably come in here just to make sure she wasn't taking unnecessary risks.

"I'm supposed to tell you," he said so quietly she could barely hear him, "that you have another twenty hours. At that point, you and your team will have to leave."

"We're not leaving until we solve this," she said.

He shook his head. "It's not your decision."

"We can't just leave this," she said. "It's dangerous. We think it's expanding."

She wasn't supposed to tell him any of this, but she figured it didn't matter. Clearance was a minor issue. Besides, he was probably reporting to the head of the station. And maybe even to the military's science commander himself.

"I know," Quint said, his voice still low. "That's what some of the others are saying."

"Then you understand why we can't leave it," she said.

"It might expand you out of existence," he said.

She nodded. "Or expand this part of space out of existence or maybe even part of the planet. We don't know, Quint."

"It doesn't matter," he said. "They're removing you all in twenty hours, whether you've solved this or not."

"And they're going to let the expansion happen?" she asked. "They're going to leave this disaster untouched?"

"They're going to blow it up," he said.

She pulled away from him. "They can't do that. It might expand the problem. It might make this thing grow faster. We just don't know. You have to tell them to leave me alone."

"I'll do my best, Rose," he said, "but I'm not in charge any more than you are."

"But it's stupid—"

"I know," he said, then kissed her. The kiss felt good. It brought her to herself momentarily, like the smell of food had. She had almost forgotten how to be alive, because she had been so busy thinking.

He clung to her for a moment, then eased back just enough so that he could see her face.

"Promise me you'll leave when the time comes," he said.

"I can't promise that," she said.

"You'll die otherwise."

"We'll stay until we finish this," she said. "You tell them that."

"I already have," he said, his voice wobbling just a bit. "And they said that doesn't matter. They're destroying the base in a little over twenty hours. With you on it or not."

She looked at him. "You'd let them do that?"

"I don't have a choice," he said. "They didn't want me to come in now. They didn't want me to warn you. I got permission for that. I might not get permission to pull you out. I'll try, Rose, but I can't guarantee anything."

"Neither can I," she said, and turned her back on him.

FIFTY-NINE

*E*ight more meals later, the door opened again. This time, four guards entered. They told Squishy to extend her arms so that she could be cuffed, and then they put something on her feet as well so that she could only shuffle instead of walk.

As if she was a dangerous prisoner.

As if they were frightened of her.

They probably were. After all, she was a mass murderer, at least in the eyes of the Empire.

The guards wore full gear including helmets. The battle gear seemed more intimidating in her cell, probably because the guards took up so much room.

She knew one of the guards was male, because he was the one who curtly gave her orders—*Extend your hands, Keep your face forward, Do not move*—but she couldn't tell the gender of the others. They were all taller than her, or at least they seemed that way, maybe because their boots gave them extra height. Just like the armor gave them extra width, making them seem like they had planet-bound muscles.

They led her—shuffling—into the main brig area, which looked bigger now than it had when they first brought her in. If that was the result of a few days of captivity, she had no idea what would happen after years.

Of course, if they put her in a real prison, she would never get out again.

She kept her head forward, not bowed like she had seen so many other prisoners do. She wondered what kind of prison they had brought her to. Some were "easy" prisons, for celebrities and people charged with crimes without violence. She was probably going somewhere high security, for people who murdered and set off bombs and used violence to make their point. Dangerous people.

People like her.

She hadn't seen Quint since that afternoon (if, indeed, it was an afternoon), and he didn't show up now. Just the silent guards backtracking the route they had taken her days ago, heading to one of the military vessel's airlocks and exits.

Her heart was pounding—of course it was; she was terrified—but she tried to keep her breathing under control. She was sweating, and she realized for the first time that she hadn't had a shower or a change of clothing in days.

They could probably smell how frightened she was.

They took her down a couple of levels. The trip to the airlock was longer just because she shuffled. She felt old and fragile and very small, probably like she was supposed to. She also felt helpless.

When they got close to the airlock, they veered toward another part of the ship, and she almost corrected them. She bit back her comment, let them continue to take charge.

They brought her to an empty wing of the ship, then pushed her into a gigantic locker area. A woman she had never seen before stood there.

She had clothes over her arm.

"You're to shower," she said, "and then put these on."

The clothes didn't look like a prison uniform. They looked like regular clothing. But she had only seen prison uniforms in news footage and entertainments. She didn't know if such uniforms actually existed or if they were the stuff of fiction.

She waited while the guards removed the thing around her feet and hands. They turned so she could take her clothes off. But the woman didn't.

"It's a sonic shower," the woman said, as if she'd had this conversation before and it exhausted her.

Squishy nodded, then walked toward the shower. She was happy to see it. She felt heavy with filth from her ordeal.

She stepped into the shower, and realized she would miss all the amenities of her life.

That was what prison was for; to make the person understand what she had given up to commit her crime.

Sonic showers were not worth lingering in, although this one did leave her feeling cleaner than she had in days.

The woman actually helped her dress, and Squishy wasn't embarrassed by this. She was already becoming accustomed to the lack of privacy.

The clothing was loose, probably to accommodate the various latches and leashes the military had to attach to her.

They reattached the things to her, but not as tightly. She could actually take steps instead of shuffle. The guards did tighten her cuffs, though, holding her hands together in front of her.

She didn't want to leave the ship. Not because she had grown attached to it, but because she wasn't sure when she would ever be on a ship again. All of her life, she had never stayed in the same place longer than a few years. Even places she had stayed for those years had allowed her to travel, to get away, to be private.

And even though she had been alone these last few days, she certainly hadn't been private.

The guards took her down the expected corridor now, to the airlock. She wasn't even sure if it was the same guards, since no one spoke, and there was nothing about those uniforms that distinguished them.

They got to the airlock, and one of the guards stepped forward, putting some command into the keypad. The airlock door slid open, revealing an airlock the size of the *Dane*'s cockpit.

This wasn't the airlock she had entered. She was turned around, or maybe all of the corridors on this ship looked the same.

The airlock was large enough for all of them—guards and prisoner—to get into together. Two guards flanked her and two followed.

She couldn't escape if she wanted to.

Her stomach tightened, and she wished she hadn't eaten that crappy breakfast—if indeed it was breakfast. (According to her mental schedule, it should have been, but she had gotten another sandwich and that weird fruit.)

She tried not to be too melodramatic inside her own head, almost smiling at herself for using the term, but she couldn't help it. She was stepping into a prison, and she was about to leave the life she had known forever.

She was entitled to feel bad about that, right? Even if she deserved it.

The main door opened, and she frowned.

She certainly didn't expect the docking bay of a prison to look like the docking bay at the research station she had so recently blown up.

"I'll take her from here," Quint said to the guards.

He was standing off to the side, in his security uniform, the one he had worn at the research station—or one just like it. Several security guards stood next to him, not in battle armor, but in standard security uniforms with laser pistols on their hips.

Squishy's head suddenly hurt. She had destroyed that research station. She had seen it explode. It was gone, and there was no way he could have rigged her ship to show that without it happening.

So she had to be somewhere else.

That other research station he mentioned?

If that was the case, then how had she ended up here? She hadn't made those promises he wanted. She had decided not to talk. She was willing—well, "willing" was the wrong word; "braced" was probably better—to suffer those interrogations.

"Come on, Rose," Quint said, extending his hand.

She couldn't take it even if she wanted to, which she did not.

"I didn't agree to anything," she said to him.

"Not yet," he said. "You will. Trust me."

She didn't trust him. But that didn't matter. She wasn't in a prison, yet. She would be after this little interlude, but every day away from total confinement was a gift.

She walked toward him, the restraints on her legs tugging at her skin and nearly tripping her.

"Does she need those?" he asked, looking down.

"It's better, sir," said the guard beside her. Male. A voice she recognized. So that was the same group of guards.

"Unhook her," Quint said.

"Beg pardon, sir, but she could kill you with those feet."

Squishy raised her eyebrows. She had no idea how to kill anyone with her feet. She wasn't even sure how to do it hand-to-hand, except maybe in theory, and the theory came from a medical, healing perspective.

"She won't try to kill me," Quint said.

"She did once, sir."

Quint smiled just a little and shook his head. "If she had wanted to kill me that day, she had plenty of opportunity. She didn't. Take those off."

"Sir, I'll have to make a note of this in the file. That we're setting her legs free on your orders."

"Fine," Quint said, and watched as one of the guards bent down to loosen the restraints.

Squishy felt an urge to kick him, just because he had given her the idea. She would kick the guard, use her slightly mobile hands to grab a nearby laser pistol, then kill everyone in sight. She would flee into the station . . . and what? Get captured again?

It wasn't even a worthwhile fantasy.

The guard unhooked her legs, but her skin ached where the restraints had been.

"Come on, Rosealma," Quint said again.

"Where are we going?" she asked.

"To meet a man who knows how to ask the right questions," Quint said. "And maybe you'll feel comfortable enough with him to give him the right answers."

Squishy didn't believe there were right answers. Not anymore. But she followed Quint anyway.

Because she had no other choice.

SIXTY

Sixteen hours after Quint brought food, Rosealma managed to shut down the experiment. It had taken all kinds of finagling. She thought she had shut it down six hours before, but she hadn't. Testing and retesting and even more testing showed her something was still pulsing.

She had to go back to the earliest experiments to figure out how to turn the damn thing off. She had to go back to that afternoon when they lost Professor Dane in one of the simplest stealth-tech experiments ever done.

Rosealma—a post-doc—had been the one to finally shut down that experiment, and she was the one who shut down this one.

And if someone asked her to explain exactly how she did it, she wouldn't be able to do so. Normally she had a very orderly mind, but not this afternoon or evening or whenever the hell it had become. Her expanded mind felt like it was becoming part of the stealth tech, like it was stretching into a variety of dimensions, and that was when she realized what the pulses were—an attempt to reach those dimensions.

She had been trying to shut down a cloak, and that hadn't worked. But when she shut down the device that could reach outside of this dimension—when she had actually looked at the experiment as something that crossed both space and time—she was able to deactivate it.

She still wasn't sure she had shut it all down—she wasn't sure they could shut it down. Not after what they had done. But she had disabled it or made it inactive, at least for the time being.

Then she had sent the others out, asked for a meeting with the head of the base via vid conference, and told him that this device, this cloak that her people had created, needed to be put somewhere far away from human beings, from any possibility of human beings ever traveling through, and certainly not any place where those human beings would colonize.

He said he understood. He said the military would find such a place. She gave instructions for transport, made him swear that he wouldn't destroy the base with the device in it—explaining, once again, the disaster—and then she left it to him.

She evacuated like everyone else had, and trusted the military to take care of it.

Only later did she realize that they had followed part of her instruction, but not all of it.

They had taken the device away before destroying the military base. They blew up the base, but first they made sure that no stealth tech was on board.

And they hadn't abandoned the experiments at all.

Instead, they moved the experiments to an even more remote site, did not let the scientists working on them have their families anywhere nearby, and made everyone who worked around stealth tech sign waivers in case of "accidental death or disappearance."

But Rosealma didn't find out about that for a year. She was too busy, testifying at the various courts-martial and being investigated herself for some kind of negligence.

Eventually, she was cleared, and then she was offered a new job: director of Stealth-Tech Research.

And that made her furious—so furious she had screamed at them as she said no.

But she did say no.

And somehow she managed to secure a retirement, and a pension. And an honorable discharge.

Somehow.

Whether she wanted them or not.

SIXTY-ONE

The layout of this research station was exactly the same as the layout of the research station Squishy had blown up. Quint was leading her through corridors that looked almost the same as the corridors on the station she had destroyed. The wall color was different, the floor a bit more scuffed.

This station was older, and had been in use longer.

And that made her furious. All of that work, all of that deception, for nothing.

She hoped the rest of her team had survived, because if they hadn't, they had died in vain.

As they walked, she didn't ask any questions. She didn't need to. She knew where they were going.

Quint was leading her to the heart of the administrative wing, which surprised her, although on second thought, he couldn't really lead her anywhere else. There wasn't a brig on a research station, no place to hold prisoners, no place to put heretical reluctant scientists whose research somehow did not measure up.

They arrived at one of the offices, bigger than hers had been on the other station. Those 360-degree views along with an open ceiling that looked at the stars. Apparently whoever had this office didn't mind being viewed from the upper rings.

He led her inside. The décor was also open, all hard edges and black lines. Even the couches were more bench than a comfortable upholstered place to sit.

Still, Quint put her on one of those couches, facing a black laminated desk so shiny that she could see the reflection of the rings above.

"Wait here," he said, and went to the desk. Then, before he touched the in-house com system, he looked over his shoulder at her. "Cooperate, okay?"

"With what?" Squishy asked.

"Please," he said. "I'm trying to save your life."

She knew that. She didn't understand it, but she knew it. And she didn't want to tell him that she didn't care about her life. She didn't care enough about it to end it, and she certainly didn't care enough about it to save it.

But she didn't say that because it would be melodramatic, and she was done with melodrama, at least for now.

He touched the desk, said, "She's here," and then took his hand off the surface. Then he walked to the door, as if he expected her to bolt.

She wasn't going to bolt. She probably wasn't going to cooperate either, but she wasn't going to bolt.

She waited. After a while, Quint smiled at someone in the hallway. Quint's phony smile, the one that he put on to be polite.

A man came into the room. He was tall, planet-born, with strong bones and sharp features. He was older and had never bothered with enhancements. His face was lined, but in a pleasant way, adding depth to his features rather than making him look like his bones had shrunk.

He had white, white hair and bushy white eyebrows, and he somehow looked familiar, although Squishy knew she had never seen him before.

"Rosealma Quintana," he said as he came toward her, hand extended. "I have heard so much about you."

She glanced over at Quint. "I'm sure you have," she said dryly.

Then she raised her cuffed hands so that the man could see that she couldn't shake his hand.

He turned to Quint. "Take those off her."

"I don't think so," he said. "She's tricky."

"She cannot do anything here," the man said.

"She destroyed an entire station," Quint said.

"And a science vessel, if I'm not mistaken," the man said with a bit of admiration. "And maybe a few other things. But that took planning and some small bombs. I trust you've searched her for weaponry?"

So that was what the shower had been about. Not just to make her presentable, but to make sure she had nothing else on her person. A sonic shower was best, because even if she had managed to squirrel away a small bomb, it would have gone off inside her as the sound vibrated through her. Tricky.

She now wondered if those showers had been reinforced to handle a blast. Probably. The imperial military didn't trust anyone.

But it seemed this man did. He waved a hand toward her, giving Quint a silent command to set her free.

She had no idea how she could get away, but she wished she could, just to prove this man wrong.

Quint's mouth thinned, and he sighed in exasperation. Then he came over to Squishy, grabbed her hands, and unhooked the cuffs.

"Try anything and I will shoot you," he said softly.

"I thought you were trying to save my life," she said.

"I didn't say I would kill you," he snapped. "I just said I would shoot you. And believe me, I'd make sure it hurt."

She believed him.

He stepped away, returning to the door. He pulled it shut, then stood with his back to the wall, so that he faced her.

The man watched with undisguised amusement.

"So Rosealma Quintana," the man said, "your husband fears you."

"Ex-husband," she said.

The man shrugged. "Relationships are supposed to be forever, aren't they?"

"Some relationships," she said. "Not this one."

The man raised his eyebrows in mock surprise, then looked at Quint to see if the barb had hit. Quint hadn't moved.

"You've angered the lady," the man said.

"Years ago," Quint said flatly. The tone sounded dismissive, almost an order to get on with things.

The man nodded. "I'm amazed, Rosealma—may I call you Rosealma?"

He didn't wait for her to answer, not that she would have answered. She had no idea what people should call her now.

"I'm amazed that you and I have never met before. You, the godmother of stealth tech, and me, the man who has brought it into a new era."

She watched him. She had no idea who he was.

"You did almost kill me, you know."

She almost said, *So you were on the base?* but she caught herself just in time. She knew better than to admit to anything.

"Your bombs are quite efficient," he said. "I'm as impressed by them as I am by the way that you completely revamped stealth-tech research twenty years ago."

"I had stopped researching twenty years ago," she said.

"You know what I mean," he said. "You completely changed the direction of the research, made us all see things we had never seen before. We were happy when you came back to us, before we realized it was a ruse."

"What do you want from me?" Squishy asked.

"Your brain, primarily," the man said. "It's a marvelous brain, capable of thinking in multidimensions, conquering a part of science the rest of us can't fathom. I'd like to turn you away from the darkness that has been holding you and get you to help us."

"Why would I do that?" Squishy asked.

"Enlightened self-interest," he said. "You're about to go to prison. Once you lose your court case—which you will, because we have footage of you setting the bombs on that base—you will be subjected to the worst kind of hell. I doubt that marvelous brain of yours will survive intact."

"That's what Quint tells me," she said. "But that could all be a lie to get me to do what you people want."

"It could be," the man said. "What an interesting risk you would be taking if it was. You'd risk everything—your intelligence, your personality, your freedom—because you believe we might lie."

"You have no guarantee that anything I told you would work," Squishy said. "I could lie to you about the things I've discovered in stealth tech."

"You could," the man said, "but you wouldn't. Because you would soon realize that we have other gifted scientists here who would figure out if you took us in the wrong direction."

She smiled just a little. "Like the gifted scientists did in Vallevu."

"Are you saying you sent them in the wrong direction?"

"Not deliberately," Squishy said. "But the research you're doing is dangerous. You're messing with things you don't understand."

"And you do?" His question had a sharper edge than she expected. He had finally gotten to the part of the conversation that interested him.

"I understand the dangers," she said. "Of course, I have a non-imperial attitude."

She looked at Quint before continuing.

"I believe that all lives have value. I don't believe any lives should be sacrificed for the greater good."

Quint glared at her, but the man was the one who answered her.

"What about your life, Rosealma? If you don't cooperate, aren't you sacrificing your own life for the greater good?"

"What good would that be?" she asked.

"You might be one of those true-believer rebels who thinks that the Empire is evil, and that you must keep all things from us at all cost."

"You're assuming I have something to keep from you," she said. "Look at my history. I quit the military, stopped doing research, and got a medical license."

"And then came back to us six months ago," he said.

"To stop the deaths," she said. "Your experiments kill people."

"Sometimes," the man said. "But the occasional life is a worthy sacrifice if it saves other lives."

"If I believed that," Squishy said, "I would never have become a doctor."

He studied her. "You're an intriguing woman, Rosealma. Does my daughter find you that way as well?"

Squishy frowned, confused. "Your daughter?"

"I believe you call her Boss."

Squishy blurted, "Boss said you were dead."

"In that science vessel?" he asked. "I thought she saw the bridge detach."

Then he glanced at Quint, as if Quint had been there. For all Squishy knew, Quint had.

"Boss probably figured I tried to save my experiment. I saved the research and have since replicated it. I didn't need to risk my life to save something I could repeat."

"She said—." Squishy stopped herself. She wasn't going to argue this. It might implicate her. But Boss had reported he stayed to save that tiny bottle of budding stealth tech. She said she had watched the science vessel, with him still on board, explode.

"She said what?" he asked.

Squishy shook her head. *She said you're evil. She said you have no soul. She said the universe was better without you.*

He smiled just a little. "My daughter and I have never gotten along. She blames me for her mother's death."

Yes, she had told Squishy that.

"She never tells people the actual truth," he said. "I'm the one who saved her life."

Actually, she did tell people that, but she made it sound self-serving. She said it was because he had tested her the only way he had known how, before they knew exactly how to find the marker for working inside stealth tech. He had put her in a stealth-tech field along with her mother. Her mother had died. Boss had not.

She had been four years old.

"I can see we're going to have to have a few discussions before you'll trust me," he said. "We only have your best interests at heart."

It was her turn to smile. "Forgive me, sir," she said. "But it's clear you've never had anyone's best interests at heart except your own."

"And the Empire's," he said without disagreeing with her. "You need to realize we have the same goal. We want people to stop dying in stealth-tech experiments. We're not going to stop the experimentation. So the best way to save lives, my dear Rosealma, is to help me. Tell me what you know. You'll save lives. I guarantee it."

The hell of it was he was right. She would save lives—at least in the short term. But probably start a war in the long term.

And she knew his answer to that as well. It was something she would have said years ago, something that Professor Dane had said in one of his early classes:

Scientists cannot control how the knowledge they discover is used. They can only search for truth and hope that others will show some restraint.

But throughout human history, people did not show restraint. She hadn't shown restraint either.

"I'm not going to work with you," Squishy said—but her voice wavered just a little, and she wondered if, deep down, she really meant it.

THE EMPIRE

SIXTY-TWO

We take two Dignity Vessels into the Empire, even though we don't have enough people to man both ships. The first ship is, of course, the *Ivoire*, with Coop in command. The second is one we found almost intact and have managed to rebuild with the help of Coop's engineers. We have named it the *Shadow*. It's my ship at the moment, although I will probably give it to Coop for his trip to the Boneyard. I have a third fully functional Dignity Vessel still at Lost Souls, and that's the one I plan to keep for myself.

Coop's original second officer, Lynda Rooney, commands the *Shadow*. With Pompiono's suicide, she had become Coop's first officer, but Coop has always said she needed her own ship.

This is her chance, and she doesn't complain.

Even though both ships are terribly short staffed, Coop wants them for possible rescue efforts should our commando raid (as he calls it) go wrong. He also wants both ships for the increased firepower.

He said that in the meeting we had with everyone who would lead this mission, mostly his people, and then he looked at me. The increased firepower thing was supposed to get me to change my mind.

I know he plans to obliterate that station. I also know he expects me to protest that. I have no idea why he thinks I would, when I'm against the Empire having stealth tech in the first place.

Of course, he wasn't around when I blew up one of the Empire's science labs.

Each ship has a skeleton crew of one hundred people who will man the support systems and maintain the equipment—all doing jobs I don't entirely understand. Fifty of my people are training with them on each ship, mostly observing.

Then each ship has thirty purely military assault teams. I wanted more people, but Coop says a mission like this needs to surprise and overwhelm, but not cause friendly fire casualties.

I didn't even know that last part was an option.

I'm on Coop's ship, but have no command duties. I have a seat to the side of the bridge so that I can watch everything as we travel. The bridge amazes me. The first time I was on a Dignity Vessel bridge, I was diving it. It was a mess of debris and it seemed smaller than this bridge, even though I know it wasn't.

This bridge is huge. It has equipment on all sides and in the center, along with Coop's massive command chair. Screens cover the walls. The screens are off when we're in foldspace, making the walls black.

Coop has his full bridge crew complement on this mission. It's his usual team, except that he has promoted someone I don't know—Mavis Kravchenko—to first officer. She's a big woman, landborn, with flaming red hair and a brash manner. It seems odd to see her in Pompiono's spot on the far side of the bridge, and as I have that thought, I realize I have only ridden on the *Ivoire* when Pompiono was alive.

It's been three years, then. Three years since I've actually flown inside Coop's Dignity Vessel. And we're not going to spend a lot of time here, or at least, I'm not.

I have insisted that I get to go with the teams when they invade the research station.

Coop doesn't like that. Not even he gets to go to the research station. He stays on board and runs the entire operation.

But my trip down there is the only condition I made when Coop said he would command this mission. I made it sound like I was protesting his decision, but I had secretly hoped he would take charge.

I have no military experience. I don't have a military brain. I know this is a military mission, and I know that on my own I would have botched it up horribly.

As we head out, I am relieved that Coop will take this mission, and I am terrified. I have never done anything of this magnitude before.

We have the map to the facility that Turtle gave us, and the map *of* the facility. Coop doesn't trust it, but I do. I've done some work on Turtle's recent past in the time since we started designing this mission, and I realize she has become someone powerful, someone who lives on the fringes, someone who believes that complete access to information is the only way to freedom.

She works in the shadows; perhaps that's why I named the second Dignity Vessel *Shadow*. After Turtle.

It was a way of bringing her on this mission. Because even though I trust her map, I don't entirely trust her. Not anymore. Too many years have gotten between us, too much life.

Besides, I actually have things to protect now. People to protect.

Coop said he didn't want Turtle along, and I let him think he won that battle. But I had made the decision long before he spoke up.

Our trip into the Empire is short. It doesn't even feel like a trip. It feels like we close our eyes and then we arrive.

Foldspace is a miraculous thing. First we are at Lost Souls, and then we are at the research station—so top secret that even its name is classified.

It sprawls like so many imperial space stations do. It has wings upon wings, rings along some of them. It's got several levels, and some of them appear to be detachable.

As we look at it on our screens, Coop says to me—softly— "Last chance."

He's asking me to abort.

"See if she's there," I say.

He scans. Or rather, orders his chief linguist Kjersti Perkins to scan. She nods.

Squishy is on board. The *Ivoire* has found her personal signature and knows exactly where she is.

"We're not aborting," I say. "We're going to rescue Squishy, and we're going to do it now."

SIXTY-THREE

The station has three different landing bays and two emergency bays. We're going to take transport to all of them while fighters provide cover.

I'm heading to join my battle team when Coop says, "Wait."

I stop, turn, and look at the screen in front of me. In addition to a bunch of science vessels docked on one of the bays, there's a military vessel. I don't know the class—the Empire has changed class names since I stopped diving—but it's one of the military flagships. Something important.

"Is that what I think it is?" Coop asks, but I can't tell if he's asking me.

"It has fifteen different weapons systems," says Anita Tren. She's Coop's tiniest officer, who usually sits on a very high chair just so that she see everything. Right now she's standing, the chair pushed against her back.

"Not to mention a variety of missiles, fighters, transports, and God knows what kind of weaponry inside," Yash says from her position down front.

"It also seems to have a full crew," says Kravchenko.

"They're probably noticing us right now," Coop says. "We can leave before this gets messy."

I swallow against a dry throat. "What's messy?"

"We were prepared for a well-guarded science station that has no exterior defensive capability," Coop says. "We weren't prepared to meet a battleship."

I don't know how these things work. "Meaning?"

"Meaning we take it out now, before you go in."

I stiffen. "With the full crew on board?"

"Yes, ma'am," he says. He never calls me "ma'am" and I realize he's in full captain mode.

"Are there other options?" I ask.

"We try limited strikes, but I don't know what we're up against here," Coop says. "That might not be effective."

"Won't a full shot on the vessel destroy the landing bay?" I ask. "Won't it hurt the station?"

"We're here to destroy the station," Coop says. "It either begins now, or we abort."

I swallow. What I was about to do was only a theory before. Now it's reality.

"Attacking that vessel is an act of war," Coop says, reminding me of our earlier conversation.

"So's attacking the station," I say, and to my surprise, my voice doesn't shake. "We're not going to abort. Do what you need to, Captain."

And with that, I leave the bridge.

SIXTY-FOUR

I don't see the results of the explosion until we're in transit. I'm in a military transport vehicle along with five other people. Our ship is protected by fighters. We're heading to one of the emergency bays.

The transport vehicle is open—just a long box. I can easily see into the cockpit and see what the pilot sees.

She sees red and orange and white light everywhere, light filled with debris. She occasionally has to steer around pieces that come flying out at her. The shields take care of the rest.

That military vessel was big, bigger than I expected. At least I'm not seeing body parts in the wreckage—or at least, if I am, I don't recognize them.

I look away.

I clasp my hands in my lap and make myself take a deep breath. I'm wearing black body armor, which feels so much bulkier than my environmental suit. The armor will act like an environmental suit, but it will also protect me from weapons' fire.

Yash says our weapons are much more primitive than any she's seen, that this body armor is built for shots that would completely destroy the body armor the Empire wears. She says the laser pistol I'm carrying now—one based on the Fleet's design—has more firing power than the laser rifle I had hidden under my cockpit in the *Business*.

I don't just have a laser pistol. I have Karl's knife, although it's under my armor, more as a talisman than anything else, a reminder of all that can go wrong with out-of-control stealth tech. I also have a laser rifle strapped to my back.

I feel like a soldier, even though I'm not one. I wear a white helmet to distinguish me from everyone else, so that no one is surprised if I don't follow a military order to the letter.

Rossetti is in charge of this mission. She sits across from me, looking serene. Apparently, she's led a dozen missions. She's handpicked this team, and I recognize two of them from our early meetings back in Sector Base V— Adam Shärf, who seems like a good young officer despite his eagerness, and Salvador Ahidjo, who is Shärf's opposite in most things, a calm older man who seems like he's seen everything. The other two—Edith Fennimore and Idina Winsor—I know mostly as muscle. They're both exceptionally strong, and when I see them (usually together) they're firing weapons or doing some other kind of training.

Having them on the team reassures me more than I can say.

I know that I'm the wild card here, and we've all tried to plan for that. I thought I might inadvertently give orders, but now that I'm sitting here, gloved hands clutched together, I'm worried more about how tense I am.

Underneath, I'm terrified.

Fortunately (I tell myself) we're the extraction team. Our job is to go in, get Squishy, and leave. If we don't succeed, there's another extraction team coming from the *Shadow*, only it arrives a few minutes later.

We dock on the emergency bay. I have no idea how the transport opened the bay doors, but it did—or maybe someone did from the *Ivoire*, or maybe someone shot it out ahead of us.

At this point, I'm along for the ride.

"You have full environment," the pilot says, which means we don't have to activate the environmental part of our body armor. When we put the suits on, Rossetti told me not to use the environmental part of the armor unless I had to.

It's the worst part of the suit, she said.

I believe her.

Still, I adjust my helmet, and follow Ahidjo and Shärf down that ramp. Rossetti is beside me, and Fennimore and Winsor follow her.

They have their weapons out. I'm clutching my laser pistol too tightly.

I can almost hear Squishy in my head, warning me of the gids.

Thank God I don't have on my environmental suit. Thank God I'm not relying on oxygen. Because I would be hyperventilating. I would be having the gids.

I'm out of my element, and I think that's truly become clear for the very first time.

SIXTY-FIVE

The bay is smaller than any we have anywhere in Lost Souls. This place truly is for medical or emergency access only. Maybe six medium-size ships can function here, with its low ceiling and its narrow landing docks.

Doors in front of us burst open and people pour in, most wearing uniforms that I don't recognize. Security guards? Military personnel in a newer uniform? I can't tell and it doesn't matter.

Shärf and Ahidjo shoot them as they appear. The weapons are as powerful as Yash said; the guards (if that's what they are) fall backward or tumble sideways or simply collapse, and not a one of them even utters a sound.

I'm shaking now. I've shot at people myself, but I have never done so like this. They've always shot first.

We rush past them—over them, really—and into a corridor. On the faceplate of my helmet, the map of the station appears, the path we're to take to Squishy outlined in red.

She appears as a tiny blue dot. Theoretically, the scanners on our suits can read her as easily as the *Ivoire* can.

I hope so.

We run up a ramp and then veer to the left. The corridors are wide, allowing us to remain two abreast. There are doors on all sides, big doors.

Everything matches Turtle's map, and somewhere inside, I'm relieved at that. Because we would be fucked if it didn't, no matter how much firepower the Dignity Vessels have.

We keep up a good pace, and I'm already getting winded. I'm not made for exercise like this in full gravity, particularly when I'm wearing extra weight. Sweat pours down my face, and I struggle to keep up.

As we round corners, Shärf and Ahidjo shoot whenever someone appears or opens a door. When it becomes clear that they've shot a few civilians, Rossetti starts yelling, "Stay back! Stay back!"

I'm not sure why she's doing this, particularly when we're going to blow the base, but I'm not going to question it. I run, hoping that I can make it the entire distance of this map without passing out.

Damn gids. I have to remind myself to breathe.

Once I do that, I'm breathing too hard, deep gulping breaths that actually hurt.

I glance over my shoulder. Fennimore and Winsor are running backward, shooting guards as they approach us. I make myself focus on the running backward, not the shooting. Because if I think about how in shape Fennimore and Winsor are and how out of shape I am, at least for this kind of thing, then I'm not thinking about all the people dying around me.

People dying because I didn't abort.

It's one thing to have an abstract mission, particularly one you believe in.

It's another to see the mission happen around you, to understand that the loss of life you agreed to in theory actually meant that people—people you didn't know and would never know—die.

We go up another ramp and this time veer to the left. The administrative wing, or so it said on the original map. Squishy's not being held in a cell; she's in some kind of office, which confuses me.

But we run to it, and when we reach it, Shärf and Ahidjo slaughter two guards in full body armor. I recognize that armor: imperial military. Only the shots go through the armor as if they're not wearing anything at all.

They slump against the wall.

Shärf turns toward Rossetti, one hand on the door.

She nods.

And we go in.

SIXTY-SIX

*T*he room is huge. It seems even bigger because of its expansive views. The other rings are visible above us as well as in front of us. Through one set of similar windows, I can see laser weapons' fire.

There are several different seating areas, and a large desk. I only make out three people: a man with tiny marks all over his face, Squishy who looks thinner than I expect, and my father.

My breath catches. That can't be my father. He died years ago in the explosion of that science lab ship. Although the cockpit did detach and fly away.

I thought he was too far away to get there, too invested in saving his experiment to try.

I should never have underestimated his powers of survival.

Squishy looks terrified, and I realize she has no idea who we are. No one does.

I pull off my helmet with my left hand. My right still clutches my laser pistol. My laser rifle remains lashed across my back. I haven't used the damn thing, and I won't unless I'm cornered.

"Squishy," I say. "Get over here."

Her mouth drops open. "I told you not to come."

"My daughter doesn't listen to anyone," my father says.

I am suddenly furious. Furious that this man survived all these years. Furious that he's standing here, with Squishy. Proof that he's taking more lives with his damn stealth-tech experiments.

I have never hated anyone before.

I hate him.

But I'm not going to let him bait me. I'll deal with him in a moment. After Squishy is secure. I keep my gaze on hers.

"Squishy, come over here now," I say.

She stands.

The man with the marks on his face watches everything. "This is the famous Boss?" he asks.

No one answers him. Squishy walks toward me. She stops beside me.

"I told you not to come," she says.

"My father's right on this one point," I say as I move her beside me. "I make my own decisions."

"I don't know if I should applaud your independence or take you to task for the lives you've cost today," my father says.

He looks no older, as if time can't touch him. His white hair is just as thick, his face just as lined.

"You have no right to take me to task for costing lives," I say. "You've cost hundreds, maybe thousands, starting with my mother."

"You have no reason to be sanctimonious," my father says. "You don't understand how important my work is."

I raise my laser pistol. I've had enough of him. He deliberately watched as dozens of people died in his "tests" at the Room of Lost Souls. He murdered my mother for his work; he murdered Karl.

My father smirks at me. He looks at the laser pistol as if it means nothing. I suppose it does mean nothing to him. After all, he hasn't died while people all around him have died in explosions, in stealth tech, in his own damn experiments.

"Move," I say quietly to Shärf.

He does, and without a second thought, I shoot.

The shot hits my father squarely. He vibrates for a moment, his entire torso turning red. Then he collapses.

His body sprawls on the floor, his eyes open. He's dead.

Finally, my father is dead.

And I am relieved.

The man with the marks on his face steps forward. "You bitch!" he says, sounding shocked.

I turn. He has a laser pistol.

He shoots—

And at that same moment, someone shoves me sideways. I tumble into Winsor, who stumbles as well. There's a grunt, and a thud.

The man looks startled, but only for a moment.

Because Rossetti shoots him. He slams into the wall, and then down. He has no armor at all. He's dead before he hits the floor.

Rossetti turns toward me, and I get the sense she's glaring, even though I can't see her eyes.

"This is exactly why you don't bring civilians on military missions," she says.

I don't know what she means until I stand.

Then I see who shoved me out of the way. Who took the shot intended for me.

Squishy.

She's lying there, and not moving, her body twisted wrong.

"No," I say, crouching beside her. "Please. No."

SIXTY-SEVEN

I pick Squishy up and carry her out of the room, even though I'm exhausted, even though I stagger under her weight. Shärf tries to take her from me, but I won't let him.

We don't run. We walk. I don't see any more guards—at least, not standing.

As we head down the corridor, Rossetti hits a wall panel, starting the mass evacuation just like we planned. Supposedly—and I hope she checked, but I'm no longer wearing my helmet so I can't hear—we have people stationed at the exits now, people who will prevent the residents of the science station from carrying their research with them as they leave.

Suddenly sirens blare overhead: *Emergency evacuation under way. Proceed to your designated evac area. If that evac area is sealed off, proceed to your secondary evac area. Do not finish your work. Do not bring your work. Once life tags move out of an area, that area will seal off. If sealed inside, no one will rescue you. Do not double back. Go directly to your designated evac area. The station will shut down entirely in . . . sixty . . . minutes.*

Some of that probably isn't true. I doubt we'll wait sixty minutes, but I don't know. I'm not in charge. I doubt the station will shut down either.

We walk, and I can barely remain upright. Squishy doesn't move.

She didn't want me here. The last thing she said to me was *I told you not to come,* and I gave her a flip answer, one aimed at my father, not at her.

I make my own decisions.

I would have explained that decision. By the time we reached the *Ivoire* or maybe once we were on the *Ivoire,* she would have understood. She would have realized there was logic in coming for her.

Instead, she probably thought it was a suicide mission.

Just like our code said it was.

And she knew I got the code: I wasn't surprised when she said *I told you not to come.*

I wasn't surprised, but she was. She really didn't expect rescue.

Halfway back to the transport, my knees buckle. Winsor takes Squishy from me and I don't fight. I let her carry my friend the rest of the way.

Around us, the sirens continue. People I don't recognize, people from the Empire, start down our corridor, see us, and then divert as if they expect us to shoot them.

We're not shooting anymore. We have no reason to shoot unless someone threatens us. And everyone is avoiding us.

I don't know what's happening with the other teams, but I know what's happening on the *Ivoire*.

Coop is waiting.

Once we all get off the station, he will destroy it.

With the station gone, and my father truly dead, stealth tech will get set back just like Squishy wanted. The Empire will lose all of its research.

At a cost I hadn't imagined days ago.

At a cost I never ever expected.

THE BEGINNING

SIXTY-EIGHT

Squishy's in the infirmary because I made them take her here, even though we all knew there was no reason for it.

I sit across from her bed, just staring at her. We'll take care of her when we get home, which won't take long. I don't want to face Turtle. But I will. That's part of my job.

The infirmary is unlike any place I've ever seen. It changes with mood, or it did until I made someone shut the damn changing thing off. Now I'm just in a white space, sitting on a white chair, staring at the body of a difficult but much loved friend stretched out on a white bed.

I accomplished her mission, at exactly the cost I once predicted.

I told her it would cost her her life.

We didn't lose any of our people on this mission. It went like clockwork. Coop praised Lynda Rooney right after they blew the station together.

We have no idea what the total death count is and we might never know, but we know that most of the people on that station survived. Their ships were headed away as the station exploded.

I wish Squishy could have seen it.

I wanted her to see it.

I want her to know what has happened.

We've stopped imperial stealth tech, even though Coop worries that we started a war.

Although I still maintain that the Empire will have no idea who attacked them. Our ships are unrecognizable, except as part of the historical record, and so are our uniforms. No one in the government of the Nine Planets Alliance has any idea that we completed this mission.

And, best of all, we leave no trail. We immediately activated the *anacapa* drives, so there's no way to know how we escaped the Empire, let alone how we arrived.

There will be theories, of course, but there won't be proof.

The Empire is crippled, just like Squishy wanted. This kind of stealth tech will take years to recover, if it ever does. I imagine—and I might be wrong—that scientists will now try to figure out how these two massive ships operated, and what caused them to disappear in the blink of an eye.

The door opens and Coop steps in. He gives me a compassionate look.

I suspect he thought I would be crying, but my eyes have remained stubbornly dry. Maybe I'm too numb to mourn.

Or maybe I'm too angry.

Squishy did force us into this position, after all.

"You have the right to tell me I told you so," I say.

He sits down next to me and takes my hand. "I won't do that."

I glance over at him. He's looking at me with compassion.

"You told me that missions don't go as planned. You warned me."

He nodded. "Everyone has to learn that for themselves."

"I should have known."

"What would you have done differently?" he asks. "Would you have left her there? Would you have left the job undone?"

He knows better. *I* know better. With the information I had at the time, I would always make the same choice.

"I've decided that when we get back, we're not heading to the Boneyard right away," he says.

I look at him in surprise. "Why not?"

"Because the Nine Planets needs protecting. We put it in jeopardy. Boss, we have planning to do."

I can't deny that. "So you're going to protect the Nine Planets with two ships?"

"Three," he says, "if you'll let the third be part of my mini-Fleet."

I want to yell at him. I want to tell him he's wrong. But I know my emotions are all over the place.

And besides, I have another idea.

"You think you can get into that Boneyard with the *Ivoire*, right?" I ask.

"Yeah," he says. "But—"

"It's your turn to hear me out," I say. "I saw that place just like you did. How many derelict Fleet ships do you think are there? A hundred? More?"

He looks at me, and frowns. He's beginning to understand where I'm going with this.

"I'm sure they're not all fixable," I say, "but some will be and the rest can act as parts."

"Do you know how long that will take?" he asks.

"Yes," I say, "but not as long as you think. You need me, Coop. You'll need me to dive those ships, to figure out which work and which don't. My people and I will do this fast and we'll be accurate. And if there's a station inside, maintaining that field, we're going to have to go into that too."

"Even if we get a dozen ships out of that Boneyard," he says, "we won't have enough crew to run them."

"Of your people, that's right," I say. "But if you're right, we just brought all of the Nine Planets in on this. That's a lot of people. That's a lot of recruits."

He lets out a small breath. "You're crazy, you know that, right?"

I nod. "I've always done things my own way," I say.

"If you can't help me find the Fleet, you'll help me build a new one," he says.

I shrug a single shoulder. "That's the idea." And then I look at Squishy, immobile. Lost forever. "Besides, you might get answers in that Boneyard."

"Yeah," he says softly. He's looking at Squishy too. "But I'm beginning to think there's merit in letting go of your past."

I almost touch her arm. But I can't quite bring myself to feel the cooling flesh.

"The past makes you who you are," I say.

"No," he says. "The past gives you a start toward your future. You choose where you go from that starting point."

I look at him. He doesn't need to say the rest. Squishy chose to go backward.

We're heading forward. To Lost Souls, and then to the Boneyard. And maybe on from there.

Into the unknown.

Which is always where I've felt most at home.

aBOUT THE auTHOR

Kristine Kathryn Rusch is an award-winning mystery, romance, science fiction, and fantasy writer. She has written many novels under various names, including Kristine Grayson for romance and Kris Nelscott for mystery. Her novels have made the bestseller lists and have been published in fourteen countries and thirteen different languages. Her awards range from the *Ellery Queen Mystery Magazine* Readers Choice Award to the John W. Campbell Award. She is the only person in the history of the science fiction field to have won a Hugo Award for editing and a Hugo Award for fiction. Her short work has been reprinted in sixteen Year's Best collections. She is the former editor of the prestigious *Magazine of Fantasy and Science Fiction*. Before that, she and Dean Wesley Smith started and ran Pulphouse Publishing, a science fiction and mystery press in Eugene. She lives and works on the Oregon Coast. Visit her online at kriswrites.com.